A whistling from the trees snapped R.C. out of his grief, and he brought his head up, looking around—

—just in time to see something leap out from the trees.

"What the—?" Instinctively he pulled back, ducking down and turning slightly, and felt a sharp, burning sting as something sliced his cheek. But there had been no sound beyond the whistling, and a thin rush of air like a narrow breeze.

An arrow!

His pistol had fallen to the leaves beside him, and now R.C. scooped it up and fired where the arrow had appeared.

Bam!

The gun's report was deafening in the forest.

He didn't hear anyone grunt from pain, so he had to assume he'd missed. Not surprising, given he couldn't actually see anything over there. Also, the cut along his cheek was stinging worse now, and the pain was distracting him.

But the shadows all around him seemed to grow deeper suddenly.

Then the whistling sound picked up, its tone growing sharper, more ominous. And it now echoed from several other spots, as if a dozen small winds were cutting through the trees ahead of him. The eerie noise made the hair on the back of his neck stand up, and his skin crawl.

Something was coming. He could feel it, even if he couldn't see or hear it. Something bad. Something . . . angry.

Incursion

Aaron Rosenberg

Crossroad Press

About the O. C. L. T. Series

There are incidents and emergencies in the world that defy logical explanation, events that could be defined as supernatural, extraterrestrial, or simply otherworldly. Standard laws do not allow for such instances, nor are most officials or authorities trained to handle them. In recognition of these facts, one organization has been created that can. Assembled by a loose international coalition, their mission is to deal with these situations using diplomacy, guile, force, and strategy as necessary. They shield the rest of the world from their own actions, and clean up the messes left in their wake. They are our protection, our guide, our sword, and our voice, all rolled into one.

They are O.C.L.T.

TALES OF THE O. C. L. T.

OTHER BOOKS BY AARON ROSENBERG

NOVELS:
No Small Bills
Too Small For Tall
The Birth of the Dread Remora
Stargate: Atlantis: Hunt and Run
Indefinite Renewal
The Daemon Gates trilogy
World of WarCraft: Tides of Darkness
Worlds of WarCraft: Beyond the Dark Portal
StarCraft: Queen of Blades
Exalted: The Carnelian Flame
Eureka: Substitution Method (as Cris Ramsay)
Eureka: The Road Less Traveled (as Cris Ramsay)
Star Trek SCE: Creative Couplings
Star Trek SCE: Collective Hindsight
Star Trek SCE: The Riddled Post

NOVELLAS:
For This Is Hell (with Steven Savile)
Crossed Paths: A Tale of the Dread Remora

CHILDREN'S BOOKS:
The Pete and Penny's Pizza Puzzles series
Knight of the Starborne
Lego Star Wars: Fly, Anakin, Fly!
Chaotic: The Khilaian Sphere
Bandslam: The Novel
Transformers Animated: Bumblebee vs. Meltdown
Transformers Animated: Attack of the Dinobots
The Powerpuff Girls: Bubbles in the Middle

Prologue

"Damn it!"

He ran, brushing limbs and branches from his face as he moved, the needles and leaves stabbing at his hands and wrists above his leather jacket and tugging at his long hair in its braid. In the dark they were mere shapes, fluttering shadows that blurred by as he moved, feet churning, his heavy boots stomping flat leaves and cones and bristles alike as he charged headlong through the night.

And behind him, the wind howled in the trees, and it sounded like screams of rage.

He'd tried to warn them, he reminded himself as he ran. He'd warned them not to do it, shown them the right way and urged them to follow it—but of course they wouldn't listen. They never did. Why had he thought this time would be any different?

But this time *was* different.

This time their arrogance might prove fatal.

And now he was caught in the middle.

"I'm sorry!" he shouted over his shoulder, the wind taking his words and whipping them away into the dark. "I tried to stop them!" That was a lie, though. He had warned them, yes, but had he really done anything to stand in their way? Had he really put forth his best effort to prevent them from moving forward with this insanity?

Or had he let them sway him from his own better judgment, and cow him into keeping silent?

Deep in his heart, he knew the answer to those questions, and the shame of it made him weak.

But was that enough reason for him to be facing this himself?

He didn't think so.

So he ran on, stumbling over sticks and roots, reeling as branches struck out at him, and crying as the wind continued to howl behind him and alongside him.

And then the tenor of the wind changed.

Its howls shifted, shortened, rose in pitch, became thin, reedy whistles.

And the whistles surged forward, circling him, ringing him in. Surrounding him.

"I'm sorry!" he called out again, the words little more than a sob. "I'm so sorry! Please!"

He raised his hands high even as he dropped to his knees.

One of the flickering shadows detached itself from the darkness and raced forward, trailing his descent. Long and slender and lightning-swift, it took him just under the chin, and he felt his life leave him all in a rush, not gently tugged free but roughly shoved aside, slammed from his body by the same lethal impact that took his last breath and made his vision go dark.

He toppled to the ground, blood bubbling up in his throat and choking him, the rich scent of the earth filling his nostrils as his head hit the thin grass and the loose soil beneath, and he spasmed, unable to control his body's last urges—

—and all around him, the whistles continued through the trees, and they sounded like laughter.

1

"**R**emind me again what we're doing all the way up ere?" R.C. muttered as he turned off Interstate 90 and ont he narrow two-lane. The sign by the road read "Flathead Indian servation" but there wasn't a gate or even a fence, and the land th were now driving through looked much like what they'd seen r the past hour since landing at Missoula International. Weste Montana wasn't known for its variety. Or its densely populated as.

"Just taking in the scenery," his partner Nick answd, waving one hand at the sights in question. "Which includesountains, rivers, a lake or two, possibly some valleys—oh yealnd a few dead bodies."

"Ah, now you make it sound interesting." R.C. gred at her, one big hand wrapped loosely around the steering wl and the other resting casually on the lip of the door just below window, and she laughed and grinned back.

"You're a terrible vacation buddy, you know," she pted out, still laughing as their rental barreled down the road, rai dust all around them in a thick cloud.

"Maybe, but I'm a good partner," he countered. T quieted them both for a second, and he cursed himself in his for not thinking before he spoke. Would he ever learn?

Probably not.

"Where're we heading, exactly?" he asked insteadd Nick looked just as grateful as she pulled the map from herse and checked where it had been marked.

"Pablo," he answered finally. "That's the home of the tribal headquarters as well as the BIA local office, the Flathead Tribal Police Department, and the Salish Kootenai College. And it's only seven miles south of Polson, which is the largest community out here, at a whopping eighty-five hundred residents. Polson's also the county seat for Lake County, and home to the Kwataqnuk resort and casino.

"Thank you, Miss Tour Guide," he told her. "But no gambling while on duty, remember?" For a second he worried that he'd strayed too close to dangerous topics again, but she smiled and he relaxed a little.

"Look at that!" she said a few minutes later, as the road crested a small rise and they spotted a wave of dark shapes moving through a valley below. "Aren't they amazing?"

R.C. glanced over briefly, and had to agree. Even from this distance the massive, woolly-coated bison were impressive creatures, and the image of their herd running full out across the plain shook the road beneath their wheels and filled the air with the pounding of their hooves. He'd never seen anything so majestic, or so powerful, at least not in person. It was truly awe-inspiring.

He wondered if the rest of this trip would prove to be as pleasant, or easily spotted.

It took them another three hours to pull into Pablo. They'd passed five or other communities along the way, none of them more than a dozen homes and buildings clustered around the main road and perhaps one cross street, and the few people they'd seen had barely bothered to glance their way. But then R.C. supposed they were used to visitors. The reservation made a lot of its money off the casino, so there were always people heading to and from Polson plus students going to the small community college in Pablo and then there were the tourists here to see the Kerr Dam, or the Flathead Lake State Park, or seeking the St. Ignatius Mission, or looking to walk through the National Bison Range.

And then there were people like them.

"Special Agent Reed Hayes, FBI," R.C. announced after he'd

parked in front of the two-story adobe council building and he had Nick had climbed the front steps and stepped into the dark, cool inner lobby. "This is my partner, Danika Frome." He showed the woman behind the front desk his badge and ID, and beside him Nick did the same. "We'd like to speak to the tribal council."

"Just a minute," she told them, and then turned away, whispering into the mic at her throat. She was short, dark, and heavy-set, though not nearly as dark as R.C. himself—he was way beyond Native American in coloring, just as Nick was nowhere near. He knew they made a striking pair, him tall and broad-shouldered and still fit even with the gray starting to show in his short dark hair, and her average height and slender but still curvy, with her blonde-brown hair cropped close and her pale skin and big blue eyes. Even in the fitted suit, Nick didn't look like any FBI agent he'd ever imagined before joining the Bureau.

But the times, they'd certainly changed.

"Special Agent Hayes? Special Agent Frome?" The man who approached them was young, maybe thirty, with the typically glossy black hair pulled back in a ponytail, and his face was round and very friendly. He wore jeans and a denim shirt, though his leather belt had a hand-tooled silver buckle, a braided rope-tie with a carved turquoise eagle hung around his neck, and moccasins adorned his feet. Tribal casual, R.C. guessed. "I'm Detective Jonathan Couture, with the Flathead Tribal Police Department. I was assigned to the murders. Right this way."

R.C. shook hands with him, as did Nick, and then they followed him through the doors at the far end of the lobby, and up the broad staircase to the second floor. Along the way R.C. set his phone to "voice recorder" mode, and spotted Nick doing the same. It was the quickest and easiest way to take notes on the situation— they'd download those to their laptops later, run them through the dictation software to translate the audio files into text, and then clean them up to use as the basis for their status reports. He did carry a small notepad and a pen in his jacket, of course, but that was more for doodling or jotting down reminders to himself than for any real note-taking.

He was glad to see that the local cops were already on the case. The FBI took charge of any situation it was in, and some local authorities didn't appreciate being ordered around. He tried to keep things on as friendly a basis as possible—he'd always believed it was better to have willing partners than grudging assistants—and the detective's friendly attitude suggested that wouldn't be a problem here, plus obviously he would be the man to ask for details about the situation.

Detective Couture led them down the hall to a wide room that took up the entire middle of the floor, the sides of which were filled with tiered wooden seats facing a long table. It was like a courtroom—or a council room.

Ten men sat at that table, most of them older if their gray-streaked hair was an indication, and all of them Native American. The reservation actually had many non-Native residents—in fact, only eight towns here were predominantly Flathead Indian, or Bitterroot Salish as the largest tribe was called—but the tribe still controlled the reservation as a whole, and non-Natives couldn't be members of the tribal council.

"Welcome, agents Hayes and Frome," one of the men announced. He didn't look like the oldest member present—that honor was reserved for the elderly gentleman to the far right, whose braids were almost snow-white and hung down his chest probably to his waist—but his face was deeply lined and his braids were adorned with feathers and beads. He was wearing jeans and a denim shirt as well, though his shirt had embroidery woven into it at the collars and cuffs and down the front panels, and his bolo tie had a silver and lapis image of a leaping trout. "I am Willy Silverstream, chairman of the tribal council. Your superiors notified us that you were coming. We appreciate the FBI's help in this matter." That was a good sign, as well—the federal government didn't have the best track record of treating Native Americans fairly, especially with regards to the reservations, and many Native Americans still resented them, but it sounded as if the council leader really was happy to have them here.

"Glad to be of service," R.C. answered, giving the old man a polite nod. He wasn't sure he could refer to him as "Willy" and still keep a straight face, and hoped it wouldn't come to that. "Why don't you tell us exactly what's been going on here, and we'll see what we can do to help?"

"Of course." Willy frowned and placed both hands flat on the table—they were lined and wrinkled, but still looked strong, the fingers thick and blunt and marked with tiny scars here and there that showed white against his weathered skin. "Men have been dying, out in the woods."

"What men?" Nick asked. "How long ago, and how often? And where in the woods?"

The old man's gaze flicked to her for half a second, and R.C. wondered if they were going to have a problem, but if the tribal elder didn't like speaking to a woman he didn't let it show in his face or his tone. "Three men so far," he answered instead, "starting a week ago. The first one, Elk in the Trees, was hunting. The second, Peter Colman, was a student at the community college, studying animal husbandry, and had been given an assignment to study the local wildlife—easy enough to do around here. The third, Roger Tanner, was a fisherman."

"All of them had lived here on the reservation their whole lives," another of the council members offered. "None of them had any enemies beyond the usual rivalries and minor arguments. Elk in the Trees was a widower with grown children, Peter Colman was engaged, and Roger Tanner was married with one small child and another on the way."

"Any connection between them, beyond being here on the reservation?" R.C. directed that question to Detective Couture, and wasn't surprised when the local cop shook his head. Of course they would have investigated that.

"How did they die?" R.C. didn't miss the pause after his question, or the way neither Willy nor this other council member would look him in the eye. He knew Nick hadn't missed it either.

It was the detective who finally answered. "They were each shot through the throat. With an arrow."

R.C. studied him, but the younger man wasn't smiling or

laughing. "An arrow? Each of them? Through the throat?" He scratched at his jaw. "So we're looking for William Tell here?"

"That was a crossbow," the oldest elder corrected, though there was a trace of humor in his raspy voice that R.C. saw was mirrored in his sharp blue eyes. "Better to say you are looking for Robin Hood. But a Salish version."

"Fair enough." R.C. considered the matter seriously. "Do you have anybody who could make a shot like that, repeatedly? I'm assuming it wasn't at close range or these guys would have run, or fought back, or something?" He knew from his time on the firing range that hitting a target as small as the human throat wasn't easy, especially if you needed that first bullet—or arrow—to be a kill shot. That took real skill.

"That would make sense, yes," Willy agreed, finding his voice again. "But we don't know for certain. There were no witnesses with any of the deaths. Each time the man in question was alone in the woods, and his body was found the next day."

"So each of these attacks occurred at night?" Good of Nick to pick up on that.

"We think so, yes."

"Where did they happen?" was R.C.'s next question.

"Along the edge of the Hog Heaven range," Detective Couture replied. There was a large map of the reservation tacked to the far wall above the massive stone fireplace that took up the space between two wide windows, and he stepped over to it and gestured toward an area near the northwest corner. Polson and Pablo itself were a bit south of the northeast corner, which was dominated by the lake.

"All three of them?" R.C. moved closer to study the map, Nick half a step behind him. "How big is the reservation, in all?"

"Almost two thousand square miles," Willy answered proudly. "We are one of the largest reservations in North America."

"And yet all three deaths occurred in one area," Nick pointed out. She caught R.C.'s eye. "I think we'd better take a closer look at this mountain range."

He nodded. "Can we get a guide to show us the way, and the

original locations of the bodies?" He made a mental note to ask about autopsy reports as well. Assuming any had been performed.

Willy nodded, but before he could speak Detective Couture stepped forward. "I can show you," he offered, with a glance at the council members, who silently nodded permission after a second. "I know the area well, and I know where each of them were found."

"Perfect." Something else had caught his attention, and R.C. figured he'd better mention it now before they really got into anything. "Where's the BIA in all this?" The FBI was tasked with investigating major crimes on Indian land, but the BIA, or Bureau of Indian Affairs, was responsible for maintaining law and order on the reservations otherwise, including police matters. He'd expected to find a BIA officer here waiting for them, and didn't want to step on any toes, especially if that could foul the investigation later.

A few of the elders made harrumphing noises, but they seemed as much amused as annoyed. "That would be Martin Proudfoot and Isaiah Fisher," Willy explained after a moment. "They're the only two manning the local BIA office—the rest are up at the regional office in Portland. But Martin broke his leg a few days back, bike accident, and he's stuck in traction for a bit. And Isaiah's wife's expecting—their first, and there's some complications, so he's sticking to her side over at St. Luke's." He removed a folded-up paper from a pocket in his vest, smoothed it out, and slid it across the table. "Isaiah dropped this off, though, says they were duly notified of your presence and cooperate fully, so you're in the clear." He was definitely holding back a grin, and though his lips only twitched his eyes crinkled and the lines around his mouth deepened so much they looked like furrows.

Nonetheless, the news was good. As long as the BIA knew they were here and didn't have a problem with it, R.C. wasn't too worried. He'd copy any reports to their regional office, of course, just to keep them in the loop, but honestly this way was probably better. Now he didn't have to worry about some paper-pusher dogging his steps along the way.

He turned back to Willy and the others. "We'll let you know what we find, of course. Hopefully we can resolve this quickly, and before anyone else gets hurt."

Willy nodded. "That is our hope as well. Thank you."

There were nods all around, and then Detective Couture led them back out into the hall. "The council's booked you into the Hawthorne House, a really nice bed-and-breakfast over in Polson," he explained as they headed down the stairs and outside. "Did you want to rest for a bit, or head straight out?"

"We should probably check in and drop off our bags," R.C. decided. "But I'd like to get going right after that. How long will it take to get over there?"

"A few hours," the detective answered. "I'll get my Jeep and meet you over at the hotel in a few minutes."

"Sounds great." R.C. shook hands with him and watched the young Native walk off, then turned to his partner. "What do you think?"

"He seems like a straight-up guy," she answered as they unlocked their car and got in. "And this could be as simple as one crazy guy staking out an area and shooting any 'trespassers.'" Her tone said she wasn't convinced, however, as did the sigh she released right after that.

"But?" he urged as he backed out and drove to the bed-and-breakfast.

She gave him a tired smile in reply. "But when is it ever that easy?"

2

"**I still don't see why they couldn't have booked us there instead,**" Nick groused for the tenth time as they walked. She'd been complaining about the accommodations off and on since they'd checked in, and R.C. knew she was only half-kidding. The Hawthorne House where they were staying seemed decent enough—big airy rooms, clean whitewashed walls, hardwood floors, high ceiling beams, nice big beds.

But Nick was stuck on the fact that there was a resort only a few blocks away. And that they weren't staying there.

"We're just government grunts," he reminded her yet again. "We're lucky the council is putting us up at all." Most of the time they had to arrange their own accommodations, and pay for them, too. The Bureau would reimburse them, of course. Eventually. After a mountain of paperwork and what seemed like an eternity. This time, they didn't have to deal with any of that. The council was covering their room and board, which was a lot more generous than most local agencies that had asked for their help.

But that still wasn't swaying Nick any.

"In for a penny, in for a pound," she grumbled. "It's not like we're asking to gamble. But a massage sure would be nice."

R.C. almost offered to give her one, then stopped and cursed himself for that impulse. Then cursed again for stopping what would have been a completely reasonable and harmless remark, but now would seem either forced or salacious. Damn it! Would this ever get any easier?

"It's just up ahead," Detective Couture called back. He was obviously at home in the woods and had quickly moved in front of them, though perhaps that was just to get out of range of Nick's complaints. "Where we found Elk in the Trees."

"Did you find him?" R.C. asked, pushing away questions of his partner's comfort level and focusing on the investigation again.

"No, it was a young family, the Singing Doves," their guide replied. He slowed to let them catch up a little so he didn't have to shout. R.C. had already learned that Detective Couture was very helpful but also very soft-spoken—nice when sharing a car ride but not good when trying to be heard while climbing a mountain.

Not that they were really climbing a mountain, of course. The Hog Heaven Range might contain some genuine mountains, but they were only in the foothills here. There were some decent peaks and valleys, to be sure, but R.C. had gotten used to Denver these past two years. Compared to the heights around that city, these were barely speed bumps.

The land did have a rugged beauty, however. They were well beyond any towns or villages out here, and as far as the eye could see there was nothing but thick grass and tall trees, broken here and there by a jumble of rocks or a narrow, swiftly flowing stream or a small, dark lake.

There were birds aplenty, their calls and cries and wing-beats echoing all around. R.C. had spotted a few deer as well, and Nick swore she'd seen wolves peering at her from behind a fallen tree. Detective Couture had assured her that wolves would never attack three armed men—he'd brought a hunting rifle along, grabbing it from the Jeep's back window probably out of reflex, and R.C. had decided not to raise a fuss about it. They were the guests here, after all.

"They were out on a nature walk," the detective was explaining, and it took R.C. a second to rein in his thoughts and return to the subject. "Their little girl, Sophie, ran ahead to pick some wildflowers, and then screamed. Her parents came running, and that's when they found him." The three of them topped a low crest, and Couture surveyed the area from beneath one hand, then pointed. "Right over there."

R.C. followed him across the small valley, scanning the area for signs of trouble or ambush. Old habits died hard. He'd been in the Army a long time, mostly Military Intelligence but you still had to serve a stint of active duty and he'd never forgotten those skills, or lost those reflexes. Which was a good thing—he was fairly sure he would have died on the job several times otherwise.

But the area seemed clear, aside from a lone falcon and a few small deer, plus the ubiquitous birds. The spot in question was right at the edge of a small clearing, the first trees of the renewed forest springing up just beyond, and R.C. crouched down to study the area better.

Much of the ground had been trampled here, unfortunately. Probably one of the local officers and whoever had collected the body, plus anyone out to help and whoever took the Singing Dove family home, and then anyone who'd heard about the incident and wanted to see for themselves.

Christ.

"Yo, check this out." Nick hadn't stopped with them, and now she was calling from just inside the tree line, some fifty feet beyond. R.C. joined her, and found her kneeling in the loose underbrush.

"What've you got?" he asked.

"This." She indicated a spot just to her side. "I figured the space right around the body would get too much foot traffic but if we were lucky the killer might have struck from back in the trees, where nobody thought to look and thus destroy the evidence." Her smug expression finally gave way to a grin. "Guess I was right."

R.C. studied the spot she'd gestured down at, and stiffened when he realized he was looking at a shape depressed into the leaves and moss and pine needles that coated the forest floor.

A shape that looked an awful lot like a footprint.

Fishing out his phone, R.C. snapped a photo of the print. Then he ran the image through a special FBI app, one that stripped out everything but the outline and a few pertinent physical characteristics.

A few second later his "Message Waiting" icon blinked on. He checked the phone's logs and found the image there, waiting.

But when he'd called it up, all he could do was stare.

"That can't be right," he muttered. He glanced down at the actual print, then back at the display, which did appear to match.

But it didn't make any sense.

"What's up? Let me see!" Nick demanded, practically ripping the phone from his hand.

"Here." R.C. showed her the image. After a second she shook her head as well.

"What the hell did that?" she wondered aloud. R.C. didn't answer. He was still trying to process what he'd seen. Even if it didn't make sense.

Just like a certain incident many years ago.

But he tried very hard not think of that anymore.

Especially at times like this.

The print was a footprint, all right. The program had rendered it out, clear as day. It was a left foot, and bare, with long, thin toes spread wide—

—and a total width of no more than two inches, but a total length of close to eighteen. Which made it half again as long as one of his own feet—and only half as wide. No way a man had a foot like that. A monkey, maybe, or some kind of lizard, though whatever had cast that print had five toes and a heel, and the general shape was a lot more like a man's than it was any sort of animal R.C. had ever seen. Still, he freely admitted he wasn't exactly a wilderness expert.

Fortunately, they were with someone who was.

"Detective!" Their guide had been studying the body's final resting spot, still, and glanced up at the call. A minute later he was crouching beside them.

"What's up?" R.C. pointed to the print, and held up the phone as well, but the young local shook his head. "I don't know—I haven't ever seen anything like that. I'd say it was a man's, but horribly stretched."

"Is it a prank?" Nick asked. "There is a college near here—could this have been some kind of game or hazing ritual gone horribly wrong?"

"Maybe, but only one of the victims was a college student,"

R.C. pointed out. "And it was the middle one. Besides, the college is in Pablo, near the tribal headquarters, right? Long way to go for a prank." He spread his hand over the footprint for a second, then rose and took a single long stride past it and into the woods. He didn't spot any marks on the ground there but the print had been far longer than his own feet so he took half another stride—and saw a second print beside a tree's roots. It matched the first one except that this was clearly a right foot.

Another step and a half brought him to a third print, this one a left again.

"We've got a trail," he called back over his shoulder. But each print had been a little shallower, and though he did find a fourth it was barely visible as an impression in the leaves. There wasn't a fifth.

So much for the trail.

Still, they had proof that someone had been here. Someone with a stride significantly longer than R.C.'s own.

Which would suggest the stranger was significantly taller as well. Almost half again as tall. And R.C. was a few inches over six feet.

That would make their quarry one of the tallest men alive.

Unbidden, R.C.'s thoughts flashed back again, back to his military days—and to the incident that had all but ended them. It had been in Uppsala, a small city up in Sweden. He and the rest of his MI team had been called in to search for a missing scientist, and for the CIA agent who'd vanished while looking for him. They'd expected to find the scientist had gone rogue, or that bike gangs had invaded the area and struck them both down, or even that someone had targeted the scientist and then taken out the agent when he'd gotten too close.

What they'd found had been something else altogether.

The official report had claimed that a homeless man had ambushed and killed both men along the riverbank, and had then attacked R.C. and his team when they'd approached his hiding place under an old bridge. He'd killed their team leader and one of the others in their first encounter, and had taken out two of the remaining three the second time they'd met.

Only R.C. had survived. He'd fatally wounded the homeless

man, but the crazed fiend had dove into the river, and his body was never recovered.

But that wasn't exactly what had happened.

Most of the report had been accurate enough. Except it hadn't been a homeless man, and he hadn't escaped into the river. It had been—even now R.C. didn't like to admit it, even to himself. But the footprints here forced him to remember it properly, and to acknowledge the truth.

It had been a troll.

Monstrously tall, with massive jaws and hands and insanely long arms, it had crushed Polo's skull with a single blow and thrown Lobo a dozen feet, shattering his spine in the process. Similar blows during their rematch had laid out both Drew and Colt. Only a phosphorous grenade had saved him from the same fate—he'd lobbed it right at the unholy creature, which had swallowed the thing whole.

And then turned to stone when the light washed over it from the inside out.

R.C. had never told anyone what had really happened, not even Nancy, who had still been only his girlfriend at the time. He'd sold the homeless-man story as best he could instead, but there'd been too many holes in it and as a result he'd been benched from active missions afterward, flagged as a possible psych case. He'd stuck it out in MI for a few more years after that, hoping to find his way back to full duty, but had eventually given up and cashed out. After he'd returned to the states he'd applied to the FBI, and they'd been delighted to get someone with his training and field experience. The past two years had been good, with interesting cases and even some dangerous ones but nothing that defied explanation.

Nothing until now.

Nick joined him by the fourth print, and R.C. glanced up to meet her eyes. He saw there the same confusion he was feeling, and a conviction that there must be a rational explanation behind this.

As he rose to his feet and brushed leaves and pine needle from his legs and hands, he wondered if his eyes still said the same.

3

"**T**hat's some weird shit right there."

The sudden pronouncement made R.C. start a bit, and for half a second as he reached for his gun he wondered who had snuck up on him. Then his brain reconnected and he let his hand brush his arm instead, as if that's what he had intended all along, as he glanced over at Detective Couture. The Salish officer had moved away from the site where the body had been found and had crept up on them and the vanishing tracks so silently he could have been a ghost himself.

"That about covers it," Nick agreed, laughing, and the sound made R.C. smile. His dainty-looking partner had a wickedly earthy sense of humor, as he knew all too well.

"What did you find there?" R.C. asked, gesturing back behind them.

Couture answered with a shrug. "Not much," he elaborated after a second. "Elk in the Trees probably died there, judging by the dried blood I found on the grass he flattened when he fell. The Singing Doves didn't move him at all, and there's no sign of him crawling anywhere, no tracks or disturbance around the spot except for his old footprints and then theirs a day or two later."

R.C. frowned and rubbed between his eyes. "What happened to the body? We didn't get any autopsy reports."

Their guide looked down at his feet, then away. "Ah—I don't know that there were any. We're a small community. There's only two hospitals on the reservation, and the closer one is a good four hours from here. Besides, he was already dead, and it was pretty obvious what'd killed him."

"Right, no autopsy. Any chance we can exhume the body?" Nick could be a sweet girl, but right now she was all business.

Not that it helped. "No body left, I'm afraid." The detective offered them an apologetic smile. "We don't go in for burial much around here, and Elk in the Trees was old-school."

R.C. could guess what that meant. "You cremated him."

"Yep. Traditional funeral pyre, dancing around the fire, drum circle, the works."

"Any chance you at least kept the murder weapon?" R.C. asked.

"I don't know, sorry," their new friend admitted. "But I don't see why they'd have left that in, so yeah, it should be around somewhere."

"We'll want to see that first thing when we get back," Nick warned him, and Jonathan nodded. "In the meantime—" she glanced around, at the tall trees surrounding them, and the looming shadows the setting sun was casting across the rocky plain. "I have no idea."

"These tracks are facing where Elk in the Trees fell," R.C. pointed out. "Which means whoever made them—"

"—came from deeper in the woods, that way." And just like that, she was back in focus. "Right. Let's check it out. Maybe we'll get lucky."

"I'll scout ahead," Detective Couture offered. He gave them both a quick grin. "Wouldn't do to have two visiting FBI agents fall into a creek or get eaten by a bear or anything." And before they could frame snappy replies he'd slipped past them and vanished between the trees, his moccasins not making a sound even on the carpet of brittle leaves.

"We should drag him back to Denver, or better yet D.C. or New York or LA, and see how he likes it," Nick grumbled as she took off after him, and R.C. had no choice but to follow her. Still, he was happy to see her complaining again. With Nick, it was when she stopped griping that you had to worry.

"Nobody likes being a fish out of water," he agreed, his longer legs allowing him to catch up to her easily—a fact her glare showed hadn't gone unnoticed.

"You at least had some training for this, Mr. Military," she reminded him, though there wasn't much edge to the retort. "I didn't." He knew that she'd joined the Bureau right out of college, where she'd majored in forensics and criminal justice. She was right, he had been trained in a wide variety of terrains, and he'd even walked his share of woods and forests when he'd been stationed in Germany, but that had been a few years ago and it had never been his strong suit.

"My training didn't include how to hike in a suit," he pointed out, which at least got a giggle out of her. Though neither of them had thought to pack jeans and flannel shirts, they did have sturdy outdoor gear in their bags—which they'd left at the hotel, rather than waste time changing. Thanks to that decision, however, they were trudging through the woods still wearing their standard dark suits. At least he was wearing low-cut boots—he felt more comfortable in them than in most shoes, a holdover from his military days, and had discovered he could get away with them when not in strictly formal settings. Nick was suffering along in loafers.

"Well, by all means, take it off if it's bothering you," she told him playfully, her teasing comment followed almost immediately by swearing as a branch caught on her jacket cuff and tugged her arm half out of her sleeve.

"You first," he replied automatically—and then wished he hadn't when he saw her eyes go wide and the color rise to her cheeks. She didn't say a word as she pulled the fabric free and readjusted the fit, then walked on.

Damn it! How long was it going to be like this, R.C. wondered as he gave her a few steps before moving to catch up. Partners shouldn't be this uncomfortable around each other, this wary of saying the wrong thing, this tense.

Then again, partners also shouldn't sleep together.

It had only been the one time. They'd been tasked with taking down a group of drug runners who peddled to the snow bunny set up in Aspen. It had taken them a week to pin down the group's location, and then they'd converged, along with two other agents and a team of ten local cops.

Which would have been fine—if one of the drug-runners' playmates hadn't spotted them and screamed.

And if the nine drug-runners hadn't all been heavily armed.

What should have been a quick sting had turned into a massive firefight. One of the agents had been killed right off, as had two of the cops. Two others had been hit and taken out of the fight, and another two had been pinned down too far away to lend any aid. R.C. had gotten off a lucky shot and taken out one of the dealers. That left eight of them, all armed with submachine guns—against three FBI agents and four cops, armed with assault shotguns and pistols.

Not very good odds.

Nick and R.C. had been trapped behind one corner of the private lodge the drug-runners had rented out, with two of the dealers opening fire on them. It was only a matter of time, they both knew, before those men started to advance, cutting off any chance of retreat and chewing away at the wood and shingles of their cover.

So they'd run.

But not far. They'd fled around the corner, and then dove through a shattered plate glass window and into a palatial living room—

—right into a pile of the drug-runners.

Nick had shot one in the head before they'd even realized they weren't alone anymore, and R.C. followed up with a heart-shot to another. By the time the other dealers understood what was happening, they'd managed to roll across the room and behind the massive oak bar.

When the dealers had turned to focus on them, the remaining cops and the other FBI agent had taken the opportunity and moved in, mowing them down from behind.

It had been a close call, and afterwards Nick was shaking. She'd never been in a real gun battle before—she'd fired her weapon before, even wounded suspects in the line of duty, but this had been kill-or-be-killed, guns blazing, shooting to kill, expecting to die any second. It was a lot to handle.

R.C. had taken her back to her hotel room and comforted her, helped her clean up the cuts and scrapes she'd gotten from glass shards and wood splinters and everything else.

Somehow comforting had turned to kissing, which had turned to sex. Not lovemaking—this was raw and powerful and demanding, the body's need to confirm that it was still alive, the system's need to work out all of that adrenaline and passion.

The next morning, they had both been embarrassed, and unsure what to say. They understood what had happened and why, but that didn't change the fact that they were partners and friends.

And that R.C. was married.

He'd never even considered lying about it. He and Nancy had been together for nine years, and married for five. They were more than husband and wife, more than mates; they were true partners, two halves of a whole. They didn't keep secrets from each other.

So, after the debriefing, he'd gone home and told Nancy exactly what had happened.

And she had forgiven him.

"Oh, I'm pissed," she assured him afterward. "Don't think I'm not. But I understand why it happened. And I know it was just a result of what you'd both been through." She'd patted his cheek then. "And I know that you know that if you ever do anything like that again, I'll cut your balls off and feed them to the neighbor's pit bull."

He had never loved her more.

The funny thing was, though Nancy had gotten past it, Nick hadn't. Their relationship had been strained ever since, like that one unthinking, primal act was still hanging over them, tainting every move they made, every word they said, every gesture.

It was maddening that he couldn't joke with her the way he used to. Couldn't hip-check her or elbow her like he had before. Couldn't even look at her half the time without her going red and flustered—like she had just now.

R.C. wondered if it was ever going to get better.

He hoped so.

He missed his partner.

Maybe if they talked it out a bit. "Listen," he started. "I—"

A sudden burst of sound from up ahead cut him off. It was loud and harsh, a series of explosives noises, and in an instant R.C. had forgotten about his relationship woes—he was down in a crouch, pistol in his hand, other hand planted against its butt, eyes narrowed as he tried to peer through the dusk and the underbrush to see what had caused that sudden barrage of noise. Two steps ahead of him, Nick had flattened herself against a tree, her gun also drawn, and she caught his eye and gestured up ahead of them. He nodded. Then he eased himself forward, trying to keep as quiet as possible as he crept toward the source of the noise.

The cacophony had continued unabated, and as R.C. got closer he realized it was a man speaking but in a language he didn't recognize. The voice sounded familiar, however, and after a second or two of listening R.C. straightened.

Detective Couture?

The trees seemed to thin up ahead, and he barreled past the remaining trunks, bursting into a decent-sized clearing. The open space wasn't natural, however—even in the fading light he saw wide flat disks floating above the ground like luminescent lily pads atop a dark pond, and after a moment he realized they were tree stumps. Off to one side were long pale tubes he guessed were severed trunks, and the air was thick with the smell of sap and of sawdust and burning wood.

The local detective was standing between him and the stumps, shaking his fists and shouting, and R.C. finally understood. The mild-mannered young cop was swearing. In his native tongue.

"I take it this isn't right?" R.C. asked finally, as Nick emerged from the woods behind him and visibly relaxed to discover their guide was the one causing all the ruckus.

"No, it isn't right!" Couture snapped, then paused and closed his eyes. "I'm sorry," he continued a few seconds later, his tone much calmer. "I didn't mean to take it out on you. But no, this isn't right. The tribe fells and sells some timber, yes, but only in very carefully designated locations. Certainly not here—this is a protected area! Whoever is doing this is not only trespassing but destroying government property!"

"And they're still around," Nick pointed out quietly. Both men turned to look at her, and she shrugged, a half-smile on her lips. Any earlier discomfort had vanished. "Smell the air," she instructed. "That burning smell? They were cutting recently. See that light rig over there?" The object in question looked like a metal and plastic sawhorse with several large industrial lights clamped to it so they could swivel at different angles. "There's still a little glow about the bulbs. They weren't shut off all that long ago." R.C. saw that she was right—the bulbs were visible even in the rapidly falling darkness, as faint pools of semi-illumination in the dark outdoors.

"Besides," Nick added, "this equipment's expensive. They aren't about to just leave it laying around."

"The little lady's got it right," an unfamiliar voice called from out of the shadows. Those same inky patches shifted and roiled, and then one of them detached, moving forward into the light until they could see it was a big, burly man who'd spoken. He was wearing jeans and an open work shirt over a T-shirt of indeterminate color, though his beard was obviously black as coal even out of the shadows.

But his skin was clearly pale as a peach, and just as pink.

This was no Salish.

"That there's our equipment," the man continued, coming to a halt a dozen or so paces away. "We'd like it back now." Around him the shadows shifted and fell apart and then there were a half-dozen other men with him, all of them dressed in work clothes and all of them looking big, mean, tired, and irritable. One hell of a combination.

R.C. wasn't in the mood to back down, however. "Who is 'our'?" he demanded. "Who do you work for?"

The leader glanced him up and down, and apparently wasn't impressed by the suit because he sneered. "Who the hell are you? You don't belong here."

"No?" R.C. reached into his jacket pocket with one hand and pulled out his wallet. "This says otherwise." He flipped it open and held it up so all of them could see the badge gleaming even in the dim starlight. "So does this." And he waggled his gun at them.

The badge had caused a low murmur to spread through the men. The gun got an even stronger reaction, as they all backed off a step. Behind him, Nick grinned and raised her own gun, making it clear they weren't facing just R.C. alone. Then Detective Couture displayed his own badge. "Flathead Tribal Police Department," he announced. "Back off or I'll arrest you all!"

For a second, nobody moved.

"Fine," the leader ground out. He waved a thick, heavily callused hand. "We'll be back to pick all of that up in the morning." Then he turned and walked away from the clearing, into the trees. His men followed him, and in a minute R.C., Nick, and Detective Couture had the area to themselves once more.

"This gets more and more complicated all the time," R.C. muttered as he sheathed his pistol and studied the clearing more closely. "First some unexplained deaths, and now an illegal logging operation—and both in the same area. There's got to be a connection."

"Definitely," Nick agreed. "But we should try to find it in the morning. I think we should really get out of here before it gets even later—and darker."

R.C. nodded. He doubted they would be able to find out much more in the dark. Plus he didn't want to assume those loggers had really left and then find out otherwise—they'd looked a lot more comfortable in these woods than he felt, and two pistols and a rifle against a half dozen or more big men wasn't great odds even in broad daylight. "We'll come back first thing tomorrow."

He didn't say it, but as they trudged back toward Detective Couture's Jeep R.C. added one more thing to his to-do list:

Find out who those loggers were, and who they worked for. Get a full list of who was involved and what was on-site.

And how they could chop down ancient, protected trees without anybody even realizing they were there.

4

"I don't know about you, but I'm done in," Nick announced as they waved good-bye to Jonathan—he'd insisted on the drive back that they call him by his first name, pointing out that "you've heard me swear, so I think formality's out the window"—and watched him drive off. It was well past midnight now as they turned toward the Hawthorne House's front door. "Think anybody'll notice if we sleep in?"

She didn't seem to notice the potential tease in what she'd said, and R.C. let it pass, but he was glad she hadn't stiffened up again. "Probably," was all he answered. "Something about a job, badges, the government, dead bodies, etcetera—they might get perturbed."

That got a laugh from his partner, and she shoved his shoulder as he held the door for her. "Spoilsport."

They didn't say anything else as they trudged up the stairs to their room. "Tomorrow, then," Nick muttered as she pushed open her door. "Sleep tight, yeah?"

"You too," he told her back, and her closing door. Then he unlocked his own—they actually still used real keys here, which he thought was quaint. He managed to strip down to boxers and undershirt, splash some water on his face, and gargle for a few seconds before stumbling to his bed and collapsing on top of it.

His dreams were filled with strange footprints, angry loggers, angrier drug-runners, and a shadowy figure with enormous hands that lurked under an old bridge.

The next morning, after his phone chirped the alarm he didn't remember setting, R.C. dragged himself out of bed and into the shower. That woke him up—apparently hot water was a rare commodity out here in Montana, or maybe early-risers had simply used it all up already—and he dressed quickly, feeling alertness kick in as he finished knotting his tie and pulling on his boots. He slipped his pistol into its holster—he'd stowed it under his pillow out of habit—and tugged open the door to find Nick leaning against the opposite wall waiting for him.

"Took you long enough," was all she said, her typical impish grin on her lips. She looked rested but her short hair was still damp, attesting to the speed with which she'd gotten ready. He wondered if her shower had been freezing cold as well, but decided it was better not to ask.

"Breakfast or council?" he said by way of answer, following her down the stairs. The smells of pancakes and bacon and eggs and most of all coffee decided that for them, though, and without a word they both turned into the little dining room off the front lobby and sat at a small empty table. There weren't many other guests—Nick grumbled that most people probably stayed at the resort instead—so it didn't take long for the woman they'd seen at the front desk the night before to come out and ask what they wanted. R.C. ordered the full spread—pancakes, eggs over easy, bacon, toast, orange juice, and coffee. Nick shook her head and skipped the pancakes and the orange juice.

"What're you thinking?" she asked him a few minutes later over her coffee cup, the wisps of steam flickering in her eyes. R.C. was busy inhaling the aroma and savoring that first sip, the way it exploded on his tongue and then all the way down his throat and into his stomach, and took a second to answer.

"Somebody knows something," he said finally. "I'd bet on it. No way those guys just wandered in there, not with all that equipment."

"You think the council's been holding out on us?"

He pictured the row of men in his head. "Not all of them. But somebody is."

"Jonathan?" The doubt was clear in her tone.

"No, he was genuinely surprised—and pissed—when he saw that gear last night." Her relieved nod matched his own thoughts. He liked Jonathan Couture.

They didn't say much else once the food arrived, just tucked in with all the appetite of two active people who'd gone hiking the night before. The fare was fresh, good, and plentiful, and R.C. enjoyed every bit of it. In the Army he'd learned to appreciate good food when he got it, and to make do when he didn't. Making do wasn't a problem here.

"Ready?" Nick stood, took a last swig of her coffee, tossed her napkin on her empty plate, and grinned down at him as he wolfed down the rest of his own food.

"You ordered less," he pointed out as he rose and followed her, calling a thank-you over his shoulder as they passed through the lobby.

"Didn't want to get weighed down," his partner replied. "Figured we might be on the move a bit today."

That made sense, but R.C. didn't regret the large meal. Besides, he was a fairly big guy. He needed a lot of fuel.

It was a pleasant morning, cool and crisp but not cold, and the sun was just rising over the buildings as they drove the few short miles to Pablo, casting rosy shadows down the street and over the sidewalks. A few people were out and about as they pulled up by the tribal headquarters, sweeping or opening stores or walking dogs or driving by on their way somewhere else, and the two of them got their fair share of looks, surreptitious and otherwise. R.C. couldn't very well blame them—it wasn't often a town this size got two FBI agents sauntering through it.

He sort of wished he had a Stetson. And maybe an old Navajo blanket draped across his shoulders.

The same woman sat at the front desk, and she just nodded and gestured to the doors when she saw them. Nick led the way, taking the steps two at a time, and R.C. hauled himself up after her at a slightly slower pace. Did she have to be quite so much of a morning person?

There wasn't anyone standing guard outside the double doors to the council room, and Nick just shrugged, so R.C. rapped twice on the doors and then pushed them open and stepped inside, his partner right behind him. The council elders were seated at the same table and had clearly been talking amongst themselves but now turned and glanced up as he and Nick approached.

"Agent Hayes, Agent Frome, good morning," Willy Silverstream greeted them. "I trust you slept well? Mabel runs a nice clean establishment." He nodded toward Jonathan, who stood off to one side and waved hello. "We understand you may have found some sort of lead last night."

R.C. had started to tense but relaxed once the words registered fully. "Some sort of lead." He glanced at Jonathan, and the young detective actually winked at him. Well, that was fine—at least he'd followed their instructions. And it was clear he, and therefore the Flathead Tribal Police Department, were willing to follow the FBI's lead. When Willy nodded as well, R.C. knew the detective had spoken to him about what they had planned, and that they had his permission to proceed. Which meant it was show time.

"We did, yes," R.C. replied. He deliberately stopped a dozen or so paces back from the council table. That way he could see all of the members at once. Nick slid to one side, giving her a clear view as well. "In particular, we found something both puzzling and disturbing." He paused to make sure all of them were watching him intently.

"Someone's been logging in the Hog Heaven range."

"What?" He didn't think Willy's shock and dismay were feigned, and instantly discounted the council chairman. Several of the others reacted the same way. The oldest one, the one who'd shown a sense of humor the night before, seemed less surprised, but more sad—like he hadn't known but could believe it.

The younger council members were a different story. There were four here around Jonathan's age, all grouped near one end of the table, and they didn't start the same way their elders had. Instead of turning pale they had flushed, and three of them had looked down and away, a sure sign of guilt.

But the fourth one—the fourth one's gaze had narrowed, and then darted around, toward R.C. and Nick, toward the elders, and finally to the double doors. The only way out.

Bingo.

"We haven't met," R.C. announced, covering the distance to that council member in six long strides and looming over him. "I'm Special Agent Hayes, FBI. And you are?" He let the edge in his voice make it clear he wasn't just making polite conversation—from casual chat to interrogation in nothing flat.

"Thomas Peel." To his credit, the man didn't look particularly cowed. But he did look guilty as all hell. He was average height and build, R.C. judged, with an angular face and a sharp nose, and his dark hair had been buzz-cut neat and crisp. That and the well-pressed suit he wore, the bolo tie his one concession to his heritage, marked Thomas Peel as a would-be mover and shaker, determined to show he was modern and hip and forward-thinking.

R.C. knew the type all too well.

"Well, Mr. Peel, what do you know about this logging operation up in the mountains?" R.C. put both hands flat on the table and leaned across it, getting right up in the other man's face. Peel gulped and edged back.

"Me? Nothing! I think it's terrible! Why?" The man wasn't stupid, clearly. But just as clearly he wasn't used to having someone come after him like this. Nor was he a very good liar.

"Don't lie to us, Mr. Peel." Nick had circled around behind him, and when she spoke just over his shoulder he jumped. "We know you're involved. Come clean and it'll go better for you." Never mind the fact that they had no authority over things like logging—that would fall to the reservation's own police force unless they could prove it was directly tied to their murder investigation. But Peel didn't need to know that.

"I don't have anything to do with it!" he insisted again, but his voice was starting to go shrill and sweat was beginning to bead across his forehead. He was close to cracking.

"You're lying!" R.C. slammed one fist on the table, making the other man jump again, and a few of the other council members as well. "Do we have to haul you in and make this official? Just tell us what we want to know!" His size, dark skin, and deep voice made him a natural choice for "bad cop," while Nick's pretty face and soft voice suited "good cop" better. They'd had lots of practice at it.

As he'd hoped, that last shout did the trick, as Peel crumpled in on himself like a newspaper that'd been tossed onto the fire. "Okay, okay." His words were barely loud enough to hear.

R.C. leaned in closer, in part to keep on the pressure and in part to hear him better. "Good. Now, tell us about it."

"They came to me, said they only wanted a secluded area where they wouldn't upset the ecosystem," Peel admitted slowly. "Offered me a finder's fee for setting things up, and promised a portion of their profits would be donated to the council." He glanced up and at his fellow members. "You see, I did it for the good of the community! The casino hasn't been making the profits we expected, and we can use the money! Think of everything we can do with it! Fix up the schools, repave the roads, update the sewer system, the electrical lines—we can get this place up and out of the early twentieth century!"

"You had no authority to do this," Willy reminded the younger member, his voice sad but stern. "Such a matter should have been brought before the council for a vote."

"What, and have it shot down?" Anger was overcoming Peel's fear. "Every time any of us suggest something new, you old-timers quash it. We can't just sit here and let our way of life shrivel up and die! We need to move forward!"

"There is nothing wrong with progress," the older member stated calmly, and everyone else quieted at his words, even Willy. "But this was foolish, and sacrificed too much for too little."

"Ah, sorry to interrupt," R.C. said loudly, to forestall another round of arguing. "You can all fight about this as much as you want, of course. I just have one more question—well, two, really." He glared down at Peel. "Who owns this logging operation, and where can we find him?"

"It's Douglas Timber," Peel answered, hanging his head as the fight left him, at least for the moment. "The owner's Salvador

Douglas. He's got offices in Rollins, just north of the reservation along highway ninety-three."

"That's right alongside Flathead Lake," Jonathan explained, indicating it on the large map. "But a bit north of us, and just a little to the west."

"And not more than a few hours above and east of the Hog Heaven range," Nick pointed out.

R.C. nodded. He glanced back down at Peel. "What does Douglas have to do with these murders?" he demanded.

This time the man's eyes did go wide, and he turned pale. "I don't know, I swear I don't!" he pleaded. He turned to his fellow council members. "I agreed to let him do some logging up there, on a limited basis! He promised he'd leave the wildlife alone, the birds, even the fish. That's all!"

"Unless each of these three men stumbled upon his setup and he knew they'd expose him," R.C. pointed out. "There's big money in timber, and logging is a cutthroat business. He may have figured it was safer and cheaper to kill them than to risk exposure and having his operation shut down."

"I didn't have anything to do with any of that," Peel insisted. He glanced around for support. "You all know me! I might argue about how we do things—particularly how long it takes for us to do them—but I just want what's best for the reservation, and for our people."

After a minute, Willy nodded. "We do not doubt your intentions, Thomas," he stated, "but your methods, and your scruples, are both suspect. We will consider the situation, and what to do about it."

R.C. took that as their cue. "We'll go speak with this Salvador Douglas," he told the council, as Nick nodded and came around the table to join him. "We'll let you know what we can get out of him, and whether he really is tied to these murders."

"Thank you, agents." The elders turned back to their own discussion at once. Even Jonathan shrugged an apology but made no move to join them as R.C. and Nick headed toward the door once more. Most likely he was remaining behind in case the council decided they wanted to press charges against Peel and he needed to be taken into custody.

"Looks like we're on our own," R.C. muttered as they stalked back down the hall.

His partner nodded, but she didn't look overly concerned. "If I remember correctly, highway ninety-three actually cuts right past here and curves up around the lake," she said. "We can just follow it up to Rollins, then GPS the office itself." She grinned at him as they pushed out through the front doors and into the morning. "Nice day for a lakeside drive, wouldn't you say?"

R.C. laughed. As usual, her cheer was infectious. "Sure, why not?" he tossed the keys to her, and she snagged them out of the air. "You drive."

5

It was a nice day, clear and sunny and warm but with a mild wind, and proved to be a pretty drive as well. Nick had been right about 93, and they followed the little two-lane highway as it curved around the southwest edge of the lake, windows open and the breeze off the water blowing in their hair. Neither of them said much, just enjoyed the sun and the wind and the scenery, and just then in that car it was easy to believe they'd gotten past the unpleasantness at last and were back to their old comfortable rapport.

All too soon they reached a sign marking the outskirts of Rollins, and R.C. sighed as he tugged out his phone and did a search for "Douglas Timber," then fed the results into his GPS. "Ahead three point two miles and turn left," he stated finally. "Looks like it's right off the highway."

"You got it."

The place was indeed right off the highway—Nick spun the wheel and cut across the opposite lane and into a wide gravel parking lot that fronted a long, low wooden building. She parked between a Tesla Roadster and a beaten-up Ram truck. A handful of other vehicles dotted the lot, most of them practical and a bit worn.

"Funny that a lumber baron would have an electric car," she remarked as they clambered out and stretched before walking toward the building's front door. "Maybe he figures he's raping the environment enough already?"

"Maybe he just doesn't like paying other people for nonrenewable resources," R.C. countered, and they both shook their heads. Whatever the reason, it was obvious the high-priced electric roadster was the boss's car. Seeing it there among the pick-ups and Jeeps and SUVs gave R.C. an idea of the kind of man they'd find inside.

Douglas Timber's interior was all done in handsome wood paneling, of course, and a large, polished wooden reception desk faced the front doors as they entered. Between that and the paneling and the hardwood floor, the place felt more like an Old West saloon than a modern lumber company. R.C. had a strong urge to order a drink as he bellied up to the bar, and he must have unconsciously fallen into a cowboy swagger because he heard Nick smother a giggle behind him.

"Can I help you, sir?" The girl behind the counter was young and pert, roughly college age, with a ruddy complexion and long brown hair that said she might have some Native in her but clear blue eyes that said it wasn't alone. Her manner was friendly enough, and R.C. didn't see any reason to scare her so he kept his own voice calm and quiet and his smile disarming.

"We'd like a word with Mr. Douglas. Is he in?"

She didn't miss a beat, proving she wasn't new to this job. "I'm sorry, I'll need to check his schedule. Do you have an appointment?"

"We don't need one," Nick declared as she reached past him to flash her badge in the girl's face. Leave it to her to get impatient.

"Oh!" The girl took a quick step back, though that might have been because Nick had practically scraped her cute little nose with the wallet. "Yes, of course. I'll call him and tell him you're here."

"Don't worry about that." R.C. put just enough edge in his voice to make her stop in mid-reach for the phone. "We'll let ourselves in. You just sit tight and don't say a word, okay?" Her nod was quick, scared, but she seemed honest enough.

Besides, though he'd prefer to surprise Douglas in order to catch him off-guard, it wasn't actually necessary. If she did warn him, they'd still manage.

Nick had already brushed past the desk and turned left, heading for the end office the girl had just pointed toward. R.C. went after his partner, and caught up to her in time to pound on the door.

Then he simply opened it and walked in.

"What the— you can't just barge in here! Janice! Janice!" Salvador Douglas was a small man, R.C. saw at once, and like many small men he surrounded himself with big things to increase his own stature. The office was larger than it needed to be, with a veritable acre of space between the massive wooden desk by one end and the overstuffed leather couch and matching armchairs arrayed around a low coffee table at the other. Framed pictures hung on the walls, showing Douglas deep-sea fishing, big-game hunting, hacking through massive redwoods—manly pursuits involving high stakes or major exertion or both. A polar bear rug R.C. suspected might be real covered a large stretch of the floor, and handsome Oriental rugs sandwiched it. No trace of Native artistry anywhere in the room, R.C. noticed.

Then again, it wasn't like Douglas had any Native in him, either.

His skin was dark enough to be Salish, but it was the wrong shade, olive rather than ruddy, and his dark hair had the rich sheen one expected from someone of Hispanic or Italian descent. He was narrow but not skinny, wiry and fit, and his long face was deeply lined, with strong, sharp features. A cigar smoldered in the marble ashtray on his desk, and the rich tobacco smell filled the room, mingling with the sharp bite of the brandy that no doubt filled the snifter beside it.

Clearly Salvador Douglas liked the finer things in life—and wanted to make sure people knew he could afford them.

"It isn't Janice's fault," Nick was already informing the man as R.C. completed his visual sweep of the room—he also registered that there were two other doors, near either corner of the wall behind the desk, and guessed that one led to a private bathroom but the other could open into a closet, a subordinate's office, or even a panic room. "We wouldn't take no for an answer."

"Who the hell are you?" Douglas demanded. He started rising from his chair—an enormous leather wingback, R.C. couldn't help noticing—but Nick shoved her badge in his face and he dropped heavily back down. "FBI? What do you want with me? I've paid my taxes." The last was said with a smirk, and R.C. resisted the urge to wipe that arrogant grin off the man's face. He had to keep his cool here.

"Mr. Douglas," he said instead. "I'm Special Agent Hayes. This is my partner, Special Agent Frome. We'd like to speak with you about your logging operation in the Hog Heaven range on the Flathead Indian Reservation."

Douglas was a smooth operator, R.C. had to give him that. The man barely flinched at the name. "What about it?" he asked instead. "We were given permission to log there. I have the paperwork, if you'd like to see it."

"We would, yes." It was clear the man hadn't really thought they'd say that, but he recovered quickly enough and pressed a button on his phone.

"Janice, bring me the paperwork for the Hog Heaven operation, please," he said. His tone was well-modulated, his enunciation crisp and clear, but R.C. thought the man had spent a lot of time practicing speaking—it had that over-rehearsed quality to it. And despite his best efforts, his voice was still thin and reedy, a narrow voice for a narrow man.

"Right away, sir," the receptionist replied. A faint quaver said she hadn't gotten over her own fright yet, but a minute later she knocked and bustled in to deliver a folder to her boss. She barely glanced at Nick and R.C. as she beat a hasty retreat.

"Here you are," Douglas told them, presenting the folder. "I think you'll find it's all in order."

R.C. flipped it open and glanced at topographical maps and logging estimates and preliminary timetables before reaching the permit. He studied that one closely, and Nick came over to peruse it as well.

"Thomas Peel signed this," R.C. pointed out after a minute. "There are some other signatures here, but most of them aren't legible."

"Oh?" Douglas acted surprised. "Let me see." He held out a hand—his nails were impeccable, R.C. saw, and a gaudy gold watch hung loosely around his wrist, peeking out beneath the cuff of his expensive, tailored shirt—and R.C. handed it over. "Oh, yes. That's Jeffrey Windborn, and Marcus Gardipe and Brian Gray and Michael Steele, and the last one is Andrew Ashley." He gave them a smile that would have looked at home on a used-car salesman. "Six signatures, which represents a quorum. All perfectly legitimate and aboveboard."

"Except that Ashley and Steele aren't on the council," R.C. countered as he reclaimed the paper. He'd taken the time the other day to learn the names of the ten council members, and those two weren't familiar at all. "I'm betting they were on the council previously, though, right? But they aren't there now, and so their votes wouldn't count. And even with a majority, the decision would still have to be ratified by the chairman, whose signature is not on here. None of these men have the authority to authorize such an operation."

The flicker of fear in Douglas's dark eyes, the way they widened and then narrowed, and the way he flared his nostrils, all told R.C. that his guess had been correct. Only Peel had been actively involved—the others had been coerced, bribed, or just misled. It had been either that or the other names were senior members but not their actual signatures, and Douglas struck him as too careful to try something that obvious.

"Really?" was all the timber man said once he'd recovered. "Are you sure? Thomas assured me that it wouldn't be a problem."

"Maybe so," Nick snapped, "but regardless, he was wrong. The rest of the council had no idea, and they most definitely do not want any logging up there. Permission rescinded." It was clear she didn't like Douglas any more than R.C. did, and she wasn't bothering to hide it.

"I'm afraid it's not that simple, my dear." Again the oily smile, this time wide enough to display a gold tooth. Could this man look more like a pimp from New York's cheesy 70s era? Maybe he had a purple striped suit and a broad-brimmed, feathered hat tucked away in the closet for special occasions. "I accepted the permit on good faith. If there were false pretenses among the council, that's not my concern."

"We can make it your concern," R.C. warned him. "It all depends on whether you cooperate."

Douglas spread his hands wide. "Of course, Agent Hayes—I'm always happy to help a duly authorized government official. What can I do for you?"

"How long ago did you negotiate with Thomas Peel for this permit?"

"You have the permit in your hand," Douglas pointed out. "It's dated and notarized, see for yourself."

R.C. put on his best tough-guy scowl and took a step forward so he could lean over the desk. "I want to hear it from you." He was pleased to see Douglas shrink back in his shadow.

"Well, that would have been a week or two ago." Douglas closed his eyes and frowned, then glanced up again. The concentration had wiped away his smug demeanor. "Yes, about two weeks ago. It took a day or two to straighten out all the details, and then to select the best spot, and then we set up our camp and got to work."

R.C. glanced down at the permit. It was dated the 14th, which was eleven days ago. That matched with the timetable in the folder as well. "So your men started logging around the sixteenth?"

"I think so, yes. Rick would know for certain." At their glance, he explained. "Rick Marshall. He's my top foreman. He's in charge of the operation there."

"Uh huh. Big guy, pale, black beard?" Douglas nodded. So that had been the man they'd met the night before, the one who'd tried to scare them away from the logging equipment. It made sense. R.C. turned to Nick, and she nodded.

"Elk in the Trees was found on the seventeenth," she said. She kept her voice low but Douglas clearly heard, and frowned.

"The dead hunter? Is that what this is about?" He leaned forward, and for once he seemed sincere. "Agents, I assure you, I had nothing to do with that man's death. Nor did any of my men."

"Yet he was found dead less than a hundred yards from your logging camp," R.C. said. "And the other two men were also found in the area."

"I know, and it's horrible." Douglas picked up his partially smoked cigar, studied it for a second, and then put it back unpuffed. "I admit there may be some . . . irregularities about my permit, but that's all. I'm a businessman, not a killer. How would it help me any to murder people who wandered near my logging operations? Especially when they're completely legitimate? That just gets me negative publicity and runs the risk of the operation being closed down for investigation."

"So your men didn't report anything strange or unusual in the area?" R.C. thumbed through the file again, studying Douglas over the papers, but the smaller man just shook his head.

"No. As I said, Rick might have more information, and you're welcome to speak to him either here or at the camp, but I haven't heard anything but standard progress reports. We're completely on schedule, no problems at all." That brought just a hint of that smirk back to his lips.

"Not anymore," Nick corrected. "You're shut down, as of right now."

The smirk widened, which was about the worst thing he could have done. "Oh, I think it'll take more than a word from you, my dear. You can cordon off our site, certainly, but we'll just move things over a few dozen yards and start again. That way we aren't disturbing your investigation, hm? But shutting down the whole operation? Even with that nice shiny badge of yours, you'll need a court order for that."

"A court order? Okay." R.C. pulled out his phone, cycled through, and dialed a number. "Hello, Judge Wilder? This is Special Agent Hayes from the FBI. Yes sir, they said they had. Well, actually there is—we need a cease and desist order for a logging operation in the Hog Heaven range of the Flathead Indian Reservation. Douglas Timber. Yes, it's part of our investigation. Thank you, sir." He hung up and turned to the timber man, unable to resist the grin that erupted across his face. "You'll have your court order within the next twenty minutes. Don't touch anything up there, and tell your men to stay away from it as well. It's now a crime scene."

"That—you—but—!" It was clear that Douglas was so angry

he couldn't even form coherent words. R.C. considered that one for the Win column. "I'll—!"

Nick cut him off there. "Now I know you weren't about to threaten a pair of federal agents who acted entirely within the course of their duty, were you, sir?" Her voice had gone low, cold, and deadly. "Because that would be federal offense, punishable by a hefty fine and some prison time. That wasn't your intention, was it?" Douglas wisely clamped his mouth shut, though the glare he gave her was nothing short of murderous. "A wise choice, my dear," she taunted, and then turned and sashayed out.

R.C. shrugged. "Never a good idea to piss her off." He pulled one of his business cards out of his jacket pocket and tossed it down on the desk, then held up the folder. "We'll be taking this as evidence." He added a grin of his own. "Have a nice day." Then he followed his partner out.

6

R.C. waited ten minutes before asking, "So, what do you think?"

"Think?" He watched Nick's hands tighten on the wheel and felt the lurch as the car shot forward. "I think he's an arrogant little prick who tries to cover up his obvious inadequacies with a bunch of macho posturing! I think he's a lowlife scum who'd probably sell his own mother if he could turn a profit off the deal! I think he's only an American because nobody's offered him more money! I think he's never had a woman he didn't pay for, and even then they laughed at him afterward!"

"That's probably all true," he conceded amiably, "but what I meant was, do you think he's got anything to do with these murders?"

"Oh." There was silence for a minute, and when she spoke again it was with less anger, though she still bit off each word. "No, probably not."

"Yeah, I didn't think so either." What Douglas had said in his defense actually made a lot of sense. Unfortunately. The man was running a legitimate business that used some semi-legitimate methods to get contracts and permits. Which meant any official scrutiny could tumble the whole house of cards. Why risk that?

"Maybe Elk in the Trees figured out what he was up to, and about the phony signatures, and tried to blackmail him?" But even as she suggested the idea Nick was shaking her head. "But he's just an old, semi-retired hunter—how would he have even found out? And wouldn't he try forcing Douglas to pack it up completely, rather than asking for a handout?"

"That would actually give him motive," R.C. agreed, leaning his head back against the headrest, shutting his eyes, and letting the sun's warmth heat his face and neck. "Douglas had a strict timetable for this project—what if he was only counting on getting half of it done before people figured out his little ruse and shut him down? He'd need to clear as many trees as possible in the first week, in order to make any money off the operation. Then along comes Elk in the Trees, threatening to rat him out if he doesn't get the hell out of Dodge. But in order to do that, Douglas has to leave early, which means little to no profit." He shrugged. "So he kills Elk in the Trees and keeps right on logging."

"Okay, but why kill the other two?" Nick asked. "Elk in the Trees was a hunter, but Peter Colman was a college student. And Roger Tanner was a fisherman. Could all three have somehow figure out what Douglas was up to? That doesn't track. And there's no evidence that they knew each other, beyond maybe saying hi at tribe functions."

"No, you're right, that doesn't make much sense." He sighed and rubbed a hand across his face. "Besides, I didn't see any weapons on those loggers last night except for a few axes. Most of them probably had knife of some sort, and I could even see a gun tucked away for emergencies. But a bow and arrow? What would one of these guys be doing with something like that?"

Nick nodded. "We should question them anyway, of course. Besides, that'll just piss Douglas off more." The grin never reached her eyes. "But right now I'd guess they weren't behind this."

"I agree." He pinched the bridge of his nose. "Which means we still don't have any real suspects. Or know what happened, except the obvious."

"Well, once we make it back I know a place that might have a few of the answers." She smiled slowly, and absolutely refused to tell him what she'd meant or even to hint at it.

R.C. hated to be kept in the dark about anything.

"How'd it go with Douglas?" Jonathan asked by way of greeting when they walked into the council room. Thomas and a few others who'd been around that morning were missing, R.C. noticed.

"He won't be logging up there anymore," he replied. "We shut that down." An approving rumble swept through the council elders. "But it doesn't look like Douglas had anything to do with the murders." He sighed. "We're back to square one. So we were hoping you might have some information you just hadn't shared yet."

The rumble had changed to a more scattered noise, which split still further as most of the elders shook their heads.

"Sorry," Jonathan offered, hands in his jeans pockets. "I looked into it after you left this morning. It was just like I thought—no autopsy reports. And all three bodies were burned."

R.C. bit back a curse, and saw Nick do the same. No sense in antagonizing the very people they were here to help. Especially since it wasn't their fault—they hadn't known they might need the bodies for evidence.

"What about the murder weapons?" he asked. And almost forgot to breathe when Jonathan smiled in reply—and then retrieved a long, thin object in a plastic bag and handed it over. Yes!

Carrying his prize over to one of the windows, R.C. held it up for inspection. Nick was right beside him.

"Okay, it's an arrow," she said after a second. "Looks homemade, too."

He nodded. Even through the plastic that much was obvious. The shaft was straight enough but it didn't look perfectly smooth or perfectly even, its surface just a little bumpier and its outline tapering here and bulging there. The feathers at the back end looked like real feathers, not fancy or fake, and though they were clean and straight there was just enough variation in them to believe that someone had fletched the arrow by hand.

The head was perhaps the most interesting part. Long and narrow, with an obviously wicked point, the arrowhead didn't gleam at all in the sunlight. It was cold, though, even through the plastic. Squinting at it, R.C. saw that the edges weren't perfectly smooth, either. They looked—chipped.

The arrowhead was made of flint.

Nick agreed with his assessment once he mentioned it, and

Jonathan confirmed that the other two arrows looked exactly like this one. So their killer made his own arrows—and from found or scavenged materials, wood and feathers and flint but no metal. That didn't help them catch him, not right off the bat, but it did mean he probably had a limited number of these on hand. That was something, anyway.

"What's the next move?" Jonathan asked R.C. once he finally returned the arrow.

"I don't know," R.C. admitted. "We've checked the scene, examined the murder weapon, and spoken to both local experts and potential suspects." He shook his head. "I think we're at a dead end—the best we can do now is wait and hope something new turns up."

"And, in the meantime, we can get some lunch," Nick suggested. R.C. decided that his partner had a point. It had been hours since their big breakfast, and hassling possible suspects took a lot of energy.

If they had to wait, they might as well do it on a full stomach.

Brrrrringgg.

R.C. fished the phone out of his pocket and checked the number. He didn't recognize it but it looked like a Montana area code. "Hello?"

"Agent Hayes?" The voice was young, soft, and familiar. "It's Jonathan, Detective Couture."

"Oh, hey, Jonathan. What's up?" The lunch had turned into dinner, and now into breakfast again. At this rate they'd be too fat to move by the time they got a break in the case.

The young detective's next words proved him wrong, and sent a jolt through him that had nothing to do with his second cup of strong, fresh coffee:

"There's been another body."

R.C. was on his feet and tossing down his napkin before Jonathan had finished talking. "Same area?" he asked, throwing down a few bills. "Right, we're on our way."

"Victim number four," Nick asked as they headed outside to their car.

"Looks that way," he answered. "But there's a difference this time. The person who called it in? Rick Marshall."

"The Douglas Timber foreman? The one who isn't supposed to be anywhere near there, along with all of his men?" Nick whistled. "This ought to be interesting."

Privately, R.C. agreed. He just wasn't sure "interesting" was what they needed right now.

It took them several hours to get up to the range, and they had to hike the last leg after the terrain got too tough for their car—R.C. made a mental note to request off-road capabilities for any similar assignments in future. By the time they got close they could follow the flashing lights and the sound of raised voices straight to the scene.

Apparently the local law was here in force.

"Hold it right there!" A man in a police uniform got in their path as R.C. and Nick emerged from the trees and strode toward the logging camp. Except the camp itself was empty. The police tape and flashing lights and people were all gathered back and to one side of it. "This area is off-limits!" The man was young and fit, R.C. noticed, and had sturdy hiking boots under his uniform pants. Smart. His tone was strong, authoritative, without being mean, but R.C. didn't have time for niceties.

"Not to us," he replied, flashing his badge. "FBI. Where's your boss?"

The young patrolman turned to let them past, and pointed at a man in the center of the commotion. R.C. followed the gesture.

"Excuse me, sir?"

The man who turned at his call was average height, stocky, and blond, with reddish skin that said he'd seen too much sun and a wispy mustache probably supposed to make him look more intimidating. "Ah, you must be the Feds." His voice wasn't any more impressive, pleasant and mellow and a little hoarse.

Probably from shouting at the burly men surrounding him, several of whom R.C. recognized.

"That's right." He gave the police officer his patented "I'm a nice guy but I'm also a Fed, don't mess with me" grin. "Special Agent Hayes and this is Special Agent Frome. You must be Detective Couture's boss."

"I am, at that." He offered a hand. "Police Captain Roy Moran, pleased to meetcha."

"Captain." R.C. shook hands with him—the captain's grip was firm, at least—and then turned his attention to the black-bearded man glaring at them both. "And you must be Rick Marshall. I didn't get your name the other night, but your boss told it to me when I visited him yesterday."

If being identified fazed him at all, Marshall's scowl didn't show it. "Yeah, so what? You gonna do something about this, or you gonna be just like the rest of these tin stars?"

Tin stars? "Well, let's talk about it and see." R.C. felt a hand on his arm and turned.

"I'm going to poke around," Nick told him quietly. "It's been a few hours, but we might still get lucky, find some fresh tracks or something. Keep them occupied?"

"You got it." He glanced down at her. "Be careful. Whoever this guy is, he's a damn good shot, and we're in his playground."

"I know. But at least this time I'm better prepared." Nick grinned and raised one foot, tugging the cuff of her pants up to show off the hiking boots there. She'd remembered to slip into them today to keep from ruining her good shoes any more than she already had.

He bit back a comment about her showing some leg and just nodded instead.

He also did his best not to watch as she slunk off into the woods. Just friends, damn it. Just partners and friends.

"Now, let's get this all sorted out," he said instead, turning back to Marshall and the captain and the others. "First off, where's the body?"

"'The body' has a name, Jeff Landis," Marshall snapped. "He's one of my guys, has been for three years now. And he's right over there."

There was a draped form on the ground next to some trees a few yards away, two more uniformed cops standing guard over it with rifles in hand. R.C. stepped between them, knelt, and flipped back the sheet. The man staring up at him was definitely Caucasian, tanned and weathered with short brown hair and sideburns, and definitely dead. He had a ragged hole in his throat, right where his carotid had been—but nothing jutting out but jagged, bloody flesh. "Where's the arrow?"

"Over here," one of the tribal police replied, nudging something with his foot. R.C. sidled across. It was a match for the others they'd found, and out of the plastic he could better appreciate the artistry that had gone into its fashioning. Whoever had made these was a master craftsman, and they were as beautiful and graceful as they were deadly.

"What's it doing away from the body?" he asked. "Who removed it?"

"I did," Marshall answered, stepping around the captain to confront R.C. across the roots and leaves and trampled grass. "I got to him first and yanked it out, but it was already too late. He died on me." Now R.C. noticed the blood spattered across the foreman's arms and chest and neck.

"You idiot." He kept his tone mild as he rose to face the bearded logger. "That arrow is evidence, and you messed with it. It could have had the killer's fingerprints all over it, but know we'll never know." He shook his head. "Still, your friend was dying and you acted on instinct. Can't really blame you for that." He registered exactly what the other man had said. "Wait, you said you got to him first? So you saw him get hit?"

"Hell yeah, we all did," Marshall answered. "We were all here together and suddenly Jeff gulps and freezes. Then he just topples over."

"What were you doing here in the first place?" This time R.C. did let a little steel seep into his voice. "There's a cease-and-desist on your operation, and the camp itself is a crime scene. You were trespassing." Or close to it, since the body was actually some forty feet from the camp's edge.

"It's our stuff!" Marshall snapped back. "We didn't want no greedy redskins making off with any of it!" Now R.C. realized that many of the loggers carried hunting rifles, though they were keeping them low and sticking to the shadows so as not to draw attention to the fact.

He shook his head. "So you and your men came back out here, armed, to a place where several people had died already? And then you're surprised when one of your own becomes the next victim?" At least that confirmed that the loggers weren't behind the deaths—why would they shoot one of their own if they were? And he still didn't see any signs of a bow among them.

"You think we're just gonna back off?" Marshall's face was turning red, and his brows had dropped so low they were starting to hide his eyes. "This is our camp, our gear, our livelihood! Nobody's gonna run us off, and what's a few dead locals to us, anyway?" His big, scarred hands bunched into fists. "But now they killed Jeff. Now it's personal."

"Now you're all under arrest," R.C. replied sharply, reining in his own temper. "For obstruction of justice, tampering with evidence, and whatever other charges I can come up with to throw at you." He nodded to the officers, who started to move forward, and then reached for his own pistol when the loggers began to raise their rifles. "Is this going to have to get ugly?"

Fortunately, Marshall wasn't completely stupid—R.C. had been counting on that, figuring Douglas was too canny to put a man in charge if he couldn't think things through. Which was a good thing, since there were at least as many loggers here as tribal cops, and he wasn't sure they could actually follow through on his threat to arrest them all if they decided to resist. "Now, hold on a second." Marshall raised both hands, fingers splayed, and the glare he sent back over his shoulder made his men pause and lower their weapons again. "Nobody wants to cause trouble here. One of our friends is dead, we're a little riled up, but that's all. We want this guy caught as much as you do. And we didn't actually set foot in the camp—we were just patrolling around it, standing guard."

"Then back off," R.C. warned. "Get your men out of here, and stay clear. I will find who's doing this, and I will bring them to justice, but if you get in my way again I'll take you down, too." He held Marshall's gaze until the bearded foreman looked away.

"Fair enough." Marshall turned his back on R.C. and summoned his men with an impatient wave. "Let's go, guys. Leave the Fed and the cops to do their thing." He glanced back at R.C. "But if you don't settle this, we will." The warning was calm, which worried R.C. It wasn't a threat, it was a promise.

He just nodded, though. "I'll take care of it."

"You really gonna let them go?" Captain Moran asked as the loggers began slipping away into the woods. "Those boys could be trouble."

"Could be," R.C. agreed, "but do you really want to haul them all in?" He laughed at the look on the other man's face. "It's not like I have a jail, Captain—you and your officers would have to handle them, not me." He shook his head. "I think I made my point. They'll stay out of our way." At least for now. He just hoped they could find something before the loggers got impatient and took matters into their own hands. There was no telling who they might go after.

His eyes flicked to the dead body again. "This is the first time one of the loggers has been killed," he mused aloud. "Why?" He turned to see what Nick thought—and realized she wasn't there.

And it felt like she'd been gone for a long time.

Too long.

"Nick?" He started away from the camp and further into the woods, listening for a reply. "Hey, Nick!"

He took a few steps, and suddenly he was in among the trees, their towering heights and waving branches cutting off the light and casting him in near darkness even though it was early afternoon. The downed leaves and branches muffled sound, making it feel as if he'd stepped into a different world, dark and drowsy and quiet.

Until a piercing scream split that heavy silence.

The thunder crack that followed galvanized R.C. into a run. He knew from far too much experience that it wasn't thunder he'd just heard.

It was gunfire.

"Nick!"

He hurtled headlong into the woods.

7

"**N**ick!" R.C. ran, stumbling over roots and branches and uneven ground, thrusting branches aside as they grabbed at his hair and arms and clothes, pistol out and held before him to shield his face. He could barely see, his eyes still not adapted to the shadows after the bright sunlight of the logging camp's clearing, and he squinted to make out shapes as he swerved to avoid tree trunks looming up at him out of the murkiness.

The shot—and the scream—had come from somewhere up ahead. He was sure of it.

The scream had been a woman's, and he was sure it had been Nick's, though he'd never heard her scream like that before, not even in that one firefight. His blood ran cold at the thought of what could have produced such a sound from her now.

The shot had almost certainly been hers as well, and he could only hope she had hit whatever—or whomever—she'd aimed for.

The fact that he hadn't heard a second shot—or another scream—was either a very good sign, or a very bad one.

He was almost afraid to find out which.

Finally, after what felt like hours, he spotted a splotchy patch through the trees on the ground up ahead and to the left. It looked too large to be most animals, too small to be a downed tree, and its paler patches were light enough to be fair skin, its darker sections easily right for a navy suit.

Nick.

Now he could see her light brown hair.

And the fact that she was curled up in a ball on the ground—and wasn't moving.

"Nick!"

He skidded to a stop beside her, and sank to his knees, rolling her over. Her head lolled in his lap, and the arrow that jutted up from her neck brushed against his side, its fletching tickling at his ribs through his shirt. There was blood pumping from the wound, spraying out around the arrowhead, and he put his hand over it, fingers around the shaft, pressing down to stop the flow, but all that did was cause it to seep out around his fingers instead. He could feel her pulse flickering, slowing.

"Nick!" he didn't dare shake her, but he put as much urgency into his voice as he could. "Hang on!"

Her eyes fluttered open and she glanced up at him, but they were already unfocused. "R.C.? Hey." Her voice was so soft he could barely hear her, even in the quiet of the woods. "I think . . . I got a clue."

"Yeah, lucky you." He tried to keep the sob from his own voice, and only partially succeeded. "Hold on, okay? We'll get you some help."

"Little late for that." Her smile was sad and barely tugged at her lips, which were already turning pale. "Hey, that night?" He didn't have to ask which one she meant. "Sorry."

"You don't have to be," he assured her. "Anyway, I'm not."

"No, dummy." Her voice was growing weaker. "Sorry . . . I don't regret it. Good thing this happened, or Nancy . . . might have had . . . a fight on her hands." The last words were barely a whisper.

"I'll tell her to be ready, once you're healed up," he told her, but it was too late. Her eyes had stopped focusing on him, staring up at something only she could see, and now they went wide, glazing over. A last breath rattled up from her chest, which went still. The wound was no longer leaking between his fingers, and her skin was turning cold, no pulse threading through it.

She was gone.

"I'm so sorry," he whispered, and kissed her forehead.

A whistling from the trees snapped R.C. out of his grief, and he brought his head up, looking around—

—just in time to see something leap out from the trees.

"What the—?" Instinctively he pulled back, ducking down and turning slightly though Nick's body hampered him from going very far, and felt a sharp, burning sting as something sliced his cheek. But there had been no sound beyond the whistling, and a thin rush of air like a narrow breeze.

An arrow!

His pistol had fallen to the leaves beside him when he'd gathered Nick in his arms, and now R.C. scooped it up and fired where the arrow had appeared.

Bam!

The gun's report was deafening in the forest.

He didn't hear anyone grunt from pain, so he had to assume he'd missed. Not surprising, given he couldn't actually see anything over there. Also, the cut along his cheek was stinging worse now, and the pain was distracting him.

But the shadows all around him seemed to grow deeper suddenly.

Then the whistling sound picked up, its tone growing sharper, more ominous. And it now echoed from several other spots, as if a dozen small winds were cutting through the trees ahead of him. The eerie noise made the hair on the back of his neck stand up, and his skin crawl.

Something was coming. He could feel it, even if he couldn't see or hear it. Something bad. Something . . . angry.

Blam! Blam! Blam!

The loud reports came from behind him, and R.C. glanced back—and stared.

A woman had emerged from the woods the same way he'd come before, and she was walking slowly toward him, her steps sure and steady through the forest's undergrowth. She had a shotgun clasped in her hands, an assault-style military shotgun rather than the usual hunting variety, and it was that she was firing at the trees.

The echoes from her shots shattered the wind, the whistling

fading, and the shadows seemed to draw back as well.

Then she had dropped to a crouch beside him.

"Here," she said, pulling a cloth from a pocket in her tailored hunting jacket and handing it to him. Her gaze never left the trees, however. "This will draw out the poison." Her voice was deep and husky, and her words were heavily accented.

Poison? R.C. realized that his cheek had stopped stinging—in fact, it seemed to have gone numb, and his jaw and brow and eyelid on that side felt heavy and slack and nonresponsive, as if they had gone to sleep. "Thanks." The word came out slightly slurred, and he took the cloth and pressed it against the cut. Almost at once he felt a tingling of pain return to his face. "What is it?"

She shrugged. "Mithridate." She stared at the trees a second longer, than lowered her shotgun. "They have gone. For now. But we must go. They will return, and they will be angry."

"Who? Who will return?" He shook his head—it felt fine now, except for the sting of the cut, and even that was no longer extreme, just a nagging burn like any flesh wound. "And I can't just go." He glanced down at Nick.

"Ah." The strange woman turned to study Nick, checking her pulse, her eyes, and the neck wound before sitting back on her haunches. "She is gone. I am sorry."

"I know." He'd already known there was nothing anyone could do for Nick. Except stay with her.

"We must go," the woman insisted again, and R.C. turned to study her properly. Strong, striking features—maybe not classically pretty, but certainly arresting, alluring. Definitely foreign, with that olive complexion, those strong cheekbones, the sultry lips, the clear green eyes at a slight slant, the thick, dark blonde hair. She handled herself well, too—she'd fired that assault shotgun like a pro, and even now she kept half an eye on the woods and one hand on the weapon's stock, ready to raise it and fire at a moment's notice. He'd had enough training to recognize a fellow soldier, and could see some of that in her poise and her combat reflexes, but at the same time it didn't match with any organization he could think of. She wasn't American, definitely, but she wasn't Mossad or MI5 or even Spetznaz or any of the other military units he knew. Who was she?

That wasn't his top concern right now, however. "I'm not leaving her," he replied, clutching Nick's body closer.

The woman studied him for a moment, then shrugged again. "Very well." She rose to her feet and paced in front of him, shotgun now raised and at the ready. "Your friends will have heard the shots. They should be here soon. I am staying at the Kwataqnuk. You can find me there."

She stalked forward, long legs carrying her soundlessly across the forest floor, and disappeared among the trees.

R.C. wasn't even sure she'd really been there. Except that he still held the cloth she'd given him, wadded up in his hand. He could smell a mild minty odor rising from its folds, along with the faintest whiff of perfume.

"Agent Hayes! Agent Hayes!" The shout came from back behind him, and he recognized the hoarse bellow as Captain Moran's.

"Over here!" he shouted back, though his voice was thick with grief and he wasn't sure just how clear the words had been.

Apparently it had been enough. A minute later Moran came barreling through the trees, one of his officers right behind him. He slammed to a halt and nearly fell over when he saw R.C. there, and even in the gloom R.C. could see the other man's eyes go wide at the sight of Nick's body splayed across him.

"We need an EMT!" Moran started to shout, but his request faltered when R.C. shook his head. "Damn." The Captain sank down beside him. "I'm real sorry, Agent Hayes." He sounded like he meant it, and R.C. automatically reevaluated the Captain, mentally moving him from "useless fool" to "decent but out of his league."

"So am I." R.C. felt his jaw tense. "But not as sorry as they're going to be."

"Did you see who did it?" That was the uniformed officer, who had hung back and now peered around with frightened eyes, looking anywhere but at Nick's body. Poor kid had probably never even seen a dead body before, and now he got two in one day. A real education, but he seemed to be coping.

R.C. shook his head. "No. I got off a shot or two, and they

clipped me in return, but I couldn't see anything." He didn't mention the woman—it was obvious from the way they were looking around that the Captain and his men didn't know anything about her, and for now he decided to leave it that way. Things were confusing enough without adding a mystery woman and an assault shotgun into the mix. He'd have plenty of questions for her later, though.

"Coroner's on his way for the logger," Moran said after a minute. His eyes strayed to Nick, and his voice was gentle. "I'll let him know to collect her, too."

"Thank you." R.C. shifted his legs slightly—they'd started to fall asleep under Nick's body, though she had never been heavy. In death she seemed to weigh more, which went against everything he'd ever heard about the body becoming lighter without the soul or whatever. Still, he wasn't about to let her go, not until he had to.

He was in shock, he knew. He could feel it insulating him, a pleasantly numb wall allowing him to function through his grief, and he knew that wasn't entirely a bad thing. Without it he doubted he'd be able to answer a question coherently, or move around, or think about what to do next.

Once the shock faded, he'd feel the full impact of Nick's death. That's when the grief would hit, and he knew from bitter experience that it could be overwhelming. He had to keep that walled off for now.

He had to hold himself together until he could catch whoever had done this to her.

As Rick Marshall had said, now it was personal.

8

"You were lucky," the doctor said as he stitched up R.C.'s cheek. "Nice clean cut, perfect edges, easy to suture. What'd they use, a scalpel?"

"An arrow," R.C. replied mechanically. They'd given him a topical anesthetic for the wound, but honestly he'd barely felt it anyway. As the doctor had said, it was a clean slice, almost a paper cut in its width and precision, and after that woman had given him the cloth and the stinging had stopped there really hadn't been much pain.

Besides, he was still numb in general.

They had collected Nick's body, along with that of the logger, Jeff Landis. Both of them had been brought back here, to the tiny regional hospital of St. Luke's, which was still the largest medical center in the area. Non-Native medicine, anyway. Moran was checking on a next of kin for Landis, and then he'd deal with the body's final disposition from there. As far as Nick—she had a sister, R.C. knew, younger and wilder and estranged for years, and he thought she'd mentioned a maiden aunt once or twice. Both of her parents were dead, as was her older brother, though his ex-wife and son were still around somewhere. Nick hadn't exactly had close ties. The FBI tended to like that in its agents—unlike the military, which actually encouraged soldiers to have families so they had a reason to survive, the Bureau found it easier to put agents in dangerous situations if they didn't have people waiting for them back home.

He'd have to report in, of course. This wasn't just a murder investigation anymore. There were five dead now, for one thing, which made it technically a serial killer case. And one of those was an FBI agent, which made this a top priority.

It also meant he'd probably get pulled from it, since it was his partner who'd been killed.

He understood the reasoning behind that, but that didn't mean he had to like it.

It also didn't mean he had to set those gears in motion right away. He had at least an hour or two—he'd been injured himself, it was natural to assume he'd get that checked out, probably get some pain killers, and head back to his room for some rest before returning to his duties.

Instead he walked out of the hospital, hopped in his rented car and drove to Polson and through it, straight toward the lake—and the Kwataqnuk resort and casino.

A small part of him, the part that could still feel such things, was amused to note that the hotel part of the complex was in fact a Best Western. If Nick had known that, she might not have griped so much about their quaint little bed-and-breakfast.

The front entrance was two stories tall, with an inward-sloping ceiling and strange fake girders above the door connecting to pale jutting beams. It was like a strange fusion of industrial and rustic, with a bit of whitewashed hotel chain thrown in. Slot machines lined the walls to either side, and past them he saw entrances to the resort's restaurants and bars. The entire back wall was windows looking out onto the patio that faced the lake itself, and he was amazed to see the clear blue sky and realize it was still only early afternoon, and a bright, sunny day. It felt like it should be the dead of night, or at least a slate-gray sky before a storm, to match his mood.

There were plenty of people milling about within the resort, trying their luck at the slots or hanging out at the bar or coming or going from the restaurants or just lounging, talking, taking in the scenery. None of them were local, of course—the only Native faces he saw here were those working. Most of the people only spared him a glance, no doubt seeing a fellow traveler though his dark suit didn't exactly fit in with the jeans and khakis and sweaters he saw in abundance. None of that mattered, though, as his own gaze swept the wide, high-ceilinged space. He was only looking for one person in particular.

He finally spotted a dark blonde mane through the windows, and made his way toward the back, skirting people as he went. Glass doors led out to the patio, and she was sitting at a small table facing the water. A tall glass sat in front of her, its sides sweating from the ice cubes within.

A second glass sat untouched at the chair across from her.

"Water," she said as R.C. came around and sank down into that seat. "I thought you might need it." Now that he was able to focus on her he could hear her accent more clearly, with its broad, rich sounds.

"You're Italian?" His hand reached for the glass of its own accord, and he took a long swallow, the cold water soothing his throat as it went down. He did briefly wonder if she might have drugged it somehow, but what would be the point of that?

"Isabella Ferrara." She offered her hand, and he shook it. Her grip was firm, strong, her fingers long and graceful, her skin supple but callused on the palm and the fingertips. "And you are Reed Christopher Hayes but you prefer Crease, yes?"

That made him start—both the fact that she knew his name and the mention of his old nickname. "It's R.C.," he corrected automatically. "I haven't gone by Crease since I left the Army."

"Ah, yes, this is good to know." He could practically see her filing that knowledge away.

"Okay, who are you, exactly?" He leaned forward. "You know my name, you knew where to find me, and you were definitely prepared for trouble, but you're not with the Bureau."

That made her laugh, a deep, rich, rolling laugh R.C. was sure most men would find utterly intoxicating. A few heads did in fact turn to admire her here and there on the patio, but after a moment they all returned to their own conversations and activities. "No, I am not with the Bureau," she agreed after a moment, her voice still thick with amusement. "I work for . . . well, perhaps now is not the time for that, no? I am not here for them. I am here for me." She shrugged. "I had heard there was a problem here. I came to see what could be done. I see you were here first, so I stay back but I do not go. I wait to see if I can help."

"Help? Well, you definitely did that." He'd turned the events over and over in his head, replaying exactly what had happened there in the woods, and he was convinced he owed this stunning mystery woman his life. That arrow should have been the first of several, but her arrival—and the hail of slugs she'd directed at the trees—had clearly driven away their hidden assailant. He or she had escaped clean—R.C. had done a cursory check after the coroners' arrival before letting them lead him away—which meant whoever had killed Nick was still out there. But at least thanks to this woman's intervention R.C. wasn't laying on a slab next to her.

He tuned in on the rest of what she'd said. "Wait, you heard there was a problem? Where did you hear it from? Who told you, and what did they say?"

She shrugged again, and R.C. steadfastly tried to ignore the things that did to her chest. He mostly succeeded. "As to what, only that something of interest was occurring here on this reservation. As to who? Occult." She watched him as she said that, and he had the feeling she was waiting to gauge his reaction. The way she studied not only him but their surroundings, the way she shifted unconsciously whenever someone passed by the window behind her or moved elsewhere on the patio—he'd seen behavior like that before. In trained and hardened soldiers, but not all of them. Just the ones with a certain approach to life, death, and combat.

This woman was a hunter.

That fit with the way she'd handled that shotgun, out in the woods. He still couldn't tell where her training had been, but he was getting the impression she was very good at what she did.

Which didn't bring him any closer to figuring out what was going on.

Nor did her answer. "Occult? You mean you saw it in some tea leaves, or in the Tarot cards, something like that?" He hadn't taken her for a believer in that sort of thing, so he wasn't surprised when she shook her head.

"Not occult," she corrected. "O.C.L.T. Occult." Something about the spelling sounded familiar, and R.C. frowned, dredging his memories. But he couldn't place it.

"Okay, this is a group or something?" She nodded. "So they sent you out here to check on this, but I beat you to it." Another nod. "And you decided to stick around and lend a hand anyway." Another nod—he was on a roll. "Well, I can't offer you any official involvement, not without knowing your credentials and running it by my superiors, but I'm probably about to get pulled from the case anyway." He took another sip of water before setting the glass firmly on the table. "Until then, though, I want to figure out who killed my partner."

"Yes, we must identify the killer," Isabella agreed. She frowned, stroking her own glass and flicking away the droplets, her gaze nominally on the beverage but her focus clearly back in the woods. "What did you see?"

R.C. frowned as well, leaning back and calling up what he remembered. "Nothing but shadows," he admitted after a moment. "I couldn't even tell you if there was one attacker or many—it felt like there were a bunch of them, but Nick only took one arrow and I only caught the one, so it might just be one guy." He thought about mentioning the wind, and the strange whistling noises, but decided against it. No reason to let his superstitions run wild.

"I, too, thought there were many," Isabella agreed. "But I did not see either. That is a shame. Seeing would have made this easier. As it is, we must narrow down from what we know." She ticked off points by tapping her nails against the glass. "One, they like the woods. Two, they like the night and the shadows. Three, they are not easily seen or heard."

"Four, they have long, narrow feet." He told her about the footprints he and Nick had found . . . good God, only two days ago! He'd thought about withholding the information—what did he really know about this woman, after all? She could even be working with the killer, trying to see how much he knew and how close he was to catching them—but decided to share it in the end. After all, she had saved his life. And he was curious to see what she would make of it.

"Good, this is good," she commented after listening. "These long, narrow feet, and the arrows—this is good." She favored him with a sharp, knowing smile. "It is not Wendigo. This was a concern for me. They are very tough, very hard to kill. But this is a different beast entirely."

R.C. stared at her, the sun and lake and the tourists around them all forgotten. "I'm sorry, did you just say 'Wendigo'? As in, mythical Indian monsters that eat people?"

"Yes." She shrugged. "This is not them. I am relieved."

"We can discount a Native American boogeyman and you're relieved?" He studied her. "We can probably rule out Bigfoot, too—does that make you feel better?"

Her frown was back, but now it wasn't merely a look of concentration—it was directed at him, and it was clearly disapproving. "You do not take this seriously."

That made him half-rise from his chair, leaning toward her. "Seriously? Lady, my partner just took an arrow to the throat! I'm taking this very seriously!" Heads turned, and he forced himself to settle back down, lowering his voice as he continued, "I am deadly serious about catching whoever's behind this. What I'm not taking seriously is your suggestion that some sort of storybook monster is behind all this."

That got a sigh out of her, and R.C. suddenly felt like he'd just failed some sort of test. "We hoped you'd be more open-minded, yes? After your experiences in Uppsala?"

A second passed in silence before he realized he was staring at her again. What she'd said had completely floored him, and when he did find his voice it was raspy. "What do you know about that?"

"I know you face a troll there," she answered without any hint of joking or dismissal. "I know you lose the rest of your team, but you kill this troll. I am impressed—they are not easy to kill, trolls." She spoke that matter-of-factly, like she'd faced a few of them herself. "This is no troll, I think, but it is something of that ilk, perhaps. A dweller in the woods, fast, quiet, deadly. We must know what it is before we can know how to kill it."

But R.C. was already on his feet, kicking back his chair. "Those files—those files are classified," he managed backing away from her until he felt the railing cool across his legs. "And it was a homeless man." At least that's what it said in the official report.

Because no one would have believed the truth. That the real Uppsala killer had been a troll, hiding under bridges and devouring those foolish enough to cross its path—and that R.C. and his teammates had turned it to stone with a phosphorous grenade.

Nobody should have known that.

But this woman did.

Nothing was making sense anymore.

"A homeless man. Of course." Her tone was clearly mocking, as was the little half-smile on her full lips. "Perhaps, then, we face another homeless man here, hm?"

R.C. shook his head. It was all too much. "I can't deal with this right now," he muttered, as much to himself as to her. "I just—I can't."

Ignoring anything else she might say, he pushed away from the railing, barreling past her and through the glass doors, back into the resort and then through there as well, until he was back out on the street. He didn't slow his pace until he'd reached the Hawthorne House, taken the stairs two at a time, unlocked his door, and slammed it behind him. Then R.C. dropped onto his bed, cradling his head in his hands, and shook as his world started to crumble around him.

9

R.C. lay like that for the better part of an hour before he got his breathing under control. He felt weak, wrung out, and his hands shook as he pushed himself up into a sitting position and then leaned forward, resting his forearms across his thighs. Several deep breaths helped clear his head, and finally he was able to reach into his pocket and pull out his phone.

No point putting this off any longer.

"Get me AD Ebling," he instructed once the call had gone through and he'd identified himself. There was a short pause, and then a familiar no-nonsense voice came on the line.

"Hayes." As always, Assistant Director Madelyn Ebling managed to make his last name sound like a barking cough. "Report."

"The situation here at the Flathead reservation has exploded," he answered, trying to keep his response crisp and impersonal. Maybe that way it wouldn't hurt as much. "There are five dead so far, and we have no leads as to the assailant's identity." He had to pause there and gulp air, steeling himself for the next sentence and hoping to keep the quivering in his chest out of his voice. "Agent Frome was the most recent victim."

"Frome is dead?"

"Yes, sir."

"I see. That changes matters, as I'm sure you're aware." She didn't waste any time. "You're off this case, Hayes. Report back here immediately. And bring Frome's body and personal effects with you."

Her tone made it clear she thought the matter was closed, but R.C. wasn't ready to give up that easily. "I request that you reconsider," he said instead. He was careful to keep his words and tone formal. He knew that was how the assistant director preferred things. "Matters here seem to be escalating, and need to be dealt with quickly. I'm already on-site and already versed on the situation, plus I already have established contact and working relations with the local authorities. I can get this done, sir."

"Maybe so, but you're not going to." There was no sympathy in her voice, not that he'd ever expected it, but there wasn't any anger or disgust either. Just calm, cool, and utterly dispassionate. "Everclean Ebling," they called her around the office—and well out of earshot. But now she was saying, "you know the drill, Hayes. Your objectivity has been compromised. In your current state you could make mistakes, put yourself and others in danger, and completely botch the investigation. We can't afford that. Any of it. Make arrangements to either bring Frome's remains or have her shipped back here, and then get back here yourself."

"What about everything that's been happening here?" R.C. asked. "We can't just leave these people unprotected."

But his boss had an answer there as well. "I'm dispatching your replacements now. You'll pass them en route—at most the reservation will be without FBI intervention for a few hours, maybe even as much as a whole morning or afternoon. I suspect they'll survive."

He started to argue that, but sighed and left the latest words unsaid.

Besides, what difference would it make? He was off the case. He couldn't disobey a direct order from a superior. All those years in the military had made sure of that. So his only reply was "Yes, sir."

He tossed the phone onto the bed behind him and just sat there staring off into space after they'd hung up.

That had gone about as well as he could have expected.

The woman at the front desk let him into Nick's room and then was nice enough to leave him alone while he packed up everything. It didn't take long—they'd only been here a few days, and neither of them had brought much beyond essentials. Besides, Nick hadn't been the type to spread everything everywhere. Most of her things were still in her carry bag, so really it was just a matter grabbing a few toiletries from the bathroom and the clothes she'd hung up in the closet, plus scanning the room to make sure he hadn't missed anything.

He tried hard not to think about what he was doing while he was casing her room. Tried to keep it at a distance, just going over a hotel room, collecting personal items, another mundane task, ho hum. That didn't work, though. He kept seeing her with everything he touched, everything he collected. Her hair brush had strands of hair still enmeshed in the bristles, the bathroom light making the gold in them shine the way her head had almost glowed in direct sunlight—he used to tease her about being the only FBI agent with a halo. Her spare shirt, freshly laundered by the hotel staff, hung in the closet, neat and clean, but there was still the faintest whiff of the wildflower scent she'd liked to wear. A sleep shirt had been tossed onto the pillow, no doubt when she'd gotten up this morning, and he fought back tears as he scooped it up and hurled it into her open bag, trying not to feel the softness of the well-worn cotton or smell her wildflowers and her mint shampoo from it, and most of all trying not to remember that time, that one time, when he had held her and caressed her and discovered just what lay beneath that shirt and those suits.

He couldn't get out of her room fast enough, but he forced himself to do a thorough job. It wouldn't have looked too good if Nick had kept a back-up pistol under her pillow and he left it there for the next guest or even the housekeepers. Nick would have laughed at that image, and he had to choke back tears when he could almost hear her throaty chuckle in his ear.

He'd packed his own things right after the phone call, and now he carried both bags down and out to the car. The Hawthorne House's manager watched him go. He'd told her why he'd needed Nick's things, of course—in a town this size, he'd figured she'd find out soon anyway—and he could still see the sympathy in her gaze.

After dropping the bags in the car, his next stop was the Tribal Council. "We are very sorry about your partner," Willy told him when he reached the council room and found the elders sitting there around the long table, as always. "She was a bright light snuffed out too soon." The old man's eyes were bright with compassion, and it was clear that his words were more than polite commiseration. He'd obviously felt loss himself, and his look said he knew what R.C. was going through.

"Yeah, she was. Thanks." R.C. tried to maintain his composure. "Anyway, I've been pulled from this case. Too much emotional investment now, too much personal interest. They're sending my replacements; they should be here in a few hours. But I need to go back now. I'm sorry." He felt like he was letting them down, these wizened old men with their braids and their tattoos and their beading. They'd greeted him and Nick, given them as much support and aid as they could, and trusted them to handle this problem. And it had only gotten worse.

But none of them glared at him, none of them cursed him under their breath. None of them seemed to be condemning him.

"We understand." That was Jonathan, who rose from his usual seat along the side and walked over. "We all wish you the best of luck, Agent Hayes. And thank you." He held out his hand, and R.C. shook it, touched by the clear gratitude the young detective radiated. Several of the council members came up to say good-bye as well, and to offer their condolences and their thanks, but finally R.C. was leaving the council behind and walking outside one last time.

Isabella was leaning against the hood of his car as he emerged onto the street again, arms folded across her chest, eyes scanning the street but locking onto him the minute he passed through the doors.

"You're leaving." It wasn't a question.

"I said this would happen," he reminded her, stopping a few feet away. "I've been pulled from the case. They've called me back to Denver."

She met that with a scowl. "They are abandoning this case?"

"No, just sending other agents to pick up where I left off." Agents who didn't just let their partner get killed, he added but didn't say. "They should be here soon."

"But they will not be you." She sighed. "This is not good. You are qualified to handle this matter. You have faced such things before."

"Whoever they send, they'll be good agents," R.C. assured her. He wasn't sure why he felt the need to convince this woman. True, she'd saved his life, but she'd shown up out of nowhere, knew way too much about him, and clearly believed in fairy tales and other nonsense. "They can handle it."

But the look she gave him told him without words to cut the crap. "They cannot. They will be good agents, yes, but not . . . open-minded. They will only see what they want to see, believe what they have been taught to believe. You know there is more out there. You can set aside old ideas, look with fresh eyes. That is what is needed here."

"Well, there's not much I can do about it." He was tired of arguing. "I've been pulled. The case's been reassigned. Now if you'll excuse me, I need to head over to the hospital and arrange for my partner's body to be returned to Denver. Then I need to head back to the office and get yelled at by my boss. It'll be a wonder if I don't get suspended."

She pushed herself off the car, arms lowering, but made no move to get out of his way. Instead, she stepped closer, her face only a few inches from his own, hands now hovering at her sides like a gunfighter preparing to draw. "Do you wish to leave?"

"What?" He tried to laugh it off, but that green gaze held him. "No," he admitted finally. "No, I don't. I want to catch this guy and put him down. For Nick. For all the others. And for all the people he could hurt if he isn't stopped."

"Good." The sharp nod said he'd passed that test, and for some reason he felt—relieved? Proud? "Perhaps I can help you with this."

"Help me stay on the case?" Now he did laugh, though it was a bitter one. "Lady, unless you've got some serious pull with the Bureau, you're dreaming."

She pulled back slightly and shook her head, though her flying golden mane didn't quite hide the small smile on her lips. "I? No, I am no one to the Bureau, and I wish to remain that way." That smile was still peeking out. "But perhaps—just perhaps . . ."

She left it at that, and R.C. shrugged. "Whatever. I need to get moving." He stuck out his hand. "Thank you again for saving my life last night."

"It is my pleasure." Her grip was still firm. "Perhaps someday you return the favor, yes?"

"Absolutely." He let go and edged past her, pulling open the car door. "Well, take care. And good luck."

"You as well, Special Agent Hayes." She pivoted to watch as he slid into the driver's seat, started the car, and pulled out. "We will see each other again."

Something about the way she said it, the absolute certainty in her rich voice, stayed with him as he drove away, her words and her gaze lingering even as she dwindled in his rearview.

10

R.C. usually enjoyed coming home. Even when home had just been a bunk at Wiesbaden, there was something satisfying about returning to your own space, to familiar surroundings, to a place where you'd carved out a niche and put your stamp upon it and marked it as uniquely yours. When whatever assignment he'd been sent on had gone well, it felt particularly good, coming home the conquering hero, success written across his face, his friends and co-workers cheering him on and congratulating him. Even when the mission had been a failure, it was a relief to go home, to have friends comfort him and support him, to know that he had people there watching his back, people who knew what he was going through and were looking out for him.

Coming home after losing a partner or a teammate, however—that was a whole different thing.

There were people offering condolences, of course. As he walked through the FBI's Denver office, which had been his home away from home the past two years, other agents stepped into his path to shake his hand and clap him on the back and tell him how sorry they were. Others nodded sadly as he moved past them, not wanting to intrude but letting him see they were there.

But those gestures of sympathy never seemed to reach their eyes. Their stares, hard and cold and mean, said something completely different. Those glares said, clear as shouts, "you let her die. We've lost a good agent, and it's all your fault." Every step he took, he could feel their eyes upon him, bearing down on him, judging him—and finding him wanting. Sentencing him for Nick's death, putting all that weight upon him, and telling him that no matter what happened from here on out, he would always be little more than a criminal to them, as if a cop killer had somehow escaped justice, put on a police uniform, and tried to hide in a police station. He was labeled now, and every false smile and fake handshake just served to remind him of that.

Walking that hall, from the front door to the AD's office, was one of the longest treks of his life.

"Come," Ebling snapped after his first knock, and R.C. pushed the door open. He slid in past it, shutting it behind him, and felt a guilty relief to have evaded his colleagues' stares, however briefly.

Then he turned to look at his boss, who was watching him the way a hungry lion watched an emaciated goat it didn't really consider worth eating but planned to devour anyway just because it could, and wondered if he wouldn't be better off back out in the hall.

"Hayes. Sit." Ebling never wasted two words when one would suffice. He sank into the chair across from her, which was as unyielding as she was, and waited, trying not to wither beneath her stare. She let him wait for several seconds that felt like minutes, and he fought the desire to squirm like a naughty schoolboy.

Finally, she frowned, the expression creating tiny wrinkles on her otherwise unmarred face. Some of the agents joked that she shrink wrapped herself at night to prevent any lines. Others thought she used spray fixative as a base for her makeup each morning. Whatever the reason, her even, bland features were usually as unexpressive as a stone, so the frown was a major departure and signaled an unusual degree of emotion. "What happened?" she demanded, leaning forward, arms folded on her desk. "This was supposed to be a simple murder investigation—find the killer, deal with him however necessary, come back. Instead I've got one dead FBI agent and four dead civilians, and not a suspect in sight. How did you manage to screw this up?"

R.C. bristled at the suggestion. "With all due respect, sir," he replied, fighting to keep his tone civil, "we didn't screw it up. It was screwed up from the get-go. There were three deaths by the time we arrived on the scene, not one. All of them were within one area of the reservation, and we investigated there. We found signs of an illegal lumber operation, which we then discovered had been sanctioned by certain junior members of the tribal council without the rest of the council's knowledge or permission. We confronted the man in charge of the operation and shut it down, but then one of his men turned up dead as well. The rest of his men threatened to riot, and it was while defusing that situation that Agent Frome scouted the area and was attacked. I caught up with her too late to save her, and was attacked myself but managed to scare off the assailant. I looked for him but couldn't find any traces of him. Then I brought Agent Frome's body back, got my own wound tended, and called in." He took a deep breath. "I don't see how anyone could have dealt with that situation any better."

If he'd thought that would make Ebling back off, she quickly proved him wrong. "Agent Frome scouted the area," she repeated, her own tone deceptively calm. "While you were dealing with a potential riot? Why wasn't she backing you up? Or waiting for you to scout with her, when four people had already died out there?"

"I figured I could handle the loggers," R.C. shot back. "So did Nick—Agent Frome. She said she was going to look around while I took care of that. She was a trained agent, and armed, so I thought she could take care of herself."

"And were any of the first four victims supposedly able to take care of themselves?" Still that soft, smooth tone. Like a jaguar pacing through the jungle, eyeing its prey, its footsteps silent along the branches. "Did it not occur to you that perhaps this killer was too dangerous for any one person to handle alone?"

"We didn't see any sign of the killer. We thought he'd probably fled the scene already, to avoid us and the local police." Though thinking back upon it, he wasn't sure they'd ever discussed it that fully. Nick had said she was going to look around, and he'd been busy with the loggers so he'd nodded, and off she'd gone. To her death. And almost his as well.

"Had you seen much sign of him before?" Ebling asked. "Or

did you already suspect he was an expert at stealth and forestry, the kind who could lay low and ambush you from the trees without you ever realizing he was there? Exactly the last person in the world you should ever assume was gone when you blundered aimlessly through the woods painting a big target on your chest!" The last words were delivered rapid-fire and loud, sharp and clear like gun reports, and R.C. blinked and shifted back in his chair, surprised by her obvious anger. He'd never heard of Ebling losing it like this. Not ever.

And, unfortunately, she had a point. "Yes, all indications pointed to him being an expert woodsman," he admitted, spitting the words out through a clenched jaw. "But nothing suggested he would attack an FBI agent. All of the other victims were local."

"Because there'd never been an FBI agent on the scene until you two started tromping about raising trouble." His boss had calmed back down, though her words were still bitingly sharp. "You misjudged him, and now Frome is dead as a result. In other words, you screwed up."

He started to say that Nick was just as much to blame, but bit that back. She was dead. He wasn't going to sully her name by accusing her of anything. She deserved better than that.

Unfortunately, that left him holding the bag. He nodded stiffly. "Yes, sir." The two short words tasted like ash in his mouth, dry and gritty and foul.

"What is this about an arrow?" Ebling asked next, switching tacks without warning. "Hand-carved?"

"Yes, sir. Flint head, goose-feather fletching, natural shaft. Definitely made by hand." Discussing the plain facts of the case helped him rein in his own temper as well.

"And Agent Frome said in her last report there were footprints?"

Damn, Nick must have sent in a status update after that first night in the woods. R.C. winced. "Yes sir, there were. But they disappeared a little ways in, so we couldn't track them."

"Did you take shoe impressions?"

"No, sir." He steeled himself. "There were no shoes, sir. These were of bare feet."

"Even better." She studied him. "Why didn't you take imprints? You could match those to any suspects."

"The prints were . . . abnormal, sir." R.C. kept his voice level. "I'm not convinced they were made by a person. They may have been some kind of animal." He saw Isabella in his head again, and heard her words: "This is no troll, I think, but it is something of that ilk, perhaps." He sure as hell wasn't going to tell Everclean Ebling that!

But apparently he didn't have to. "An animal?" One eyebrow quirked so slightly he thought he might have imagined it. "Are you saying an animal killed your partner and these four men?"

"No, sir."

"Do you mean that the killer has an animal with him, and those were the tracks you saw?"

He ground his teeth together. "No sir, there was only the one set of tracks."

"Perhaps this man killed an animal and is wearing its feet to throw you off the scent?" Her upper lip curled up ever so slightly, showing clear as day her opinion of this possibility.

"No, sir. I do not have an explanation for why the prints do not look normal, sir." Unless it's some kind of supernatural creature, he thought bitterly. But not a Wendigo, because I have it on good authority they don't use bows. For half a second he considered simply showing her the print and letting her draw her own conclusion, but knew there was a strong chance she'd simply say he'd bungled taking the picture in the first place. Even if she conceded it was abnormal, what then? That didn't excuse his letting Nick get killed. Nothing did.

"I see." For a second, judging from his boss's expressions, R.C. wondered if he'd said that last bit out loud. "So, to sum up, you found tracks you can't identify or explain, you knew the killer was dangerous but let your partner go off alone, and now she's dead and he's still on the loose and we don't have any real leads?"

R.C. found it hard to swallow suddenly. He could practically hear the axe falling, and the dull thud of his career's severed head hitting the ground and rolling away into a deep, dark pit. But there was no way out that he could see, not without her thinking he was crazy instead of just incompetent and stupid. "Yes, sir," he finally managed to mutter.

"Very well." Ebling pushed herself up from her desk—she was not a tall woman, but standing she still looked down on R.C. as he sat, which he knew had been the desired effect. "Agent Hayes, you are hereby placed on administrative leave, effective immediately, while I order a full investigation of your conduct and of the circumstances surrounding your partner's death. Please surrender your gun and your badge."

"Yes, sir." He detached his pistol, holster and all, from his belt and set it on the table. His badge holder and ID he placed in Ebling's outstretched hand. "Will that be all, sir?"

She ignored the sarcasm. "For now. I suggest you go home. Someone will be in touch to go over your reports and your statement. You will also see a department-appointed psychologist, starting next week, to work through your partner's death—the sessions, and the psychologist's report on your state of mind, will be taken into account as part of the investigation." She glanced at her office door. "You can go now."

"Sir." R.C. pulled himself to his feet, a tiny part of him enjoying the way she shrank back ever so slightly as he loomed over her instead, and then he turned away from her and reached for the door. He stopped, however, with his hand on the knob. "What about Nick?" he asked.

Ebling had already moved back to her seat, and she glanced up at him when he spoke, seemingly surprised to find him still in her office. "What about Agent Frome?"

"She didn't have any close family," he explained, though Ebling would already know that from Nick's file. "Nobody to—no one to claim her body or make the necessary arrangements." He hated to think of her that way, as a tagged body on a slab.

"The bureau will handle it," Ebling told him, waving away the matter as she sat back down.

But R.C. wasn't about to be brushed off so easily. Not about this. "Yes sir, I know they will. What I meant was—I'd like to be kept apprised, sir. Of the arrangements."

She looked up at him, and for a second he thought he saw a glimmer of sympathy in her eyes. Then it was gone. "You will be notified," her words were as crisp as ever, "but I would advise you not to attend. Going to the funeral of your partner when you are being investigated for her death—I don't think that would be a very good idea."

In other words, she didn't want him there. Which meant no one else would either. R.C. barely managed one final "yes, sir" before letting himself out. He didn't slam her office door behind him. The sense of despair her decree had laid upon him crushed out even that last little act of defiance.

That was it, he knew. He was done. Even if the investigation proved him blameless, he'd never live this down. In the eyes of his fellow agents, he would always be "that guy who ignored the danger and got his partner killed as a result." And if the investigators decided he was to blame, he'd be facing civil and criminal charges on top of everything else. Most likely his leave would become suspension and then either forced retirement or outright dismissal. Even if he somehow kept his job, he'd be sidelined, given deskwork or crap assignments—just like what had happened to him in the Army.

Damn it! He was out of the office now, in the elevator heading down to the parking garage where his truck waited, and he slammed his fist into the elevator wall. It didn't budge, didn't even dent, but the flare of pain along his knuckles and through his hand and arm were satisfying anyway. Why did this keep happening to him? Back in Uppsala, that . . . thing had killed his entire team and he'd lost his career because all he could tell anyone was "some homeless guy jumped us" and so they all thought he was an idiot or worse! Now something in the woods had killed Nick and tried to kill him and he couldn't tell anyone so he looked like a moron all over again! Every time he got his career back on track, some unexplainable threat appeared and ended it!

But it could be worse, he reminded himself as he paced through the garage to his battered Nissan pick-up. He could be dead. Like

Nick. At least he was alive, and going home.

He tried to convince himself that was more important than any job, or his reputation, or any of those other things he was pretty sure he'd just lost. Again.

By the time he pulled into his driveway, he almost believed it.

11

"**N**ance?" The sun had set on his way from the office, and it was fully dark out now as he eased the front door open, but the porch light was on and so was the kitchen light, a mere square of dim illumination at the far end of the hall. The stairs were dark— when he'd gotten the job with the Bureau and been assigned out here they'd decided to take advantage of the more affordable real estate and splurge on a big, two-story, three bedroom house, which they hoped to fill some day—but he thought he caught a glimmer of light up and to the left, where the master bedroom lay. Nancy was usually up well past this, but he closed the door quietly behind him just in case she'd gone to bed early.

A big, bluff-colored shape detached itself from the shadows atop the stairs and charged down them with all the noise of a rampaging elephant, then launched itself at him. The force of the assault, and the weight of his attacker, slammed R.C. back against the door, and he instinctively raised both arms to defend himself.

"Down, Polo!" he told the golden retriever, but as usual his dog didn't acknowledge the command, continuing to lick his face and arms and to swipe at him with those enormous paws. As usual, R.C. gave up the attempts to discipline the beast and settled for patting his head instead. "Yes, good boy." Polo's tail thumped wildly in response.

He was so busy saying hello to his dog that R.C. almost didn't notice the second figure that glided down the stairs far more quietly. This form didn't make a sound until a pair of slender but strong hands reached out and grasped the dog by the collar, tugging him backward. "Polo, sit." The soft voice nonetheless had steel to it, and the dog immediately sank back on his haunches, tongue lolling out, tail in full spin.

"Hey, honey." R.C. reached out and pulled her close and just held her tight. He inhaled her familiar scent, cucumber and green tea and a hint of mint mixed in a way that was uniquely her, and reveled in the feel of her in his arms, of the familiar warmth of her cheek against his shoulder, and the soft brush of her hair on his cheek. They stood like that for a minute, not speaking, just embracing and swaying slightly, as if dancing.

Finally he pulled back just a little, and so did she, not letting go but loosening her grip enough that she could lean back and they could see each other's faces. Nancy looked as lovely as ever, her long dark hair just starting to come out of its customary braid, her caramel skin flushed from their embrace, her green eyes bright with their usual love and compassion. And a whole load of fresh sympathy as well.

"You okay?" she asked softly, running a hand across his forehead, her fingers caressing the worry lines stamped there.

He nodded, but the gesture became a headshake instead, and then morphed into a shrug. "I don't know," he finally admitted. "I really don't." He'd told her about Nick, of course, and about being pulled from the case.

"What did Ebling say?" Nancy led him down the hall and into the kitchen, which was one of the best rooms in the house. Rough red tile covered the floor, warm wood made up the cabinets, copper gleamed on the oven hood, and whitewashed pressed tin made up the backsplash. It was a warm, cozy space, and he gladly sank down into one of the spindle-backed chairs in the breakfast nook while she grabbed food out of the fridge and set about building him a sandwich. His stomach grumbled as he watched her work, reminding him that he hadn't eaten today except for a quick burger grabbed on the way to the airport, and he eagerly took the food when she brought it to him, along with a glass of iced tea.

"I've been placed on leave," he answered after he'd inhaled half of the sandwich in three big bites. "Which is about what I expected. She thinks I got Nick killed." He swallowed, forcing the food down his suddenly dry throat, and took a gulp of tea. "She might be right."

"She isn't." Nancy slid into the seat across from him and took his free hand in both of hers. "Sweetie, she isn't. You didn't do anything wrong. Neither did Nick. Bad things happen sometimes."

"I shouldn't have let her wander off alone," he argued. "I should have told her to wait—we knew we had a killer on the loose, knew that was his hunting ground, knew he'd have the home court advantage. But I didn't stop her, or go with her, and now she's gone." He was still coming to terms with the fact that he'd never see his partner's face or hear her laugh or trade quips and mock-slaps with her ever again.

"Nick was a big girl," Nancy reminded him firmly, using her now-you-listen-to-me voice. "She knew the risks, and she would not have appreciated you talking about protecting her like some baby doll. Don't take all the weight for this."

He shrugged, taking another bite and washing it down. "I've got it, whether I want it or not." He swallowed. "Ebling will probably have my job for this."

"Then you'll find a different job," his wife told him firmly. "Something even better."

"Like what?" There weren't exactly a long list of intelligence agencies and militaries operating in the United States. At least, not legally.

"I don't know, but you'll find something if it comes to that." She patted his hand. "In the meantime, you said you're on leave?" The gleam in her eye, and the lingering letters in her voice, along with the way she was stroking his hand now, made him smile.

He polished off the last of the sandwich and most of the remaining tea. "I am indeed."

"Well then." Now her fingers were marching their way along his forearm. "I seem to remember some other times you were on leave, back in the Army."

"I remember those, too." He could feel his lips and cheeks twitching in a grin.

"So maybe, since you're on leave again, we should follow the same pattern we used to back then?" Her fingers were at the junction between upper arm and chest, tracing along there, and she was biting her lower lip just a little, which he'd always found both adorable and alluring.

R.C. laughed and wound his fingers in his wife's hair, tugging ever so slightly to bring her face closer. "You don't have to go in to work tomorrow?" he asked as he leaned in and kissed her. This was a long, slow, deep, powerful kiss, a real let-me-tell-you-how-I-feel-without words kind of clinch.

She responded eagerly, lips parting slightly, tongue darting out to meet his, fingers now kneading his chest and then gliding down along his abdomen and finally stopping at the waistband of his pants, tracing their way around that edge, trying in vain to slip past the pants and the shirt tails to what lay beneath.

With a sound somewhere between a growl and a chuckle, R.C. rose to his feet, both hands slipping under and around Nancy. His arms tightened slightly as he stood, and his wife found herself suddenly being lifted off her feet and hoisted up, her lower legs draping over one arm and her arms, shoulders, and head over the other. Her own arms slid around his neck in response, and she clung to him, stealing hungry kisses every few seconds, as he carried her out of the kitchen and upstairs to their bed.

And for a little while, Nancy made him forget about Nick, about his badge, about the dead Native Americans and their strange hunter. She made him forget about everything.

"I hate this," R.C. said some time later. He was staring up at the ceiling, watching the shadows there slide by as the ceiling fan rotated lazily a few feet off to one side.

"Really?" Beside him Nancy raised herself up on one elbow, the sheets slipping back and offering him a tantalizing view of the lovely chest he had been fondling just moments before. "That's certainly not what you were saying a minute ago."

He laughed, and then laughed harder at her gleeful, kid-getting-away-with-murder expression. "No, I definitely didn't hate that," he agreed. "Not even a little bit."

She flopped down against him, her head on his chest. "Good. I didn't hate it either."

"Glad to hear that." He kissed the top of her head and began stroking her hair, his whole body relaxed for the first time in days. "I just hate being benched like this."

"I know." She had one arm across his stomach and that hand was tracing lazy circles over his palm. "But you know why she had to."

"Yeah, I do. I just—" The phone interrupted, its harsh ring shattering the drowsy contentment that had settled over them, and R.C. fumbled for the handset. "Hello?" He didn't recognize the number flashing on the display.

"What did they say?" That rich, husky voice took him by surprise. How had she gotten this number?

"I'm on leave," he explained. "Pending a full investigation."

He thought he heard her snort. "And you trust this?"

"It's not about trust," he argued. "It's about doing what you're told. Always respect the chain of command."

"To hell with the chain of command," Isabella replied. "Do you wish to return to your investigation?"

R.C. sighed. "They'd never let me. I'm probably not supposed to be anywhere near the crime scenes now. If I did interfere they'd arrest me for obstruction."

"Do not worry about that," she assured him. "Do you wish to return?"

"I've already probably lost my job," he argued, shrugging a tell-you-later motion at Nancy when she gave him a querulous frown. "I don't think I want to go adding criminal charges to that."

"Yes or no?" she asked again, her tone a little sharper now.

"It's really not that simple." He wondered again where she'd been trained and how such matters were handled there.

"Do not worry about simple, or possible, or dangerous," she insisted. "Just yes or no, do you wish to be involved again?"

He sighed. "Yes," he admitted. "Yes, I wish I could finish what I started."

"Very good." The line went dead, and after a second he returned the receiver to its base.

"Who was that?" Nancy asked. "Is Ebling reconsidering?"

"Not likely." He told her about Isabella, how she'd saved his life in the woods and how she seemed convinced that only he could deal with this case. He left out the Italian hunter's whole "this is a supernatural creature like the one you fought in Uppsala" claim, though. No sense breaking out the crazy.

Nancy listened, as always, and nodded when he was done. "I know you'd go back if you could." She leaned up and kissed him, even as her hand stopped circling his abs and slid lower and lower, beneath the sheet. "But since you're not going anywhere right now, what say we forget about phone calls and weird women and all the rest?"

He smiled and kissed his wife on the top of the head, on the forehead, on the tip of the nose, and finally full on the lips. "I like the way you think."

The doorbell's chime jolted him awake the next morning. It was 7:03, according to the clock on his bedside table, and Nancy was still asleep curled up beside him—one of the nice things about being an optometrist was that she kept regular bank hours, so she didn't need to get up until a little after eight most days. The doorbell sounded again, and R.C. sat up, swinging his legs over the side and shuddering slightly as his bare feet touched the cool wood floor. Then he was levering himself to a standing position and stumbling toward the door, grabbing his robe off its hook on the door back as he passed. He had it wrapped around him and loosely tied by the time he pulled the front door open.

"Reed Christopher Hayes?" The woman standing there giving his bare legs a frankly appreciative glance was short, slight, and Asian, and couldn't have been more than early twenties. She was wearing black and purple right down to her bike helmet and gloves, and the satchel slung across her chest and resting against one slender hip was black but for the words "Denver Delivery" emblazoned in purple across the front. She was holding a thin packet.

"That's right." R.C. stifled a yawn and blinked away some of the fuzziness. Who was sending him a delivery at this hour? Could it be Ebling's "investigators," starting already? Regardless, he signed for the package and thanked the messenger as she turned away toward the trim racing bike propped against the tree in their front yard. It had been detailed in matching colors.

Stepping back inside and shutting the door behind him, R.C. traipsed back upstairs and sank down onto the bed again, still holding the packet. Behind him, Nancy stirred.

"Whassit?" she mumbled, peering at him and the item through her tousled hair. She never understood why he thought she was so adorable in the mornings.

"Delivery," he answered, his own voice still as bleary as he felt. He tore it open and extracted a standard-size letter envelope, unsealed and with his name written across the front. There was a single page folded inside, and as he read it he snapped to full alertness, though a part of him wondered if this wasn't some bizarre dream.

"What's wrong?" Nancy had felt the shift in his posture and came awake herself, leaning up against him and trying to study the letter over his shoulder, but he knew her vision hadn't fully focused yet.

"It's from the Department of Justice," he answered, hardly believing the words he was saying. "It grants me official consultant status on the Flathead Reservation case, and authorizes me to work alongside the bureau and local law enforcement officials and receive their full cooperation." He stared at the signature down at the bottom. It was a name he recognized, but not someone he'd ever encountered directly—the FBI was part of the Department of Justice and this man was a senior member of the DoJ itself, which meant mere FBI field agents like R.C. were well below his notice. So why was he signing off on something like this?

Maybe it was a joke. R.C. checked the time again. 7:24. Which meant it was 9:24 in D.C. She might be in. He grabbed the phone and dialed from memory, then waited impatiently as it rang.

"Federal Bureau of Investigations, counterterrorism unit, Catherine Assera speaking." She sounded the same as ever, brisk, words slightly clipped, voice a little too sharp and thin to be truly sexy but a welcome sound to him nonetheless.

"Hey, Cat."

"Chris? Hey, how are you? How's Denver?" Cat was one of the few people who could get away with calling him "Chris," but that was because she'd been using that nickname since they were both kids.

"Denver's fine," he told her, which technically was true. The city itself seemed to be doing okay. "But that's not why I called. I need a favor."

"Name it. As long as it won't get me fired." Though he knew, if he asked, even that risk wouldn't necessarily stop her. They'd been friends a long time.

"There's a current case out in Montana, at the Flathead Indian Reservation. Can you pull up the file for me?" He recited the case number for her.

"Sure, hang on." He could hear her fingers tapping the keys. "Okay, here we go—whoa! 'Official consultant'? Really? Why aren't you just listed as the agent in charge?"

"Long story, and I'll explain it later," he promised. "But that consultant status, it's legit?"

The sound of more typing. "Oh yeah. Very legit. Very high-level, too—you been holding out on me?"

He had to laugh. "Would I do that? Okay, thanks. I'll talk to you later."

"You'd better. My love to Nancy."

"You got it. My love to . . . whatever his or her name is this month."

"Ass."

"Wench."

He hung up and studied the letter again. "It's real?" Nancy asked. She'd heard his side, at least.

"It is." He stared down at the phone, frowning, then dialed

another familiar number. "AD Ebling, please." She was always the first one in and the last to leave, though he knew at this hour he had maybe fifty-fifty odds.

She answered a few seconds later.

"Sir, it's Hayes." He had to struggle not to include the "Special Agent" in front of his name. "Did you receive a notification about me this morning?"

"I did." She spat those two words out like they were poison. "I won't ask how you managed that. Just try not to mess up my crime scene, or get in my agents' way." The way she emphasized "my agents" made it clear that, no matter how things shook down from here on out, he'd probably just kissed his FBI career good-bye. Ebling didn't take well to people stepping on her toes—or cutting the rug out from under her.

But he couldn't worry about that now.

"I will. Thank you, sir." He hung up and swiveled to face his wife, who was now propped up on both elbows, face cupped in her hands.

"You're going back." It wasn't a question, and it wasn't said angrily. That was one of the many, many things he loved about her. She understood him and didn't try to change him, just accepted him for who he was.

"I am." He leaned back and kissed her cheek, then her lips. "I need to finish this."

"I know." She kissed him back, then rubbed at his forehead again. "Just be careful."

He caught her hand in his and kissed each finger and her palm. "I will." He paused. "I love you."

"I love you too." She pulled her hand free and swatted him across the chest. "Now get packed—you've got a long ways to go."

12

The lady at the Hawthorne House looked surprised to see him but covered it well enough and said that yes, his same room was available. R.C. put it on his credit card—no way the Bureau was going to pay for it, and he doubted the DoJ had a stipend for "official consultants," though he made a mental note to check on that later—and dropped his bags, then made a beeline for his truck, intending to drive back to the tribal headquarters. With his hand on the door, however, he changed his mind and turned away, setting his steps instead for the Kwataqnuk. She was sitting out on the back deck again, at the same table as before. It gave her a perfect view of anyone approaching, and her smug smile as he approached made it clear she'd not only seen him coming but fully expected him.

"Okay, what did you do?" R.C. asked as he dropped into the chair across from her. There wasn't a glass waiting this time, but a waiter appeared after a few seconds and set out water and a place setting. R.C. ignored it, however. He was too intent upon this mysterious woman and her answer to his question.

What he hadn't expected was for her to laugh in his face. "Me? I did nothing," she replied easily, her humor seemingly less at his expense than just at the idea in general. Then she shrugged. "But I have friends. I might have mentioned you."

"You mentioned me?" He shook his head and picked up the water glass, pressing it to his forehead and feeling the beads of condensation sink into his skin. "So these 'friends,' they wouldn't happen to be senior members of the DoJ, would they?"

"I do not know for certain." She didn't appear to be lying, or at least her voice was level and her gaze direct and unflinching. "Not directly, I suspect. But they have friends, too. And those friends have friends. And—"

"Yeah, I get it," R.C. interrupted. "You're one big network. And, what, all of you decided to help me out? Though that help probably cost me my job for real this time."

"You are needed here." She said that bluntly, leaving no room to argue. "This is more serious than you know, and only you can handle it. I am sure of this, so I tell my friends. They believe me. Now you are here, where you should be." A simple hand wave dismissed matters as mundane as career and paycheck. "These other things we will sort out later."

"Right. Fine. Swell." He lowered the glass to his lips, took a sip, feeling the icy water numb his lips and tongue and throat as it washed down, and set the glass on the table as he stood. "Well, thanks. I don't know about 'needed,' but this is definitely where I wanna be right now. At least until I find out who killed Nick—and make him pay."

"Good. Revenge is a strong motivator. As long as it does not blind you." She didn't stand, merely tilting her head back to meet his eyes. "Do not be blind, R.C. Hayes."

"I'll try not to," he promised, not even sure what he was agreeing to right now, but the answer seemed to satisfy her. Then he turned away, cutting back through the resort-casino and out onto the street to return to his truck. From there he made his way to the council building.

He didn't bother to announce himself at the desk, just nodded and kept moving, straight to the stairs and up and down the hall. The council members were there as usual—it was early afternoon and the conversation was a steady, slow murmur droning out as he tugged the door open and entered the council chamber. Many of the elders looked half-asleep, though a few eyes widened as people registered his presence. The first to react, predictably, was Jonathan.

"Agent Hayes!" The young detective came around the table and offered his hand. "We didn't expect to see you again so soon!"

"I know, sorry." R.C. shook with him, scanning the room at the same time, but didn't see anyone new. "Did my replacements arrive yet?"

"Oh, yes. Agents Neill and Ambry are down the hall. I can show you." Jonathan slid past him toward the door, but another voice called out before R.C. could follow.

"Agent Hayes." Willy Silverstream was watching him closely, those eyes still sharp in the mid-day lull. "Have you returned to rid us of this menace?"

"I mean to do my best, sir," R.C. replied. And it was true. He was determined to find out what was really going on here and see justice done. Not just for Nick but for Elk in the Trees and Peter Colman and Roger Tanner and even Jeff Landis. They all deserved that.

The council chairman nodded as if he'd heard all of that. "Good." That settled, he returned to a low conversation with the elders around him, and R.C. went after Jonathan.

"Do you know these other agents?" Jonathan asked as he led the way down the hall. It was quiet here, and R.C.'s footsteps echoed along the smooth planks.

"Yeah, they're good guys." Which was true. R.C. would never have said he was friends with either Sean Neill or Ted Ambry, but "friendly," at least. They were good agents, too, solid and competent and honest. He was glad they'd been assigned the case in his stead.

"Good, good—yes, they both seem very nice," Jonathan agreed. He paused just a few paces from a lone door. "But I would have said that they lacked your and Agent Frome's . . . instincts." He gestured to the door and then moved away, his moccasins quiet as a whisper, leaving R.C. to ponder what he'd meant.

Well, might as well get this over with, R.C. decided after a second. He reached for the doorknob, twisted it and tugged sharply, and pivoted in through the gap.

The space beyond was a small office, he saw, or perhaps a spare meeting room. It had no risers, only a rectangular table in the center with chairs around it and a small desk off in one corner. A map of the area had been tacked up across one wall, and the two men studying it both started as he entered, one of them sliding off the table edge where he'd been perching and the other lurching to his feet from the desk chair.

"Sean. Ted." R.C. tugged the door shut behind him and nodded to each of them in turn. Sean was typical Black Irish, short and a little bow-legged, with pale skin but jet black hair and dark blue eyes, while Ted was taller and narrower, his long face only a few shades lighter than R.C.'s and his hair almost as short. Both of them were wearing standard Bureau-sanctioned dark suits, and he saw their jealous glares as they took in his own clothes. Since he was only here as a "consultant" he'd decided to dress for comfort and utility instead of authority, wearing jeans and a flannel button-down under a heavy canvas coat. Only his boots had stayed the same.

He'd also brought along his Beretta 96FS, since Ebling had taken away his Glock 22. The 96FS was chambered for .40 ammo, just like his Glock, but otherwise it was a match for the 92FS, which he'd called an M9 when he'd had one during his MI days. It felt strange to carry the older, heavier pistol again after being so used to the Glock's lighter frame, but he'd kept the 96FS in perfect working order and he wasn't about to go back out in those woods unarmed.

Sean moved first, which wasn't surprising. Of the two he was the more outgoing one. "Hey, R.C. Heard you might be joining us." He offered a hand, small and chubby and a little sweaty, and his smile seemed strained but genuine. "Glad to have you back. Sucks about Nick." It was clear he was trying to play down what had happened, rather than dwell on it, and R.C. actually appreciated that. He knew he'd grieve plenty later, but right now he had a job to do.

"Yeah, thanks." Ted had sauntered over by then and also offered a hand, so R.C. shook with him as well—Ted had long, slender, piano-player fingers, and his hand was almost oddly dry compared to his partner's. The grip was also more perfunctory, and contact only lasted a few seconds. "Sorry to horn in on your case like this,"

R.C. told them. "I actually didn't ask to be brought back—I just got my orders like everybody else."

"Yeah?" Ted chuckled a bit dismissively as he returned to his roost. "From whom? Ebling was pissed!"

"I wish I knew." R.C. rubbed the back of his neck. "All I know is, memo showed up from the DoJ at the crack of dawn, ordering me back down here as a consultant." Which wasn't strictly true—the letter had authorized him to consult but hadn't required him to comply—but he figured it'd go over better with these guys if they thought he was just somebody's pawn rather than actively trying to take back the case.

"Well, somebody likes you—or hates you." Sean's laugh was higher, less forced, and less mean-spirited. "I'd hate to be you when Everclean gets done with you!"

"Tell me about it." He studied the map, and saw with a pang that they'd added two new pushpins—one for Jeff Landis and the second for Nick. He tried not to obsess over her name written there in spidery black ink. "Anything new?"

"Nothing. We were figuring we'd head on up there, take a look around for ourselves," Sean explained. "Since you're here, though, can you run it all down for us? We've got your reports, of course, but better to hear it direct."

"Yeah, of course." R.C. looked away from the map and began pacing in front of it as he recounted what had happened. He started with what the council had told him and Nick when they'd arrived, and then went on with what they'd seen and done themselves. The two other agents listened intently, occasionally stopping him to ask questions. Ted's were sharper, more brusque but also more insightful, whereas Sean's were just to get extra detail or clarify something in his own head. And R.C. quickly noticed that every time he came to a detail that didn't make sense in the real world, like the footprints or the whistling in the trees, both agents rolled their eyes a little bit or glanced at each other as if to say "right, here he goes again." He started glossing over those elements, hurrying past them and downplaying them, just to avoid those looks.

"So this Salvador Douglas," Sean asked after R.C. had finished, narrating Nick's death as clinically as possible. "A dead end, you think? Or could he be behind it all?"

"We did consider him," R.C. admitted, remembering the conversation in the car, "but really these murders only called attention to him, not the other way around. I don't think he's involved. Especially with one of his own dead now."

"No locals with grudges?" Ted spoke up. "No wild hermit-men hiding out up there with a hunting rifle and an attitude?"

"Nobody the council could name," R.C. answered. "And they keep tabs on everybody around here." He frowned. "Which doesn't mean someone couldn't have wandered off and nobody's reported them gone yet. Or that it couldn't be some crazy from outside who snuck onto the reservation specifically because it's so cut off from everyone else. But we don't have any names to go with that theory yet."

"I'm liking the crazed local scenario," Sean offered, taking a swig from the coffee cup on the desk beside him. He raised it to R.C. in a mute offer, but R.C. shook his head. He'd driven straight from Denver and had already consumed way too much caffeine to make it through the long trek awake. Any more and he'd vibrate right out of his boots. "He'd know the land, obviously, and how to hunt and track and trap. He goes out there, sets himself up his own little fiefdom, and shoots anybody who trespasses on 'his land.' All we have to do is identify the bugger, then catch him and haul him off."

"The bow and hand-made arrows certainly lend themselves to an anarchist personality," Ted commented, steepling those long fingers in front of his face. Rumor around the office was that he'd been a college professor before joining the Bureau, and his big words reinforced that image. "Somebody who's divorced himself from everyday society and even from its trappings, hearkening back to the morals and methods of the past." A tight grin touched his thin lips. "He's 'gone Native,' in other words."

R.C. frowned, and not just at the bad joke. "Maybe," he conceded, "but I thought most people like that loved to lecture others about the error of their ways? This guy doesn't even fire warning shots. He aims for the throat every time." Reflexively he rubbed at the bandage over his own cheek wound, and repressed a shudder thinking about Nick in his arms with her blood spurting from her throat.

"They do like to rant usually," Sean confirmed. "But maybe this guy's all talked out? I'll check with the elders, see if they've had anybody like that around—and especially anyone fitting that bill who suddenly dropped off their radar."

"Sounds good." Ted unfolded himself from his spot on the table. "Think I'll talk to the local police, touch base, introduce myself, so forth. I also want to see if they've had any reports about outsiders wandering in, maybe locals who've had beefs with the Reservation residents."

R.C. nodded as the two agents stepped toward the door. "I need to think a little bit," he told them when he realized they were waiting on him. "You guys go ahead. We'll catch up and compare notes later. The 4 B's Restaurant, up in Polson, is supposed to have great food."

"Dinner and notes—it's a plan." Sean slapped him on the back in passing. "Later, man." Ted contented himself with a nod, and then they were gone and the door swung shut, leaving R.C. alone.

He stared at the map again, though he wasn't really seeing it. Instead he found himself thinking about what Isabella had said. "You are needed here," she'd insisted. And before that, when she'd heard he was leaving, "They will be good agents, yes, but not . . . open-minded. They will only see what they want to see, believe what they have been taught to believe."

He was starting to worry that she might be right.

Sean and Ted were no fools. They were experienced agents, and they knew how to handle themselves, how to work a case, how to narrow down a suspect list, all the usual things.

But they didn't know how to deal with something outside the norm. He thought back to their reaction to certain aspects of the case. They had footprints in the woods that didn't match any human print he'd ever seen, but both Sean and Ted had dismissed that detail as conjecture and exaggeration and possibly outright delusion. He still wasn't sure he bought into Isabella's claim that the killer was a supernatural creature, but at the same time he did realize there were things here that didn't fit with a normal, human murderer. Neither agent seemed willing to even consider that, however. And that meant they were cutting themselves off from certain possibilities, ignoring possible explanations because they didn't fit neatly into conventional reality.

Which could make them miss evidence entirely, and even put them in danger themselves.

Just like Nick had been.

Well, R.C. decided, he wasn't going to let that happen. No more friends and co-workers were going to die on his watch. If Sean and Ted couldn't study the scene objectively, he'd do it for them. He'd figure out what was going on and deal with the killer himself— they could play back-up, but he wasn't going to trust them to spot any clues or even to recognize danger right in front of them.

He would protect them from themselves, if need be—or die trying.

13

"All right, now what?"

R.C. glanced around, the sound of his words fading quickly as the trees and underbrush swallowed them eagerly. He'd driven back up to the Hog Heaven range, hiking the last leg back toward the logging camp just as the sun began to set, but had turned aside a short ways before crossing the last ridge to that site. He wasn't sure if Captain Moran had left uniforms posted there—he certainly would have, and he thought he remembered the Captain saying something about doing that, but everything was too much of a blur for him to be sure—and if so he didn't feel like talking to them right now. Instead he'd split off from the narrow trail, circling the ridge and entering the tree line a little northwest of the camp, and then had continued to work his way around and through the trees until he'd found the spot he'd unconsciously been seeking.

Any blood had already soaked into the ground—and in only two days, which was staggering—but nonetheless he was sure these were the same trees, the same branches, the same vines and leaves and bark.

This was where Nick had died.

Sinking to his knees amid the crunch of dry leaves, R.C. stared down at the ground, seeing again his partner and friend lying there, the arrow jutting from her throat, her own blood staining her white shirt and her dark suit jacket, the light already fading from those big blue eyes. He still couldn't believe she was gone. It had only been two days ago that they'd been joking and talking and working, just as always. He still expected her to emerge from the forest and crouch down beside him, resting a hand on his shoulder and telling him, "Buck up, man. Come on, we've got work to do."

For a second he thought he could even smell her, and feel the warmth of her fingers, the tickle of her breath on his ear and against his hair.

"I'm sorry," he whispered, and he thought the woods rustled in sympathy, or perhaps in acceptance. Was Nick listening? Was she somehow nearby? He'd never been much of a believer, but if the world could contain trolls and other monsters why not ghosts or angels or whatever? Still, he wasn't sure he'd want that for Nick. Better she was in some afterlife, relaxing and just being happy, than lingering out here in the wilderness, far from friends and loved ones. Surely she deserved that much?

He wished she was still here with him, though. He could really use her help right about now. Ever since they'd been partnered together they'd been each other's sounding boards, there to bounce ideas around and consider suspects and motives and evidence, to hone theories or dismiss them and to point out holes in the inevitable hypothesis. R.C. felt like he was flying blind without her guidance, spinning crazy notions with no one around to make him stop. Being blind to the possibilities was bad, Isabella was right, but so was not grounding yourself or your theories in reality. It didn't do anyone any good to have a dozen theories about what happened if all of them required magic and demons and sentient lightning or bears with human language and human hearts, or some other completely implausible notion. But without Nick he could no longer gauge the realistic possibility of such things happening. Was he going crazy, or were elements of reality really starting to twist and blur and bleed over into the fantastical—or vice-versa?

Blam! Blam! Blam!

The unmistakable sound of gunfire shattered his contemplation, and before his brain had even fully registered the noise R.C. had rolled to one side, drawing his pistol in mid-tuck, and regained his feet facing back to the south with the weapon out and aimed. Nothing moved toward him, however, and no bullets came zinging from the shadows. A second later he realized the shots had come from a short distance away, beyond this tiny clearing or the trees around it, which had to mean—

—the logging camp.

He was up and running even as that connected in his head, pistol still clasped in his hand.

It was a good two minutes before R.C. burst from the trees and into the clearing, gasping for breath, his shirt soaked with sweat, his fingers starting to cramp from their tight grip on his gun. He'd counted another eight shots during that all-out sprint, and guessed from the timing and the slight variation in pitch that he'd heard at least four different weapons. Despite his focus on reaching the source of the gunfire quickly, R.C. had retained enough presence of mind to realize that charging into the midst of a gunfight might not be the wisest move. Fortunately he'd taken the precaution of cutting west again after the first minute of his run, and so he emerged to the side of the logging camp rather than directly in front of it. Even so, he had to slam in his heels, stopping his headlong flight and simultaneously raising both hands and shouting, "Federal agent, don't shoot!" to avoid being gunned down by the handful of rifles and pistols that instantly swung in his direction.

He spotted a single tribal cop among that group of frantic-looking gunmen. The rest were definitely loggers, and he suspected a few of them might have opened up on him anyway and simply claimed it was an accident if the officer hadn't raised a hand for them to hold their fire. R.C. recognized him as one of the policemen he'd seen that other night with the Captain, and he made a beeline for the man, keeping his own pistol low and against his leg as he moved. No sense waving a red flag in front of the bulls, but he didn't feel safe holstering the Beretta just yet either.

"What the hell?" he demanded instead as he reached the men. "What happened, somebody spot a thirty-point buck?"

"The hell it was!" one of the loggers shouted, stepping forward from the group, his hunting rifle held across his chest in a ready position. R.C. remembered seeing him here as well. "That murdering bastard's out there, same one as killed Jeff, and he was gonna go for us next! We saw him first and cut 'im down—you should be thanking us!"

R.C. turned to the cop, who shrugged and looked a little embarrassed. "I don't know, sir." He was young, maybe late-twenties, well-built and blond, and probably would have been pale if not for the tan that said he spent as much time as possible outdoors. "There was definitely something in the trees, and it didn't answer when I called for it to stop and identify itself, but whether it was a man or some kind of bear or something, I don't know."

"Did you shout before or after these yokels opened fire?" R.C. asked, letting some of his anger and, yes, delayed fear bleed over into his words. A few of the loggers snarled at the slur but quieted down when he gave them his death-eye stare. He was definitely not in the mood for their crap right now. Especially when the officer glanced down at his feet but didn't otherwise answer. Great.

"So for all you knew you were blazing away at me, or at Agent Ambry or Agent Neill, or at some local who blundered into the area completely by accident?" The officer looked ashamed enough, and R.C. reined in his temper. "Don't let civilians take control of a crime scene," he warned the younger man more softly. "You're the law—you're in charge. Make sure they know it or they'll walk all over you."

"Yes, sir." The cop—his uniform bore the name "Deegan"— nodded quickly. "Um, should we check for . . . well, for signs that we hit something, sir?"

That got derisive hoots from a few of the loggers. "I sure as hell hit something!" one of them hollered. "Filled his sorry ass full of lead, too!" His friends laughed and slapped him on the back and added their own brags, but R.C. noticed none of them were volunteering to go look. He wondered if they might be worried about what he'd said, and afraid they'd shot some innocent by mistake.

"I'll go," he told Deegan, who visibly relaxed. "You keep them here, and nobody else shoots at anything, you hear me?" That last was directed more to the loggers themselves, and a few sneered or muttered but no one openly challenged him. Fine. That should hold them for a few minutes, anyway. With a conscious effort R.C.

turned his back on them, stepped over the caution tape now ringing the logging camp, and stalked across the grass to the edge of the trees where they'd been unloading a moment before.

It was getting dark now, the sun starting to vanish behind the hills, but there was still enough illumination to make out the start of the woods, and the rough shapes around and among them. R.C. squinted at those outlines, trying to make sense of them in the tricky light. He was still a few yards from the tree line when he realized what he'd initially thought was some fallen branches might in fact be a pair of legs.

Breaking into a fast jog, he covered the rest of the distance, finally holstering the Beretta and pulling a small flashlight from his pocket instead, and dropped down beside what was definitely a body.

But not like any body he'd ever seen before.

It was human, or close to it, but tall, really tall, over seven feet easily and almost impossibly thin, its long limbs spindly to the point of emaciation but with no bones sticking through the dark, roughened flesh, as if the bones themselves were narrower than normal. The skin wasn't just calloused and weathered it was bumpy, almost ridged, and such a shade of brown that, well, it looked more like tree bark than human skin. The man—he definitely looked more male than female, and his thin chest was flat—wore only a small leather breechclout, and his hands and feet were long and narrow, possibly enough to match the prints R.C. had found out here previously. His eyes were narrow, suggesting Native blood as did the flat cheeks and the sharp nose, but the mouth hung open in death and was filled with tiny, triangular teeth that would have been more at home in a shark's mouth than a human's.

Across one shoulder was slung a long leather cylinder, open at the top end and filled with bristling, feathered sticks. He felt a chill wash over him as he recognized those outlines, and felt again the sharp sting along his cheek.

A quiver of arrows.

Sweeping the light in an arc around him, R.C. noticed a long stick or branch just a few feet away, and managed to hook it in with one hand and tug it closer to where he could grab it properly. It proved to be a bow, assembled from trimmed but otherwise unshaped branches and what appeared to be a twisted, knotted vine, and despite its rough construction the weapon felt both sturdy and efficient.

For once, the loggers might have been right. They'd said they'd cut down the murderer, and it was starting to look that way.

Footsteps crunched faintly on the ground behind him, and R.C. glanced over his shoulder in time to see Isabella cross the clearing. The loggers watched her move away from them, their eyes openly tracing her curves, and R.C. could see from her expression and the way she carried herself that she was well aware of their stares and didn't dislike the attention. If anything, she seemed used to it, almost to assume it as her due. Which he supposed it was—a woman as striking as she was, it was hard to deny that she deserved admiration. Even the cop was staring, though at least he had the decency to blush as he ogled her. He didn't say anything to stop her from entering an active crime scene, either—or perhaps he had tried and she just hadn't obeyed. Isabella didn't strike R.C. as the kind of woman who obeyed others much. She didn't acknowledge the men behind her at all, in fact. Her attention was focused on R.C. and his recent find. She stopped a few paces from him, angled off to one side so that she could see him but still keep the loggers and the bulk of the clearing in her peripheral vision, her body turned slightly so she could quickly face anyone who might cause them trouble from across the clearing but just as easily pivot toward the deeper woods if a threat arose from that corner instead. Her hands were empty at the moment, but she was tense, on edge, prepared, and R.C. thought he saw her nostrils flare slightly, the way a big cat's eyes might narrow before it lunged. Her gaze flicked from R.C. to the bullet-ridden body before him, and he thought he saw pleasure in her eyes but a frown touched her lips.

"You?" was all she asked. It was hard to gauge her tone but he thought she sounded a touch disapproving, or perhaps disappointed. Was that because she was annoyed that someone had beaten her to the punch, he wondered, or because a gunman had faced off with an archer rather than choosing to make it a level playing field?

Regardless, he shook his head. "I just got here myself." He gestured back toward the loggers. "They spotted something in the woods and opened up." Much as he hated to admit it, he added, "looks like you were right about it being a creature of some sort." Because whatever this narrow figure might be, he definitely wasn't entirely human.

"Yes, but what sort?" she said, though he didn't think she was speaking to him, exactly. He was surprised when she pulled a small phone from a pocket in her coat. Then she punched in a number and raised the phone to her ear, its sleek outline disappearing beneath the waves of her hair. She started speaking rapidly, and though he couldn't make out most of what she was saying he caught enough stray words to guess that she was relaying details of this strange body before them. But to whom?

She finished speaking and waited, turning in a slow radius as she did, her eyes canvassing the area again, her free hand resting on her hip comfortably close to the bulge of what he was sure was some sort of large handgun. A different look crossed her face at one point, a look of less derision and possibly even a little respect, and R.C. followed her gaze to see Jonathan Couture step up beside the uniformed cop. He wondered if Deegan had called in the incident and the detective had been sent to report on it, or if Jonathan had merely decided to stop by and check on the site at random. Either way, R.C. was glad to see the levelheaded local, and nodded hello when Jonathan glanced his way. That was apparently all it took, and the young detective said a few last words to the officer before ducking under the tape and making his way across the clearing toward them.

Which was right when Isabella's phone contact apparently began talking again. "Are you sure?" R.C. heard her ask. "Yes, all right." She hung up, pocketing the phone, and looked down at him. He couldn't quite read the expression in her eyes or on her brow and her lips—concern? Annoyance? Displeasure? Worry? But all she said was a single word:

"Tsiatko."

14

"**T**siatko?" R.C. squinted up at her. "**What's that mean, exactly?**"
But Jonathan had gasped, and now he was staring at her
without any regard for her good looks. "Tsiatko?" he echoed.
"That's impossible! They're only a legend!"

"Well, fill me in on this legend real quick," R.C. rose to his feet
and all but growled up at them, hating to be the only one not in the
know, "because it looks like one of your living legends just got shot
up, and it also looks like he may be the one who killed my partner!"

"'Tsiatko' means 'stick Indian,'" Jonathan explained slowly,
closing his eyes for a second as if dredging up old memories, or at
least old stories. "They're a folktale parents tell children to frighten
them into staying out of the woods at night. They're really tall and
really thin, like sticks, and their skin looks a lot like tree bark so
they're almost invisible in the forest. They like the dark and most
people never see them but you can hear them talking sometimes—it
sounds like the wind whistling through the trees. They're hunters
and fisherman and"—he gulped and glanced down at the body
beside them, and at the weapon laying nearby— "expert archers."

R.C. closed his eyes and squeezed the bridge of his nose between
forefinger and thumb, trying to hold back the pounding there.
"And why didn't you tell us any of this before?" he asked when
he was sure he had his voice—and his temper—under control. "It
might have been useful going in."

"They're not real!" Jonathan protested. He stared at the body
again. "At least, I didn't think so! Nobody did, except maybe a few

of the real old-timers! They're just stories, like the boogeyman, or Bigfoot, or monsters under the bed!" He gulped—his skin was too ruddy to ever truly go pale, but beads of sweat stood out across his forehead, and his hands were shaking slightly. "I swear, I thought they were just stories!"

"I know you did." R.C. felt bad for the young detective, and for bullying him. Jonathan had been nothing but pleasant and helpful the whole time. Was it his fault he hadn't thought to mention some old wives' tale about a local race of monsters and half-men?

"Bigfoot is difficult," was Isabella's contribution to the conversation. "Tremendous strength, tremendous reach. Difficult to bring down." Her eyes met R.C.'s, and somehow he knew exactly what she was thinking. Bigfoot was difficult to bring down—just like a troll.

At least this "stick Indian" had proven vulnerable to normal gunfire.

"So that's it?" he asked, nudging the body with the tip of one boot. "This tsiatko is our killer? Do they usually go after people—in the stories, I mean?"

But Jonathan was shaking his head. "No, the tsiatko aren't usually violent. The old tales tell of them playing pranks on people all the time—they like to steal people's clothes, sew the openings of their tents shut, put holes in their canoe bottoms, stuff like that. Sometimes they make off with small children, or young women, either to become their wives or their slaves—or both." His face scrunched up as he struggled to remember. "But they don't attack people much"—then his eyes flew open wide—"unless someone attacks one of them first."

R.C. frowned. "What happens then?" He had a suspicion he already knew the answer, and it was matched by the sudden sinking feeling in his gut.

Sure enough, Jonathan gulped, then answered, "If someone kills a tsiatko, the rest of the tribe goes after them. All of them, everyone they hold responsible. And they don't stop until they're all destroyed or all of the people they targeted are dead."

"Got it." R.C. looked over at that dead body again, then across the clearing at the loggers. He was mentally rearranging his time-line, shuffling the order of events and adding in this new information. He wasn't happy with the result he got, and his long legs were already carrying him across the clearing in swift, strong strides before the thoughts had settled fully.

Officer Deegan stepped forward to meet him, hands locked on his belt, but R.C. brushed past him without a word, leaving the stunned officer standing there staring at his back. Instead he zeroed in on the logger who'd told him about how they'd spotted the killer and opened fire. The man glared at him but R.C. continued forward until he was mere inches away and got up in the man's face. The logger was big and burly but so was R.C., and he actually had an inch or two on the other guy—he took advantage of that, leaning in so he was glaring down at him, eye to eye.

"There's a body over there," he said softly, watching as each word hit the other man and eroded his bravado. "Tall, too tall, and skinny, real skinny. Bow and arrow at its side. Dark, rough skin, almost like bark. And it isn't the first one you've seen like that. Is it?" He threw those last two words out like bullets, hard and fast, and the logger flinched and took an involuntary half-step back, almost a stumble. R.C. moved forward to stay on him, his voice rising and growing sharper, whip-like. "Is it?"

The logger continued to match his stare for a few seconds before finally breaking and glancing down and away. His response was little more than a mumble, but R.C. heard it nonetheless:

"No."

"Talk to me," R.C. demanded, putting all his authority behind that order. "You guys have been holding out on me this whole time, and look what happened. Your buddy Jeff? Dead. My partner? Dead. Who's next? Me? You? All of us?" The logger was curling in on himself, not meeting R.C.'s eyes, so he poked the man in the chest with one forefinger, making him glance up automatically. "Tell me!"

"Yeah, we've seen one before," the logger finally admitted. "Okay?"

"How long ago?"

"A week, maybe." The man looked away again, and R.C. could tell he was still holding out.

"What else?" He shoved the other man with an open palm, making him stagger back. "What aren't you telling me? You saw him. How? What happened?"

Nothing. The guy was clamming up. And all of his friends had that same stubborn, mulish look about them. They weren't going to talk either. Not unless this one did. He was the key.

Fortunately, R.C. had a lot of experience with hostile witnesses and recalcitrant suspects. In Military Intelligence those were about the only kind he ever got, and he'd gotten very good at pressuring them into revealing information. His time in the FBI had only honed those skills. Now he frowned as he quickly rifled through what he knew about these men, their inclinations—and their loyalties. And just like that, he changed tacks. A quick step and a slide through the long grass took him beside the logger, and one arm went up around the other man's shoulder, pulling him close in a friendly, confidential gesture.

"Listen," R.C. told him quietly, letting all the steel vanish from his tone, now nothing but friendly concern. "This thing already killed Jeff, right? And I know you don't want to lose another friend in case it's still out there. Help me out here. The more I know about how this all started, the quicker I can fix it all. Before someone else gets hurt."

The logger shot him a sideways glance, still wary but softening. "How do I know you ain't gonna just arrest us all?" he asked, but he sounded less belligerent now, and more concerned.

"Right now I'm only interested in whoever's killing everyone," R.C. assured him. "That's it. I just want to make sure there aren't any more murders."

A motion behind him caught his eye, and without taking his arm from around the logger R.C. glanced over. Isabella and Jonathan had stayed near the body, but now they were headed his way. Neither of them looked happy, and Isabella kept spinning around and walking backward for a few steps. He noticed her hand was still hovering on her hip.

"Come on," he cajoled, focusing on the logger again. "Look—I don't even know your name."

"Pat," the logger answered reluctantly.

"Pat. Right. I'm R.C. So come on, Pat, give me a hand here, okay? You could be a hero, help me keep all your buddies safe. What do you say?"

The appeal of getting the others' gratitude and respect seemed to do the trick, and Pat straightened up. "Okay, yeah, we saw one like that guy before," he said finally. "A week ago, day after we started working this site. Only"—he glanced down at his feet again, but kept talking— "we didn't see him in time."

"Meaning what?" R.C. shot a glance at Isabella, who'd stopped a pace away. She opened her mouth, about to say something, but he shook his head ever so slightly and she paused. Pat was finally opening up. He couldn't take the risk of his shutting up again, and any interruption could disrupt the bond he'd forged between them. He had to get this now. Isabella glowered, clearly ready to argue, but he shut her up with a sharp glare of his own. Whatever she wanted could wait.

"We were just cutting down one of the trees," Pat was saying, not noticing the silent exchange. "You saw that guy, he's practically invisible. It's like he's a tree himself!" Pat gulped. "It was an accident, I swear!"

And now R.C. understood. "He was up against the tree, probably trying to avoid being seen," he guessed, "and you and your friends cut him down."

"We had no idea until he toppled over, dead," Pat insisted. "Honest! We didn't want to kill nobody—why would we? All it'd do is slow down the work, or shut us down completely." Which was exactly what R.C. and Nick had realized after talking to Salvador Douglas. Having his logging site labeled a crime scene and closed down—as it had been—was the worst thing that could have happened to him out here.

It just hadn't occurred to them that the loggers could have killed someone by accident.

Then again, they'd never counted on men who looked like living trees, either. He could see how a tsiatko would be almost impossible to spot. And with those big chainsaws the loggers used—they'd saw right through a body before they noticed.

"So what happened after that?" he asked Pat. "You killed him by accident—I believe you. But then what? Did you report it?"

Pat flushed. "Naw," he admitted after a second. "I mean, we told Rick and Mr. Douglas. But they said not to call the cops. Said there wasn't much we could do for the guy now, and we'd just get shut down. I need this job! 'Sides, the way he looked we figured the guy was a hermit or something, living up here all alone." R.C. could see where they'd think that, and where from a business standpoint it made more sense just to sweep the whole incident under the rug. Which didn't mean he wasn't going to have some harsh words for Douglas when he was done here. The man had known about this all along, and had lied to them. If he'd told them the truth when they'd been in his office, Nick might still be alive.

R.C. had to remind himself that it wasn't entirely Pat's fault to keep from taking out his rising anger on the clearly guilt-stricken logger. "So you hid the body and kept working."

"We buried him," Pat agreed. "Dug a proper grave and every-thing. Then—yeah, we kept working."

"Where's the grave?" R.C. asked. He wasn't surprised when the logger gestured past them, over to near where the second tsiatko lay. Right by the edge of the woods. Right where all of the killings had happened.

"We'll need to exhume the body," he thought aloud, releasing Pat from his grasp and taking a step back toward the trees. "Then we'll be able to—" A strong but elegant hand clamped down on his wrist, stopping him in his tracks.

R.C. glanced up to see Isabella beside him. Her face was taut, mouth tight, and she had a pistol in her other hand. "We must leave at once," she told him softly, her rich voice carrying easily across the feet that separated them.

"I can't," he argued. "I've got to find the first body. That's the key. We can—"

But again she cut him off. "Later. Right now we must go.

Quickly." It wasn't fear he saw in her eyes as she glanced back at the trees, but it was definitely a healthy caution, and that stopped him more than her strong grip had.

"Why? Did something new happen?" He looked around, but everything looked much as it had. The loggers were clustered nearby, now surrounding Pat who was no doubt telling them how he'd helped the law in order to save their necks. Deegan was keeping an eye on them but standing a little ways apart to distance himself and show his authority. Jonathan was beside Isabella, and if she looked calmly alert he looked ready to bolt right out of his skin. The poor local was terrified, his eyes enormous, his whole face now shiny with sweat, his shirt soaked as well despite the cool night air. Other than the soft buzz of Pat's words and the wind in the trees and Isabella's warning, it was quiet.

Very quiet.

Too quiet.

And the wind in the trees sounded a lot like whistling.

"How many tsiatko are there?" R.C. asked Jonathan, who shook his head.

"I don't know. Nobody does. They're just stories." His voice was shaking. "But the old tales tell of them surrounding men foolish enough to hunt for them."

Surround them. Now R.C. was looking to the trees as well, where the shadows suddenly seemed deeper, darker, more alive with menace. And the whistling continued.

Also, he wasn't sure, but he couldn't seem to see the dead tsiatko's body anymore. Either the creature had revived and crawled away—or something had dragged him deeper into the woods.

Oh, this was not good.

"We must leave!" Isabella urged again. "We are outmatched now! We can return later, when we are better prepared!"

R.C. found himself agreeing. "Deegan!" he called, making the cop jump. "Get everybody out of here! Now!"

Deegan nodded. "Let's go, folks!" he told the loggers. "Time to clear out!" The air held a definite chill now, and the shadows of the trees were reaching across the clearing like hungry fingers eager to snatch and tear, and everyone seemed to feel the increasing sense of menace because for once the loggers didn't put up any resistance. They let themselves be herded away, and R.C. motioned for Jonathan to follow them, too.

Just as he was turning to go himself, he heard a faint but rapid hissing in the air, coming from the trees. "Get down!" he shouted to Isabella, and she threw herself to the ground as he did the same. Something slender and straight passed overhead, followed by another and another, the night alive with their swift flight. One ended its deadly arc right by R.C.'s head, and the hand-made arrow quivered in the ground beside him, its point buried deep in the hard earth.

"Are you hit?" he called to Isabella as the flurry ended, dragging himself to his knees and then his feet.

"No," she replied, rolling to her feet in a smooth motion that left him envious. "You?"

He checked again. "No. And I'm not sticking around to let them improve their aim."

She nodded, and together they hurried after Jonathan, who was waiting for them a dozen paces away. The clearing behind them and all around was littered with arrows now, a score at least, and R.C. felt the pounding in his head begin again, keeping pace with the rapid beat of his heart and the bellows of his breath. There were definitely a lot of tsiatko out there.

And they were clearly out for blood.

15

"Hey man, thought you stood us up or something," Sean said as he answered his cell. "Tried calling but it went straight to voicemail so we headed over here once it got dark. You're right, though—the food's damn good."

"Glad you didn't wait on me," R.C. replied as he drove, his Bluetooth earpiece snug in his ear, his cell phone open on the dash in front of him. "I decided to take another look at the scene, see if I noticed anything new."

"You went up there without us?" The other agent sounded a little annoyed now. "Damn, man! Thought you weren't horning in?"

R.C. rubbed at his forehead. "I'm not, I promise. I just—I hadn't been back since . . ."

When Sean spoke again, his voice was softer, sympathy obvious even over the phone. "Oh. Yeah, I get it. Sorry."

"Thanks. But turns out it's a good thing I was up there. There's another body—but it's no local."

"What?" Now Sean sounded excited. "What happened?"

"A bunch of the loggers were back up there, along with one of the local cops, Deegan. They saw someone moving in the woods and opened fire. I saw the body." He left out the part about it being clearly inhuman. He also debated whether to mention the hail of arrows, but decided against it. That would just make Sean and Ted go looking for a whole clan of crazies, which would lead to a lot of bloodshed. Of course, if they got there and saw the clearing littered with arrows they might wonder about his omission, but R.C. had a feeling those shafts would all be gone by the time they arrived. Just like the body itself. The tsiatko might leave arrows in the men they'd killed, but he doubted they would waste shafts that had missed and could be fired again.

"Really? So the killer came back, looking for more targets, and got a taste of his own medicine?"

"Looks that way." Not really, R.C. amended in his head. It actually looks like a race of mythic "stick Indians" live out there in the woods and decided to open season on any trespassers—there's still a bunch of them out there, armed and angry, and there's no telling which ones actually killed any of their victims, since they look more like walking trees than regular people.

Yeah, he could just see Sean including that in his report. Most likely after the words, "Then former agent Hayes began spouting wild delusions, saying that. . . ."

He could hear Sean relaying the information to Ted, and waited patiently for him to finish. "You still on the scene?" was his next question.

"No, cell reception's spotty out there," R.C. explained. "I needed to let you know but couldn't get a clear signal, so I'm driving back to Polson." He checked his odometer. "I'm about halfway there."

"Right. Listen." He heard the sound of chairs being pushed back. "We're on our way. Turn around and wait for us—we'll need you to show us the clearing, since we haven't been yet." There was an unspoken recrimination in those last words, which R.C. had to admit was justified. They'd wanted to see the site but had gotten sidetracked, and he'd let them delay so he could go out there alone. "Got it?"

He considered arguing, but decided there wasn't any point. Besides, if their positions had been reversed he would have demanded the same thing, and probably wouldn't have been as nice about it. "Got it." He hung up, checked his mirrors, braked, and then did a three-point turn to bring himself around. He briefly wondered where Isabella had gotten to—she'd disappeared, claiming she had her own transportation, once they'd topped the rise away from the clearing, and by the time he'd reached his own car he'd been alone. Was she already back in Polson, waiting for him to return so they could talk about what had just happened? Would she wonder when he didn't show?

Well, he'd worry about that later. He still wasn't completely sure where things stood with her, anyway. It's not like she was his partner, exactly.

It's not like she was Nick.

There was no sense in hurrying now, and narrow dirt roads like this could be treacherous at night with only his brights to cast fickle beams upon their ruts and bumps and swerves, so he took his time on the drive back. Sean and Ted, on the other hand, must have floored it, because their rented sedan pulled up beside his pickup only ten minutes after he shut off his engine. R.C. was leaning against the driver's side door when they arrived, and waited until they'd climbed out of the car to greet them.

"This way," he told them after they'd exchanged nods. He'd pulled the heavy Maglite from under his car seat and switched it on now, the powerful beam cutting a swath through the dark and showing rocks and roots and scrub brush. "Watch your step."

Both Sean and Ted had flashlights at their belts, smaller versions of the monster he held, and secondary beams lanced out behind him as they walked, his boots making crunching sounds and their loafers following with slicker noises. A few times one or the other cursed as a foot slipped, but otherwise the next hour was quiet.

"Where'd the loggers go?" Ted asked finally. Out here, his words carried through the clean, crisp night air, echoing faintly off the higher peaks just beyond them.

"I cleared them out," R.C. answered over his shoulder. "They were all keyed up, liable to shoot anything that moved including me or each other, and I didn't want a bloodbath. Figured you could just as easily take statements later."

That got a grunt from Sean. "I'd have liked them all corralled," he admitted, though without any apparent rancor, "but if they were as hair-trigger as all that, yeah, better to catch them later. Preferably without guns in their hands."

"We'll have to collect all of their weapons, of course," Ted pointed out. "Compare ballistics to find out which one fired the kill shot, though I'm guessing there won't be any charges filed. Self-defense and all that."

R.C. didn't reply. They'd reached the top of the rise, and he paused to let his two companions catch up to him and take in the view. Even in the dim starlight it was breathtaking, the way the valley fell away before them, the trees marching away across the gentle slope to vanish into the shadows of the mountains. The yellow caution tape showed as a faint ribbon against the dark grass and darker sky, snaking its way around the small clearing like a loose coil of rope, and R.C. felt a sudden shiver as he realized how much that resembled a snare set out for some unwary animal. He just hoped he wasn't the prey—or the bait.

Just in case, he loosened his pistol in its holster as he led the way down the hill and toward the clearing itself.

"All of the bodies were found here, except for Nick?" Sean asked once they'd stopped by the tape and studied the scene. He met R.C.'s glare for a second before glancing away. "Sorry, man. You know I've gotta ask."

"All of them were around here, yeah." R.C. heard the words emerge, sharp and bitten off, and reminded himself that none of this was his fellow agent's fault, and that yes, he did have to ask. "But not right here in the clearing. Jeff Landis was right over there near the tree line"—he gestured with his Maglite—"but Elk in the Trees, the first victim, was maybe two hundred yards south, back on the other side of that ridge we just crossed. Peter Colman was a little east of here, by a small creek, and Roger Tanner was several hundred yards west. Nick"—he had to swallow a few times before continuing—"was maybe three hundred yards north of here."

"Okay, so it's a definite epicenter but they were spread out," Ted commented, surveying the area. "And where's our body?"

"Right over there." For the second time tonight R.C. stepped over the tape and crossed the clearing. Well, third, really, counting the controlled jog away after the arrows had fallen. As he'd guessed they were all gone now, and nothing worse than a few rocks and a couple empty beer cans and of course the logging equipment itself barred their path.

Reaching the trees confirmed what he'd thought he'd seen before the earlier retreat. The dead tsiatko was gone.

"He was right here," R.C. said nonetheless, indicating the spot where the body had been. "Tall, crazy-skinny, wearing nothing but a loincloth, had a bow by his hand and a quiver of arrows on his back. Dark skinned, weathered, with matted hair. Native, I'd say, but he'd been out here a long time." All of which was more or less true. The tsiatko were native to the area, after all, since Jonathan had said they featured in his people's legends. If people assumed he meant "standard Native American human" by his description, well, that was their own damn fault.

Ted and Sean had crouched down and were studying the ground, the light from their flashlights pooling to create a circle of almost blinding radiance as set off by the inkiness all around them. "We've got blood," Ted confirmed, waggling his light so its beam swept around the dark stains. "Looks like multiple shots."

"I've got drops leading away here," Sean added as he turned and studied the space just beyond, a few paces deeper into the trees. "Looks like maybe he dragged himself off to die."

"This much blood, he's definitely dead or dying," his partner agreed. He shook his head. "I'm surprised he had the wherewithal to collect his bow, but who knows? Perhaps the weapon had deep personal significance, maybe even a quasi-religious importance. Living out here all alone, an item like that could easily be seen as the source of life, and therefore worthy of veneration."

R.C. decided he'd better explain a few things, at least. "He wasn't alone," he offered, keeping his voice quiet and his eyes on the woods beyond. "The loggers were acting funny, holding out on me, so I bullied them into admitting they'd killed another a lot like him about a week before. It was a logging accident, took him out with the chainsaw before they even knew he was hiding against the tree, and they figured he was a lone crazy so they buried the body and pretended nothing had happened."

"Leaving his partner to go on a mad killing spree seeking revenge." Sean slapped his knee. "That'd do it. Love, rage, and grief, all tied up together and handed to a nut-job with a bow. No wonder he started shooting people!"

"And now he's been shot himself, by the same people who killed his friend and whom he'd been trying to kill in turn," Ted murmured. "Poetic justice, or just irony?"

Sean laughed and shook his head—it was obvious he was used to his partner's strange ways and apparently morbid sense of humor. "Either way, we need to find his body," he pointed out. Amusement turned to disgust as he studied the trees towering up just beyond them, and the impenetrable darkness beneath their interwoven boughs. "No way we're doing that in the dark, though. We'll need daylight, and the Captain and his men, too."

Ted rose to his feet, grunting slightly as he swiped long fingers at his pants legs. "If there are wild animals out here, they might find the body and savage it during the night," he argued. "That would destroy a great deal of potential evidence."

"Sure, and if he's still alive he could bandage himself up and come gunning for everyone tomorrow," Sean countered. "I'm not really expecting that, though." He glanced over at R.C. "What do you think, man?"

"I think walking these woods at night is a bad idea," R.C. answered honestly. "There could be wolves, bears, bobcats, all sorts of things, and they're used to hunting here at night. We aren't." He shrugged. "Yeah, we could lose some trace overnight, but better that than adding ourselves to the casualty list."

He didn't miss the pitying look Sean and Ted exchanged, and knew what the other two men were thinking: poor R.C., his partner gets killed out here and now he's worried he's going to be next. Sounds like the big bad ex-military is losing his nerve. Well, whatever. If thinking that meant they'd agree to come back tomorrow, he was fine with that. Because walking into these trees now, with the tsiatko out in full force? Was a guaranteed way to get all three of them killed.

Finally Sean nodded. "You're right. If I broke my neck tripping over a tree root in the dark, I'd never live it down." He grinned. "We'll come back at first light, bring patrolmen and dogs, the whole nine yards, and track this bad boy down. Sound good?"

R.C. relaxed a little. "Definitely."

They traipsed back to their cars without another word. It was only as R.C. was pulling open his door that Sean stepped up beside him. "If you want to sit tomorrow out," the shorter agent offered quietly, "we totally understand." There wasn't any mockery in his voice or his face, just sympathy.

"Thanks," R.C. told him. "But better to get back on the horse, right?" He managed a smile. "Besides, Nick'd kick my ass if I took the easy out like that."

"Right on." Sean slapped him on the shoulder. "See you bright and early then, big guy. Don't be late or we'll start without you." He waved and marched over to his car, where Ted was already buckled up and waiting. R.C. waved back, climbing into his pick-up as the agents' sedan roared to life and then began rumbling its way back down the hill toward the dirt road which would lead to the real road and from there back to Polson. He followed after them, keeping their headlights at the edge of his vision as he drove, thinking about what tomorrow would bring. If the tsiatko were truly nocturnal, the searchers might be safe. It occurred to him that he actually didn't know what time of day the first three victims had died. Landis could have been at night, since he was found in the morning, but Nick had been killed a little before noon, so that didn't track. Then again, there'd been lots of lights and loud noises for hours at that point, so maybe the tsiatko were night owls but got woken by all the commotion. And weren't too happy about losing their beauty sleep. That didn't bode well for tomorrow's all-out search, though the sheer numbers involved might keep them at bay, at least for a while.

He shrugged and stifled a yawn. It wasn't like he could stop Sean and Ted now, especially as a "consultant." All he could do was lend a hand, keep an eye out, and hope for the best.

But first he was going to need a good night's sleep.

As soon as he found out if the hotel's dining room was still open. With everything that had gone on, he'd never gotten around to eating today, and at the moment he thought he might be in more danger from his growling stomach than from the tsiatko and their arrows.

16

"**A**nything?"

R.C. shook his head as he dropped to his butt on the ground beside Sean and accepted a bottle of water from him. "Nothing."

"Damn." Both men were quiet for a minute as they drank their water and watched the cops and tribesmen still traipsing through the forest. "Well, that's probably that, then."

R.C. nodded. They'd been out here for four hours already, starting at dawn. The search had been careful, methodical, relentless—and ultimately useless. They hadn't found the dead tsiatko—not that R.C. had expected them to—or even any further trace of where it could have gone. The drops of blood they'd found the night before dwindled to nothing after a dozen yards, and they had yet to spot any other clues. The day had dawned cool and clear and slate-gray, perfect conditions for a search, and expectations had been high among the assembled men when they'd started, but now the general mood had cooled and gone as leaden as the sky. At least the tsiatko seemed to be hiding from the men and dogs combing the trees, so the woods hadn't erupted into violence as he'd feared. But they hadn't yielded any bodies, either.

"Let's get back and see if Ted's had any better luck," Sean suggested, and R.C. followed him toward his pickup. Ted had drawn the short straw and gotten stuck taking statements from the loggers. Or maybe he'd offered to take that task, in exchange for not having to clamber around in the wilderness again. R.C. wasn't sure.

Either way, Ted had taken the rented sedan, so he'd ferried Sean out here that morning to coordinate everything. Not that Sean had stood back and watched others work, though—he'd been out there clomping over leaves and branches along with everyone else. R.C. respected that, and not for the first time he'd found himself wondering why he and the shorter agent weren't closer. But then he hadn't really been all that close to anyone in their office—except for Nick. Friendly, sure, but not genuinely close. It had been the same way in the army, really—he'd been tight with his unit and one or two others, but only on nodding terms and casual hellos with everyone else. Which was fine, until you lost your unit and realized nobody else had your back, not really. R.C. shook his head as he neared the truck, trying to shake the dark mood before it could settle over him fully. Things were tough enough without adding depression into the mix.

"So where do we go from here?" he asked once they were in motion, after Sean had officially thanked everyone else involved and dispersed them to their own vehicles and homes and they'd pulled away and started down the dirt road again.

Beside him, the shorter agent frowned. "I think this just leads right back to the main road, doesn't it?" His quick grin showed that he knew what R.C. had meant, and after a second he sobered. "I think we're good, honestly. Yeah, I'd wanted to find the body, but with the coroner's report we're still in decent shape." Captain Moran had brought along the local medical examiner, a tall, raw-boned woman named Wendy Garrett, and she'd confirmed that the amount of blood at the scene would be fatal for anyone, even someone as tall as the footprints suggested. "Lots of animals drag themselves away to die, and manage to hide from their attackers until long after they're dead and rotting. Looks like our guy has the same knack. He's down a rabbit hole somewhere, or in a bear's den, or up a tree or something. Important thing is, he's dead and not coming back."

R.C. didn't disagree. Sean was right, after all, at least insofar as that particular body was concerned. There was no sense pointing out how many tsiatko were left, not unless he wanted to see another one of his colleagues get a fatal throat piercing.

They drove in silence for a while, the truck's shocks absorbing most of the tumult but the ride still far from smooth until they switched back to the regular road, at which point the difference was like night and day, bumpy to silken. After the ground noise had subsided, Sean asked quietly, "So, how're you doing?" He was looking out the window, watching trees and hills roll by, which R.C. suspected was just an easy excuse not to face him.

"Managing," was the best he could reply at first. After a few seconds he added, "it's tough. You know, I keep expecting to see her when I glance over, or when I turn around. I keep thinking she's gonna answer me when I ask a question, or be on the other end when I pick up the phone." He shrugged and spoke past the tightness in his throat. "But that's just the way it is. She's gone and I've got to get used to that fact. It'll take time. Right now it's still all raw."

Sean nodded. "You gonna come back after this?" And R.C. knew he didn't just mean "back to Denver once we're done here."

"I don't know," he admitted. "Not sure Ebling'll let me, and not sure I wanna without Nick there, too." He sighed. "I like the work. I like the group. I just—it might be too weird, is all. Especially working with somebody else." Some FBI agents worked solo, but Ebling frowned on that. She felt that most agents worked better in pairs, and R.C. actually agreed—it was good to know somebody had your back, and to have someone to compare notes with and tag-team witnesses with and so on. He just wasn't sure he'd be able to develop again the kind of rapport he'd had with Nick. He wasn't sure he wanted to try.

"Well, we're pulling for you," Sean told him, "me and Ted. The rest of the squad, too. Nobody blames you—this shit happens, it's a damn shame, but it's not your fault. And any one of us'd be happy to work with you." He did turn slightly then, and smiled, though the expression was tight. "I'm glad you're out here with us, though not for the reason why."

R.C. nodded and half-smiled back. "Thanks. That means a lot." There wasn't much else to say after that, and they drove the rest of the way with nothing but the thrum of the wheels on the road and the rush of the wind moving past for company.

"They confirmed what you said last night," Ted told them both once they'd returned to the little office in the council building, directing that first remark toward R.C. They'd found the other agent sitting hunched over the small desk, scribbling notes in a tight, neat hand, and had briefed him first on the coroner's professional opinion and then on their lack of other findings. Now it was his turn to catch them up on how he'd spent his morning. "They accidentally killed a local hermit a little over a week ago," he continued, referring to his notepad, "didn't realize he was plastered to a tree and cut him in half with one of those industrial chainsaws, then panicked and buried the body. The first death didn't happen until after that, and those continued until last night when they spotted another local who looked a lot like the first one—'they coulda been twins,' was the exact phrase—and mowed him down, this time with shotguns and hunting rifles." He flipped the pad shut and drummed his long fingers on its top. "None of them saw the body clearly, nobody could confirm whether he was dead or not, but they definitely saw him fall." He glanced over at R.C. "They said you examined him, along with Jonathan Couture and some woman they'd never seen before." That last one was left hanging.

R.C. nodded. He'd perched on the table edge again. "Yeah, she's a tourist or something, she was out hiking and heard the commotion, came to check it out. Completely ignored the crime-scene tape, typical hot chick figuring she could go anywhere she pleased, lost it a bit when she saw the body but didn't scream at least, just started quietly freaking. I escorted her out of there, haven't seen her since." He made a mental note to look for Isabella and warn her to play along in case Sean and Ted wanted to talk to her, and hoped like hell she'd go for it. If she refused, and acted her usual calm, confident, too-knowledgeable self, that could open a whole other can of worms.

Fortunately, Ted was shaking his head but not in a "no, I think you're full of shit way," if the little, knowing smile on his face was any indication. "Yeah, they all said she was hot," he agreed, "and that she just waltzed on in like she owned the place. Then she apparently backed off quick and started trying to use her cell phone—good luck with that out there!" He shrugged. "I'm not too worried about her."

Sean nodded. He'd taken up a post leaning against the closed door, but now he pushed off from it and started pacing. "So, are we good?" he asked, the question mostly aimed at his partner but widened to include R.C. as well.

It was Ted who answered, and R.C. found himself holding his breath as he listened to the tall, thin agent's response. "I think so. No body but an expert medical opinion that he can't have survived those wounds. A clear timeline, from his brother's death to his. Clear motive, revenge for his brother's death. We can't ID either of them, but it's obvious they were local, knew the woods, probably grew up out there and never strayed so there's no official record of them. Two guys who officially never existed, now both dead." He nodded. "I don't think anyone's going to have any more trouble out of them, so those woods should be perfectly safe now."

R.C. opened his mouth to argue, then shut it again. Why bother? He knew the danger was only just beginning—with the second death the tsiatko had gone from mere revenge to full-blown hatred, and if anything they would be stepping up their attacks, but he had no way of proving that. Even claiming the brothers were part of some backwoods clan wouldn't help because he had no way of confirming it, or even of explaining where he'd gotten that information, not without dragging Isabella into this and sounding half-crazy himself in the bargain. And he was worried about what Sean and Ted would do if he did manage to convince them. Call in reinforcements and go in there guns blazing, most likely. Which would just mean a lot more good men dead. R.C. wasn't about to let that happen. He had to admit, Isabella had been right. The other agents weren't equipped to deal with something like this. And, much as he hated it, he was. Which was why he opened his mouth again a second later, but only to say, "Sounds about right to me."

Sean was only a few feet away at that point, and stepped over to slap him on the back. "They got him, man. Those loggers took out the guy who killed Nick. Might help a little, right?"

He nodded but couldn't manage a smile, not even a little one. "Yeah, it should. Thanks."

"All right then." Ted rose to his feet, unfolding himself like a praying mantis levering itself up into attack position, all its long limbs extending, narrow head wobbling atop its elongated frame. "Time to pack it in. I'll call it in to Ebling if you want to tell the council. Then we can hit the road and head back to civilization. I would kill for a proper Danish!" He stretched, and R.C. clearly heard joints pop.

"I'm on it." Sean turned toward the door but stopped to eye R.C. "What about you, man? You gonna head back with us? We'll tell Ebling you were a big help, put in a good word for you, all that. She's gotta see there was nothing you could've done different."

I doubt that, R.C. thought to himself, and he saw from Ted's expression that he knew it, too. Sean was the more optimistic of the pair, Ted the more realistic, and R.C. could tell that the taller agent understood how unreasonable their boss could be once she'd set her mind to something—and perhaps, too, how she wasn't entirely wrong on this one. But all he said was, "Naw, you guys go on ahead. I think I might stick around for a little bit, go hiking somewhere that doesn't involve dead bodies, maybe do some fishing. It *is* really pretty out here, and I *am* on leave." He allowed some of his very real grief to show through. "I just need a little time, you know?"

That worked like a charm. "Sure, sure," Sean said quickly, pulling the door open as if eager to escape such an emotional display. "We get it. You take it easy, clear your head. By the time you get back, your gun and badge'll be waiting for you."

R.C. nodded, though he was fairly certain reality wouldn't back Sean's claim. "Thanks." He did stand and follow Sean to the door, but continued on down the hall when the shorter agent turned to the council chamber's door. This wasn't officially his case anymore, so he didn't need to be there when Sean told them it was all over. And he wasn't sure he'd be able to keep quiet, listening to such a blatant, if unaware, lie.

Instead he took a walk, enjoying the quiet bustle of the little town. People were driving past or walking or riding bikes, and there was a hum of activity, but none of the constant noise or tension of Denver or any other big city. The pace was simply different here, and because of the much smaller population whole minutes could go by without the sound of a car engine, during which you could hear the soft pounding of feet somewhere, or the sharp clack of tools on metal or wood or stone, or even a few times a murmur of someone speaking or the smoother sounds of humming or song. R.C. loved the hustle of big cities, but there were times when it was nice to get away from all that, and he took a deep breath now, enjoying the scent of the lake bordering town and the smell of fresh-baked bread and the slight bite to the air, and appreciated the momentary quiet.

He turned after a block or two and made his way back to his truck, then drove over to Polson, reaching the Hawthorne House just as Sean and Ted were tossing their duffels in their car. "All right, we're outta here," Sean called out as R.C. approached. "Take it easy, man." He offered his hand, and R.C. shook it gladly. He still liked the short, cheerful agent.

"Talk to you soon," was all Ted said, but his handclasp was a little warmer and lasted a little longer than his first one had the other day, and his tone was less stiff as well.

"Thanks, guys." R.C. stepped back to let them climb into their sedan, then stood by and watched as the engine came to life and the car pulled away. He couldn't shake the sudden feeling that he'd just seen the last of them, and wondered why that didn't make him sadder. It was the end of one chapter of his life, but he felt like there might be another chapter opening right behind it. He just wasn't sure yet what that was.

He knew one thing, though—he couldn't move on until he'd made sure the danger here really was eliminated. And that meant dealing with the real problem, not accepting the convenient little story Sean and Ted had spun. R.C. didn't waste any time. He headed straight for the Kwataqnuk resort. As he'd expected, Isabella was sitting at the same table out on the patio. The glass across from her had lost all of its condensation by now, and the water was only lukewarm, but R.C. still smiled as he sat down and took a sip.

"They are gone?" she asked by way of greeting.

"They are," he confirmed. "And as far as the FBI's concerned, this case is closed."

She nodded. "Good. I stayed away while they were here. I have no desire for the Bureau to notice me."

"You're a hard woman not to notice." That got a short smile and a small nod of thanks or at least acknowledgment from her, and R.C. bit back a laugh. She was an odd one, but he found himself starting to like her. Still, they had other things to think about right now. He took another sip, then set the glass down and leaned forward. "Now we need to deal with this for real."

17

Isabella nodded and took a drink from her own glass—white wine, he noticed, in a tall, delicate wine glass—then returned that to the table, pushed back her chair, and rose to her feet, graceful as a cat and seductive as a summer breeze. "Follow me."

R.C. didn't have any better ideas, and it was clear she had something in mind, so he did as she said, letting her lead him back into the resort and then up the wide, open-slatted stairs. A long balcony looked out over the main room, and Isabella led the way to the far end, then through a connecting door into what was clearly a hotel hallway.

I'm letting a strange but gorgeous woman take me to her hotel room, R.C. realized as they walked, his eyes involuntarily drifting to the glorious view of her backside swaying a few paces in front of him. How the hell am I going to explain this to Nance? But despite Isabella's strong, sensual appearance, he knew sex was the last thing on her mind. Nor was he interested in anything from her beyond whatever suggestion she might have to solve their current problem.

Finally they reached a door, labeled 3011, and she extracted a keycard from her jacket pocket and slid it into the door's built-in reader. After the faint beep and the blinking green light she shoved down on the door handle and then in on the door itself, causing it to swing wide. As R.C. followed her in he made a mental note never to arm-wrestle with her. He knew how stubborn and heavy these hotel doors could be, but she'd pushed it open like it was a flimsy summer curtain. There was definitely a lot more to Isabella Ferrara than met the eye.

Once the door had slammed shut behind them, Isabella latched it and drew the chain. Then she slid the closet door open and lifted a heavy, extra-long black canvas duffel from the floor within that dark alcove, hefting it and heaving it onto the king-size bed. R.C. eyed the bag warily. He'd lugged his fair share of those exact same bags in MI, though they'd all been khaki or olive drab. But he knew the type. It was a portable weapons locker.

Sure enough, when she removed a small but sturdy lock from the zippers and hauled down on them, then flung the bag open, he could see a veritable armory inside. There were handguns and submachine guns and shotguns and some sort of sniper rifle, very high-tech-looking with a folding stock and a sleek body. But there were other weapons in there as well, knives and swords and axes and clubs and even an honest-to-God crossbow. It was like Dirty Harry meets King Arthur, and all in a seedy motel room!

"Take your pick," she said after the silence had stretched on for a minute. She reached in and extracted a military-style assault shotgun with a fold-over stock and a pistol grip. "This is a good choice." With her other hand she selected a compact machine gun. "So is this. You will want something with good range, of course, and good rate of fire—we do not know how many we face, but I suspect it will not be less than a dozen."

"And this is your plan?" R.C. asked, finally finding his voice again. "To just wade in there with guns blazing and kill every one of them?"

She studied him, and if her pursed lips and furrowed brow were any indication, she wasn't kidding when she replied, "Yes, of course. You have some other idea? Because we must act quickly."

"Yeah, okay, maybe, but not like this!" His gesture encompassed all of those weapons, and her for good measure. "This is crazy! You can't kill an entire . . . what are they, a tribe? A clan? A race?"

"Of course you can." Isabella's offhand shrug confirmed the easy, almost careless confidence behind her words. "All it requires is a little planning, and enough firepower to do the job." She raised both the shotgun and the machine gun. "These should do admirably."

R.C. shook his head, then reached across the bed to take the guns out of her hands. She didn't stop him, though the stare she gave him did make him wonder if he'd gone insane. It was clear she was starting to think so. "These would definitely take down the tsiatko," he agreed slowly. "But I'm not sure they need to die at all."

If he'd expected a passionate response, he was disappointed. Isabella did nod, however, apparently in response to his half-question. Then she added, "They are killers. Killers must be dealt with, otherwise they continue killing," but from the almost disinterested calm in her voice she could have been talking about the weather or a TV show she'd seen recently or what to have for dinner. There wasn't a single hint of bloodlust there, or in her eyes. Either she didn't actually enjoy killing—possibly because she was so inured to it that it was just another everyday activity—or she was simply one of the best actresses he'd ever seen. In many ways her casual attitude was more unnerving than if she had been frothing at the mouth for blood, blood, and more blood. He'd known both types back in the Army, and it was the stone killers that scared him, not the crazed violence-seekers.

"What about those who kill in self-defense," he countered, "or out of revenge or rage or some other strong emotion? Do you put them down too? There's a big difference between a stone-cold killer, a crazed sociopath, and somebody who's out of his mind with grief."

"Not in the results," she replied. "The people they killed are just as dead, either way." She fixed R.C. with a long, searching stare. "I thought you wished to solve this problem, protect these people, and avenge your partner. Was I mistaken?"

R.C. felt his temper rise at the dig. "Listen, lady," he said, dropping the guns back on the bed and taking a step partway around it so only a few feet separated Isabella from him, "don't try feeding me that crap. You know perfectly well that I'm in this for the long haul, and that I'm not walking away until I'm sure everybody here is safe." No more Nicks, he added in his head, but bulled past that. "And if they try anything with me, I'll send those tsiatko back to whatever hell spawned them." He took a deep breath and let it out slowly, forcing the anger back down. "But I'm not gonna start shooting the instant I see one, either. I've heard what everybody says happened here, but none of the stories exactly match up. Something's missing, or somebody's lying, or somebody's covering something up, or maybe even all three. And the only people who would know for sure are the tsiatko themselves. I wanna talk to them, assuming that's even possible—see what happened from their perspective, make sure nobody's carrying some blame that isn't his, and that nobody's gonna get shot for something they didn't do."

"You do not understand yet, I think." The way she said each word, slowly and concisely, lingering over each syllable, R.C. could tell how hard it was sometimes for her to speak in English instead of her native Italian. Or maybe it was just that she thought he was an idiot. "These are not people. They are monsters. You cannot reason with monsters. They do not think like people, because they are not people. All you can do is hunt them. I hunt monsters—this is what I do. I hunt them, and then I kill them. All of them. That way no one escapes, and no other innocents get hurt afterward." A slow, sultry smile spread across her lips, her long lashes partially obscuring her enticing gaze. "Now, you wish to hunt these tsiatko, these monsters, with me?"

A part of R.C. was chomping at the bit, eager to leap into this strange woman's invitation and wallow in the violence it offered. Why not go after these tsiatko and make them pay? Blow them to smithereens, cut down their trees, leave the forest where they'd hidden nothing but a smoking ruin? The part of him that loved this idea even offered the tantalizing prospect of staying at Isabella's side afterward, the apprentice to her master, learning everything it was obvious she could teach him. He would have a partner again, possibly in more ways than one, and a clear new path for his life to take, from agent to monster hunter. That same part of him loved that idea, and felt that such a career smacked of justice and protection, just as his now-former job had. But the rest of him recognized that all of this sounded like some twisted fairy tale. Monsters? Really? The other problem was that he was letting his emotions take over, which was never a good idea when discussing the death of an entire species *or* when deciding what to do with his life. He needed a clear head before he could make decisions properly. He was too old to let his hormones—or his anger—do the thinking for him.

Besides, if the monsters didn't kill him, Nancy would.

Pushing past Isabella and trying hard to ignore the heat she was radiating, R.C. strode to the far side of the room and the glass door set there. One swift tug yanked it open and he stepped out onto the small balcony, taking a deep breath and letting the cool lake air wash away the haze Isabella had been casting over him. When his skin was tingling just shy of a shiver and his scalp was buzzing and his thoughts and heart were calm again, he ducked back inside. He left the door open, however, so the crisp weather could continue to keep him under control.

"No, I don't want to hunt them," he told Isabella, whose lovely features settled into a faint pout for just a second before hardening into something closer to anger. "I want to protect the people here. That's not the same thing. If it turns out the only way to do that is to kill every tsiatko in that forest"—he sighed—"then so be it. But I'm not accepting 'razed earth' as our only option. Not yet. I need to know there isn't some other way to do this." He glared at her, matching her stare for stare until she finally glanced away. "You may be okay with killing these things and calling them monsters, but so far all they've done is proven they want to be left alone and they'll demand payback for the death of one of their own. That makes them violent and ill-tempered, but it doesn't mean they're out of control. One of theirs got killed first, remember? They didn't start this. We did. So who are the real monsters here?"

"You cannot ascribe human thoughts or feelings to monsters," Isabella insisted, but she didn't meet his eyes when she said it, and she no longer sounded as certain. "They are not like us. They will not stop to talk to you—they may not even understand the concept."

"Maybe not," R.C. acknowledged, moving over to the weapons strewn across the bed. He scooped them back into their duffel, tugged its sides together, and zipped the heavy canvas shut again. "But I can at least try." Hoisting the heavy bag, he turned and offered it to her. "Now, you can get in my way or you can watch my back. Which is it going to be?"

She glared at him, her hands automatically reaching for the duffel, but after a second her gaze softened and a small smile touched her lips. "Very well," she agreed, accepting the weapons back. "We will do this your way." She set the bag back in the closet and pulled the doors shut around it. "I will help you, and I will make sure they do not take you without a fight." Some of the previous sharpness returned to her eyes. "But if there is no other way, you will admit it, and do what is necessary." It wasn't a question.

He answered it anyway. "Yeah, I will. One way or another, the innocents here will stop getting hurt." He knew his own glance was just as stern. "All of the innocents."

When she nodded, he felt a weight lift from his shoulders. And as he strode to the door and tugged it open to reach the hallway beyond, R.C. thought to himself that he might have the makings of a new partner after all. But if they were working together, it was going to be on his terms, not hers. He might not be an FBI agent anymore, not exactly, but he wasn't ready to throw away all propriety or due process, either. He might not need to assemble a case for a judge, but he had to be sure at least for himself that he was doing the right thing before he took any drastic action. As they walked down the hall, Isabella beside him, R.C. could feel that the balance between them had shifted. Before, she had been holding back. Then she had tried to take command. He was in the lead now, but only by agreement. It was a good feeling—not as good as it had been with Nick, but still comforting, and he could feel a little of his old confidence in his step as he set out to get some answers to the questions that were still hanging over him. Answers that he hoped would tell him what he needed to do next.

18

"Agent Hayes?" Jonathan, unsurprisingly, seemed puzzled when R.C. intercepted him coming out of the council building that evening. "I thought you had left with Agent Neill and Agent Ambry?" His gaze shifted past to Isabella, and R.C. thought he saw a faint blush touch the young councilman's cheeks as his eyes widened and he unconsciously stood a little straighter. "Miss Ferrara."

She nodded back, her eyes barely touching on the poor man before skipping past to scan the street around them, and R.C. repressed a smile. If Jonathan was smitten with the tall blonde monster hunter—as it seemed he might be—he was in for some bad luck.

"It's just R.C.," he said, drawing Jonathan's attention back to him. "I'm not currently with the Bureau, remember? I thought I'd stick around for a little longer. Is there someplace we can talk?"

"Of course," Jonathan replied. He frowned for a second, clearly thinking, then brightened. "Have you eaten yet?" The growls emanating from his own midsection made it clear he hadn't. "I know you've been staying at Mabel's, and her food is excellent, but if you like ribs and steaks Moonstalkers is amazing. Come on."

He led them a few blocks away, to a low, nondescript square adobe building with shuttered windows and a heavy oak door. The minute he tugged the door open, however, a wave of sound and heat and smells hit them, all at once. It was a heady mixture, muted conversation and even softer music mingling together and overlaid with the toasty warmth only a fire could produce, and the rich scent of grilled meat with just a hint of tang to it. R.C. found his mouth watering as he ducked his head to follow the young detective down the two steps and inside.

The floor was several more steps down from the door, clearly carved out of the ground rather than set upon it, and R.C. assumed that helped it retain heat because the entire place was warm almost to the point of sweltering. There were plenty of other people here, many of whom called out greetings to Jonathan, and the lights spaced around the walls produced enough illumination to see your way through tables and chairs clearly, and presumably to eat without stabbing yourself in the eye or drinking the barbeque sauce by mistake, but it was dim enough to not be obtrusive and to provide a little privacy if you wanted. Likewise the general hubbub was loud enough that, while you could hear conversation all around, you couldn't make out any specific words unless you were seated at the same table.

A young woman materialized in front of them, short and slender with her raven hair back in a single loose braid, and she smiled as she greeted them. "Three?" Jonathan nodded, and she led them through the maze of other diners to an empty booth near the back. "I'll be right back with water and menus," she promised as they sat, Isabella on one side and Jonathan on the other—R.C. debated who to crowd but finally settled on presenting a unified front and slid in beside his new partner-in-crime.

"So, what's going on?" Jonathan asked once the waitress had gone. "I thought Agent Neill said everything was over."

"He did," R.C. agreed, sitting back as the waitress returned with their waters and the promised menus, then leaning forward again. "But you know as much as I do that it isn't over. Agent Neill thinks a pair of reclusive hunter brothers caused the problem, and that one's dead and the other's dead or dying. He doesn't know a thing about the tsiatko, and I didn't tell him." He held up a hand to forestall the questions he could already see on Jonathan's lips. "They wouldn't have believed me. All it would have done is convince them that I've lost it. And even if they'd accepted the idea that there were more out there, so what? They'd have gotten themselves killed too, because they wouldn't be prepared." He tapped his fingers on the rough, heavily scarred tabletop. "But we're prepared. So we're going to do what they couldn't, and take care of the real problem."

Jonathan nodded. "I think you're right," he admitted. "Both agents seemed very competent, and they were perfectly pleasant, but I doubt either of them would even believe a tsiatko existed, let alone was hunting us." He frowned. "That means you won't be getting any extra help though, is that right?"

"It is." R.C. took a sip of water. "That's fine, though. I'm not worried about them outgunning us, or getting the drop on us—we know where they are now, and how they like to attack, so we can stay ready. I need to know more about what we're dealing with, though. I need to know everything I can about the tsiatko."

To his surprise, Jonathan laughed—and started looking around the restaurant. "I'm not the one you wish to speak with, then," he warned them, and suddenly grinned, an expression that made him look ten years younger. "But he is."

R.C. turned, as did Isabella, and glanced where Jonathan was pointing. A man sat by himself a few tables away, methodically working his way through a prodigious number of ribs, and when he saw the long, snowy white braids R.C. realized it was the elder from the tribal council.

"That's Nathaniel Bearwalker," Jonathan explained. "The oldest member of the council, and one of the oldest Salish here on the reservation." He beamed with pride. "He's also my great-uncle. If anyone would know about the tsiatko, it would be him."

"Excellent." Isabella made to stand, and frowned down at R.C. when he didn't move. "We must go and speak with him," she pointed out, but he shook his head.

"Not right now." When she didn't sit back down, he explained. "Look at him. He's sitting by himself, but he's nodding and exchanging hellos with people around him. The guy's not a hermit or anything—he is on the council, after all—but clearly he wants to eat in peace. We go barging in on his rib-time, he's not gonna be too happy with us. And that means he's not gonna be feeling too cooperative." He smiled. "So we let him eat, and we do the same—those ribs look amazing!—and then, when we're all done, we go over and talk to him. He'll be in a good mood from eating, so he'll be a lot more likely to be chatty."

For a second Isabella continued to glower down at him. Then she nodded once, sharply, and sank back into her seat. "That makes sense," she admitted. "I am not used to dealing with other people much anymore. And especially not thinking about what they want, and how to get what I want out of them without bloodshed." She graced him with a warm smile that he knew made Jonathan squirm with jealousy. "This is why we are working together. You know how to work with people."

"I'm not bad at it," R.C. replied modestly. "You had to be at least decent at talking to people in order to be on active duty for MI. Same with the Bureau. If you can't talk to witnesses and liaise with local law enforcement and all that, then you shouldn't be doing this job." He rubbed at his jaw. "Maybe half of my cases could've turned ugly if we hadn't talked the guy—or woman!—down right from the start, kept him calm and civil, found out what we needed to know." Nick had been brilliant at that, he remembered, accepting the now-familiar stab of guilt he felt lance into him at the memory. She'd always known how much was too much, how much was just right, when to come on strong and when to be friendly and approachable or even a little flirtatious.

Fortunately the waitress returned just then, and he was able to shunt aside those memories and order the ribs and a few sides and a beer. One other advantage to being "on leave," he decided. He didn't have to worry about not drinking on duty, or even about showing up in the morning drunk. Not that he planned to overindulge, but it was nice to know the option was there if he wanted it.

They made small talk while they waited for their food, and then again while eating. Jonathan was a good dinner companion, comfortable and almost chatty but totally respectful of other people's silence and of course perfectly happy to worship his own mound of steaming-hot ribs in silence. Isabella was a bit stranger—the more R.C. watched her the more he wondered if she'd been raised by nuns or something, because she didn't seem to quite know what to do or say in normal situations. She joined in on their conversation here and there, but she also sometimes just stared out across the room, lost in thought. He got the definite impression she'd rather have been out in the field tracking something than sitting at a restaurant, and even while eating her eyes flicked from face to face and corner to corner, and if her hands were free they were tapping or fidgeting, or her leg was bouncing when her hands were occupied. She definitely wasn't a fan of inaction.

Finally they finished their dinner—and Jonathan had been right, it was truly excellent. Nathaniel had apparently been taking his time, because even though he'd had a head start and no chatter to distract him his plates had been cleared away at about the same time as theirs. Which was when R.C. rose from the booth and led the way over to the tribal elder.

"Mr. Bearwalker?" he asked once he'd approached, Isabella and Jonathan right behind him. "Sorry to disturb your meal, but we were wondering if we could talk to you for a minute?"

"Of course," the old man replied, and his voice was like an oak tree itself, deep and rich and full of depth and resonance, powerful but not heavy. Then his face crinkled around his eyes and at the corners of his mouth. "After all, you waited so patiently for me to finish." He indicated the seats across from him.

"Well, I didn't want to distract you from the ribs," R.C. answered, impressed that Nathaniel had spotted them. "Besides, it gave us time to eat ours, too."

The old man eyed the three of them in turn as they sat, giving Isabella a cheeky grin that had probably charmed more than a few ladies in his time, and Jonathan a fatherly nod before turning back to R.C. "Now, what can I do for you, Agent Hayes?"

"It's just R.C., thanks." He wondered for a second if he should have business cards printed up saying that. "What can you tell us about"—he glanced around and lowered his voice, despite the way the other diners insulated them already—"the tsiatko?"

"Ah." Nathaniel nodded, his eyes bright but his mouth pursed into a thin line. "I'd feared that might be the case, after all this. When Agent Neill told us it was only a pair of hermits, I was relieved to know I'd been wrong. But I thought it strange you didn't join him to tell us the good news, consultant or not. Now I know why." He shook his head, waving off the justification R.C. had been about to make. "Some men cannot see things beyond their own beliefs," he said, and again his eyes studied R.C. "But you can, hm? You have before, I think. You have that mark about you." His bright gaze moved to Isabella. "And you, young lady, for all your beauty you're practically steeped in it." The nod and half-smile she retuned were more than ample confirmation.

"Well. The tsiatko." The elder leaned back in his chair, gnarled hands woven together on the table in front of him. "I am sure Jonathan has already told you the basics, hm? The stories of them, the 'stick Indians' who haunt forests and play pranks on tribes and speak in whistles?"

"He did," R.C. confirmed. "And we saw one of them ourselves, so we know they're real and this is them. But can you tell us anything else?"

Nathaniel's eyes sought his great-nephew. "Did you tell them of the seatco?" he asked. At first R.C. thought he was talking about the tsiatko again, but then realized the word the old man had uttered was close but just a little different.

Jonathan started. "No," he admitted. "I didn't think of it." His tone was that of a schoolboy who'd just been corrected in front of the class.

"Hmmm. The seatco is another figure from our old tales," Nathaniel explained. "He is a demon, some say. He looks like one of us, but taller, thinner. Very fast, very quiet—and very nasty. The tsiatko are mild enough as long as you don't cross them. The seatco is vicious and cruel. It likes to hurt people, especially those foolish enough to wander the woods alone at night. It sleeps during the day and hunts at night, and menaces any people it finds."

R.C. frowned and shared a glance with Isabella. "Okay, that's interesting, but what does that have to do with this? I thought we were dealing with the tsiatko here?"

The elder nodded. "Yes, but there are some stories that claim the two are related—or even one and the same. The seatco are the tsiatko's dark side, their anger and hatred and rage. The descriptions are close enough, and so are their actions. The difference is that the tsiatko only play tricks on people most of the time, while the seatco enjoy hurting and killing."

"So you're saying, once that first tsiatko was killed, the rest of them went into seatco mode and now they're badasses hell-bent on vengeance?" R.C. could see how that would work. Even the names were similar, "tsiatko" and "seatco."

Nathaniel was nodding again. "Exactly right, exactly right. And if anything would trigger that change, it would be killing one of them. Now that two of them are dead—" He shook his head. "They won't back down. In fact, they'll probably get worse."

R.C. tried to ignore Isabella's triumphant smirk. "Can you remember anything else about them? Like, is there any way to talk to them? Would they even understand us?"

"That's the other reason to worry about the seatco," the elder responded. "All the stories about the tsiatko, they're almost like overgrown children. They can throw temper tantrums, but that's all it is, and usually it passes fast. Most of time they're content to hunt and fish and roam the woods and play their little jokes." He frowned, a network of wrinkles spreading across his cheeks and brow. "But the seatco, they're clever, cunning. They lure people into the woods, to their death. They evade traps, and set ones of their own. They're smart, smarter than the tsiatko. As smart as men."

"So when they're calm enough to talk to, they're not really bright enough to answer," R.C. summarized. "And when they're pissed off they get smarter, but then they're not interested in talking." He sighed. "Great."

"This is useful information," Isabella put in. The smirk had faded, and she was serious again. "Now we know that we do not face dumb animals. We must treat them like men—clever, nasty men. Underestimating them could well be fatal."

"Yeah." That didn't make him feel a lot better, though he knew she was right. Better to know their opponents, and know what they were getting into. "Thank you," he told Nathaniel, pushing back his chair and standing up. "We appreciate the help."

"Of course." The elder watched them get ready to leave. "Good luck, Mr. Hayes. And be careful. Tsiatko or seatco, they will not stop until their thirst for vengeance is satisfied."

With those portentous words ringing in his ears, R.C. headed back to his hotel, pausing only long enough to argue when Jonathan informed them that dinner was on him. His resistance was only half-hearted, however. In his head he was already parsing what they'd just learned, and trying to see how they would deal with this situation before it got any worse. To her credit, Isabella didn't push her solution again, but he could hear her thinking it even after they'd parted ways, and he was uncomfortably aware of the weapons waiting patiently in her hotel room, ready to be used. He still hoped it wouldn't come to that, but right now he wasn't seeing a lot of other options.

19

The next morning R.C. woke to find that the water in the pitcher by his bed had frozen during the night. The windows were coated in frost, and his breath steamed as he hopped out of bed and quick-walked to the bathroom, wincing as his bare feet touched the icy tile and a minute later trying to keep from spasming as he twisted the shower to full and was blasted by a torrent of stinging cold water. What had happened to the heat during the night? He stayed pressed against the shower's back wall until the water finally warmed up, then showered quickly, toweled off thoroughly, and dressed as fast as he could. Layering several shirts restored a modicum of comfort, and by the time he headed down to breakfast only his hands and his face were still cold.

He was enjoying a large mug of fresh-roasted coffee and a bowl of steaming oatmeal with generous dollops of real butter and equally real maple syrup when his cell phone went off. He'd had both hands wrapped around the mug, happy to feel some sensation in his frozen fingers again, and had to juggle it into one hand while he groped out the phone in the other. The number it displayed was local but didn't look familiar.

"Hello?"

"Agent Hayes?" The voice was unmistakable—slick, syrupy, and self-assured, its crisp pronunciation desperately trying to mask its innate lack of timbre. Which was particularly ironic in this case.

"Mr. Douglas," R.C. replied. "What can I do for you?" He didn't bother to point out that he was no longer here under the FBI's auspices. If Douglas knew that he might try to get the cease-and-desist lifted, and more logging up in Hog Heaven was the last thing they needed right now.

"I just got a call from Rick Marshall," the Douglas Timber owner answered. "Another one of my men is dead. I thought all this nonsense was going to stop! I thought you and that partner of yours were supposed to fix it!"

R.C. felt himself bristle at the mention of Nick, but refused to let this man goad him into losing his temper. Especially over the phone. "We're working on it," he said instead, keeping any bite from his voice. For now. "We thought the matter was settled, actually. Who is this man of yours, and what was he doing at an official crime scene when we've already warned you not to go near it?"

"His name is Gary Ostling," Douglas told him. "And I have no idea what he was doing up there—I told my men to stay clear of the entire area until you concluded your investigation." Yeah, sure you did, R.C. thought, but the little lumber baron was still speaking. "I've been having Rick check on the site at dawn every day, just to make sure none of the others get in the way—he just found Gary's body, and called me immediately."

"I see." R.C. was pretty sure that wasn't how things had gone down, but there was no point in pushing it. "I assume he didn't touch anything, beyond checking Gary for a pulse?"

"No, I don't think he did, but I'll call and remind him," Douglas offered. For once he didn't sound smug. Just tired, and irritable. "Can you fix this? You need to fix this!"

R.C. ignored the plea. "Mr. Douglas, I need you to keep your men away from the logging site altogether, starting right now. That's two of them dead in the last few days, and I'd rather not see a third. I'm sure you wouldn't, either."

"No, of course not!" That, at least, sounded somewhat genuine, though whether it was for any real concern for the men or just because he didn't want any more delays and any bad publicity R.C. wasn't about to hazard a guess. "But I don't know how much I can control them. We suspended our operations there, as ordered, but if they wander up there on their own time . . ."

"Just inform them that they're trespassing on a federal crime scene," R.C. said, starting to lose patience. "They can be arrested, fined, imprisoned, and even shot for interfering in this investigation. Maybe that'll encourage them to steer clear."

There was a pause, and he knew that Douglas had heard the threat implied in those words—a threat that wasn't limited strictly to the loggers themselves. "I'll speak to them again," he promised finally.

"Good." R.C. stirred absently at his oatmeal, watching the butter dissolve into a pale swirl. "I'll notify the Captain about Mr. Ostling—he'll send someone to collect the body. I assume you can handle contacting his next of kin and making the necessary arrangements?" Douglas confirmed that, and R.C. nodded. "Fine. I will let you know as soon as I have anything, Mr. Douglas. But please, keep your men away. For their own safety."

After hanging up, he took a long swallow of the hot coffee, and then spooned up a hefty gob of oatmeal. He was going to have to go back out there, obviously—he wanted to see the latest victim for himself, and at the scene rather than after the coroner fetched him back. But first he was going to finish his breakfast. He had a feeling he was going to need the extra heat before he was done.

"Brrr." R.C. wrapped his arms around his torso, which blocked the stiff breeze slightly but not enough. This was ridiculous—it was just into fall and he was wearing a medium-weight coat and gloves and even a hat but he was still shivering! It was like the weather had decided to jump forward a solid month, maybe more. Then again, he was in Montana—maybe it was always this cold up here?

Doing his best to ignore the temperature, he trudged across the logging camp toward the trees. He hadn't thought to ask Douglas for specifics on where the body'd been found, but if the tsiatko were operating true to form it wouldn't be too far from this clearing. He just hoped it was still within site of the open space—he'd feel better if he wasn't completely enveloped by the trees and their long shadows.

Nearing the far edge where they'd found the dead tsiatko, R.C.

slowed to a stop and glanced around. His Beretta was in its belt holster, and he slid his gloved hand up under the back of his coat to loosen it, feeling a little more secure knowing he could get to it easily. He'd decided against the shoulder holster for now—with him all bundled up, reaching that would have been difficult, especially if he was in a hurry. And it wasn't like the tsiatko were likely to sit around and wait for him to unzip his coat so he could draw his weapon on them.

"Okay," he muttered to himself, "now if I was a brain-dead logger tromping around where I shouldn't and getting myself shot through the throat by a bunch of angry woodland spirits, where would I be?" A part of him regretted not bringing Isabella, both to have another pair of eyes and to watch his back, but he'd decided against it. From what he'd seen of her so far, the stunning Italian was likely to shoot first and ask questions later, and he still had a whole mess of questions he needed to get answered. Her trigger-happy habits might keep him alive if they were attacked, but he thought they were just as likely to make them fresh targets and piss the tsiatko off even further. Right now he needed to just gather evidence, and so he'd decided to do that alone.

He could have brought Jonathan with him, of course—the young councilman wasn't likely to get in his way, or to advocate genocide. But R.C. had worried about putting the easy-going Salish in danger. This way he didn't have to worry about anybody but himself.

He was turning a slow half-circle, scanning the area ahead of him, when a flash of blue caught his eye. R.C. picked his way through the tangle of logging equipment—some of which had pulled free or been pulled free from the tarps that had been used to cover them when the operation was shut down. Was that was Gary Ostling—and possibly Rick himself, and any others—had been doing? Sneaking in to continue the job, even though that meant messing up the crime scene? Douglas had said that they were still on-schedule, back when they'd talked in his office that day which felt so long ago. Back when Nick was still alive. He stood to lose a lot of money if the project got delayed or cancelled, and his men probably got bonuses for finishing a job on time, and even more of they managed to tie it up early. Could some of his men have decided the money was worth the risk?

Well, R.C. thought as he left the equipment behind and made his way between the first few trees of the forest there, keeping that tuft of bright blue in sight, if Gary Ostling felt that way, he found out that sometimes the risk is real. And paid the price with his life.

As he'd suspected, the blue proved to be a bright, cheery down coat. The man wearing it was laying face up on the ground, the leaves clinging to his body here and there, and a long, slim shaft jutting from his throat.

"Mr. Ostling, I presume," R.C. murmured, then berated himself silently. Was he actually losing it now, that he talked to himself all the time? Was all of this in his head? But he needed to talk to someone, and without anyone else around, talking to himself would have to do. At least this way he didn't have to worry about someone overhearing him. It was quiet as a tomb out here.

Moving carefully, R.C. inched the last few feet to the body. No sign of Marshall or any of the other loggers—maybe Douglas had been able to get through to them, or maybe they'd just scattered before being found out here with another one of their friends dead. He would want to talk to them later, but for now he just wanted to get his own first impressions.

Gary Ostling was average height, round face with a ruddy complexion, and his thin, flyaway hair offset his soft features. He looked very, very young. His hands were heavily callused, however, and his clothes looked a little worn but still comfortable and plenty serviceable, especially for outdoors work. The arrow in his neck looked like a match for the ones they'd taken from some of the other victims. No blood spurted from the wound, and for a second R.C. figured that meant he'd been killed several days ago, but then released a plume of "smoke" when he breathed and realized. Of course! Ostling's blood was too cold to spurt, which meant death could have occurred any time before Marshall's morning sweep, including mere minutes before his friends and co-workers showed up. So TOD was almost impossible to determine, which screwed with the timeline of events big time. But Marshall claimed he'd been through here at the crack of dawn and there was no sign of a body then—so if he was telling the truth, Gary had been killed somewhere between that first sweep and the second one, which only give them a small window of opportunity. And meant he'd only been dead a few hours.

"Fine," R.C. grumbled, fishing out his cell phone again. He had a signal, at least for now, and hoped it would last long enough as he dialed the number Captain Moran had given him after their last encounter.

"Captain?" he said once the call connected. "Special Agent Hayes here. We've got another body out here at Hog Heaven. Can you pass the word to the coroner? We'll need the body brought back. Great. Thanks."

Now he had a narrow window of his own, R.C. thought as he hung up. It would take them at least half an hour to get here, but still he'd need to hurry it up a bit if he was going to hope to find any clues before the spot was crawling with cops.

First he studied the body again. No defensive wounds, which wasn't surprising—the tsiatko didn't close with their quarry, they shot them down from a distance. A single arrow, so they didn't like to waste their ammo, either. Made sense, given they had to carve each one by hand. Gary was facing north and it didn't look from the ground or his clothes like he'd been rolled over—his blue down jacket was pristine on the front except for a little blood spatter, whereas the back when R.C. rolled the body slightly was covered with leaves and bits of bark. So Gary had been shot and fell backward, and died. Which meant he'd been more or less facing his attacker when he died—R.C. glanced up and across from the corpse, in the direction he figured Gary would have seen as well. Deeper into the woods.

What is it with these guys, he wondered as he rose to his feet again, dusting off leaves. They only kill in the trees or under their shadow. Do they have one of those light allergies where they get hives and rashes if it touches them at all? Were they agoraphobic, unable to tolerate wide-open spaces? Were they just terrified of being seen? Was something keeping them in the woods, or out of the open, or both?

A sound made him tense, and R.C. reached for his gun, all his senses going on high alert. It was a soft, thin noise, like a breeze stirring the leaves—or like someone whistling just enough to be heard. Warily R.C. scanned the area. Was it just the wind? Or was it the tsiatko, closing in on him?

"Hello?" he called out, keeping his voice friendly but holding his Beretta down and low by his thigh, out of easy sight but ready for use. "I'm not here to fight you. My name is R.C. Hayes—I'm with the FBI. I'd like to talk before anyone else gets hurt."

The leaves rustled with more vigor and the fainting keening picked up, but that was all. If it was the tsiatko, they were keeping their own counsel. He found that strange as well—why go after Ostling but avoid him? They weren't afraid of being discovered, they'd proven before that they would attack from less cover than they had now, and would attack whole groups at once. So what was the difference between him and Ostling? Had they had some specific vendetta against the logger? But they couldn't have had grudges against Elk in the Trees and Jeff Landis and everyone else they'd killed, all of those people they'd shot down. So why attack them—why attack Nick?—but not go after him now? What was making the difference? Was it because he'd tried talking to them? Did such a little, easy thing make all the difference?

Whatever the reason, R.C. knew better than to push it right now. He had no idea how many tsiatko there were, but judging by the arrow storm that one night he'd have to say there were at least a dozen of them. And only one of him—sure, he had backup en route in the form of the captain and his men, but involving them would only mean opening more people up to the strangeness that was occurring, and he'd rather avoid that. Which meant the only people he could rely on at the moment were Isabella and Jonathan—and neither of them were here. There was nothing to be learned by charging in among the trees, and he could easily blow whatever grace was causing the tsiatko not to attack him yet, and become a human pincushion in about three seconds flat. Not worth it.

Instead he holstered his pistol. Then he took hold of Gary's jacket at the collar. "I'm going to drag him a little ways away from here," he called out. "There will be more men coming to collect his body, and if I get the feeling you'd rather they didn't come in among the trees. So I'm going to move him, so they can reach him more easily. Okay?"

Did the wind shift slightly? Did the trees rustle more? Were those shapes flitting through the shadows of the branches? He couldn't be sure. But R.C. had never felt as exposed as he did right then, hunched over and dragging a dead timberman's body out of the woods, knowing there might be a dozen not-quite-human archers with their arrows trained on him.

When he reached the edge of the clearing, R.C. let go of the corpse and dropped to his butt on the cold, hard ground. He was drenched in sweat, the tip of his nose was cold, and he had that strange combination of fatigue and nervous energy that came from an adrenaline high. He sat there, keeping one eye on the woods, until flashlight beams and raised voices heralded the captain's arrival. The woods stayed silent.

20

"They will not believe you," Isabella told him a few hours later. They were climbing the stairs in the council building, back in Pablo. R.C. had given Captain Moran a full statement explaining how he'd known about Ostling's body and his observations when he'd found it, and then he'd been allowed to go. He'd lied, however. He'd told the local cop that the corpse was right where he'd found it, and that he hadn't touched him. They had no way of proving otherwise—the ground was too frozen to have yielded to the weight when he'd dragged the body, and the underbrush was too hardy to crush, so there weren't any tracks to indicate the original location, and most of the blood from the wound had apparently fountained up onto Ostling's face, neck, and upper chest, so there hadn't been much spatter around him or any blood pooled below him. As far as the police were concerned, he'd died right where they'd found him. It didn't really make much difference to them, but R.C. suspected it made a world of difference to the tsiatko. He just hoped they appreciated—or even understood—his trying to keep any more people from traipsing through the trees. Then again, the fact that no one had shot at him while he was waiting suggested they did.

After speaking with Moran, R.C. had wanted nothing more than to head back to the Hawthorne House and immerse himself in a tub for an hour or two—he was aching, and spattered, and grimy, and most of all cold. But that would have to wait. On leave or not, he was still an FBI agent, and he was still working a case.

The question of his official role on that case—and the FBI's continued involvement—was exactly what he was about to discuss.

Isabella had been waiting outside the council building when he'd pulled up. He hadn't bothered to ask how she knew—she clearly had a lot of experience working around local law enforcement, which meant she had to have a police-band radio on hand. She'd heard Captain Moran mobilizing his men, most likely, and probably heard his name get mentioned somewhere along the line. From that she'd guessed where he'd go next. And she'd spent the past two minutes trying to talk him out of it.

"I don't care," he told her yet again. "It doesn't matter if they believe me or not. They need to know at least something about what's going on—and why they can't just call the FBI back in." He stopped at the council chamber door and glanced down at her. "You coming?"

She sighed, but nodded. "Yes. I do not agree, but you are the lead and I will support your decision."

"Thank you." He pushed open the door, then held it so that she could enter first. That brought a quick smile to her full lips, and she curtsied before sashaying past him. She was certainly a bundle of contradictions, R.C. thought as he followed her in—bloodthirsty hunter one minute, cold-blooded killer the next, and sultry seductress the minute after that. Strange.

The sight of the men arrayed along that long table brought him back to the moment at hand, and the problems before him, and R.C. nodded hello to the assembled council members. Willy Silverstream held his usual chair of leadership right in the center, and he was relieved to see Nathaniel Bearwalker a few seats farther down and Jonathan Couture leaning against the railing that ran along the side wall. "Gentlemen."

"Mister Hayes." Willy inclined his head slightly by way of greeting. "Forgive me for saying so, but we thought we had seen the last of you—at least, in any official capacity, though of course you are welcome to stay and take in the sights." A frown crossed his seamed, tanned face. "But I hear there has been another murder in the Hog Heaven range?"

"Yes, sir." R.C. had debated how much to tell them—true,

Nathaniel had believed him right off the bat, and Jonathan as well, but he wasn't sure the rest were quite as open-minded about ancient legends being real. So for now he stuck with the more mundane facts. "It looks like the loggers didn't manage to kill all of the people responsible after all."

"Do we need to request that Agents Neill and Ambry return?" was Willy's next question, and R.C. took a deep breath before answering.

"I don't think that would be wise, sir," he said slowly. "Sean Neill and Ted Ambry are good men, and good agents. But they're . . . limited. Or maybe hamstrung would be a better way of putting it. They have to abide by the rules, fill out all the forms, and they tend to think along those lines. If something doesn't fit the FBI play-book, they push it and prod it and ignore parts of it until it does." He shook his head. "That's not what you need here."

"And what do we need?" He was sure he saw a twinkle in Willy's eye.

"You need someone to figure out what's going on and stop it as soon as possible, before more people get hurt," R.C. told him and the other council elders. "You need someone who cares, and who's seen these deaths firsthand, but who doesn't have to play by the rules. Somebody whose first priority—his only priority—is stopping the killing, not avoiding an incident or preventing a scene or anything like that."

"And where would we find such a man?" The council leader was smiling now, and several of the others were laughing and nudging each other, but R.C. carefully kept his own face and voice serious.

"Right here, sir. I started this case, and I'd like to finish it. I won't waste my time making reports or requesting permission, and I won't look for an easy excuse or a plausible explanation. All I'll do is find out what's really happening and stop it once and for all."

Willy nodded, making his grey braids whip about. Then he glanced up and down the table. "Does anyone else wish to say anything on this matter?"

Nathaniel stirred himself. "I have every confidence in the young Mister Hayes," he announced, his deep voice carrying across the room though his tone was soft. "I believe he is the man to solve this problem and protect our people."

"I agree," Jonathan offered from his perch on the side. "I've worked with Agent— Mister Hayes since he arrived, and I trust him to take care of this for us."

Willy nodded again. "Very well," he announced. "Mister Hayes, we will abide by your recommendation—you will investigate this matter for us, and do whatever is necessary to end this problem before it spirals completely out of control. But we will not call the FBI back in, nor will we tell them about this latest death—we will trust you to decide when and how and what they will be told."

"Thank you, sir." R.C. looked around at the elders. "I promise you, I will handle this."

Willy's eyes skipped past him then, and R.C. saw them brighten as they fell upon the statuesque blonde behind him. "And who is your new companion?" His tone had become lighter, more playful.

"This is Isabella," R.C. answered. "She is helping me."

The elders all nodded, and many of them leered at her. She didn't seem to mind the attention. "Welcome to the Flathead Indian Reservation," Willy told her almost formally. "I am sure Mister Hayes is lucky to have your assistance." From the chuckles that sprang up here and there, it was clear what most of the elders thought she might be doing to "assist" him. Isabella just nodded. Then she shot Willy a scintillating smile that hit him as hard as a sunburst and washed over him like a sudden thundershower. The council leader looked flustered for a second, then recovered enough to beam back at her, his face looking for all the world like that of an ecstatic child despite the wrinkles.

"If I might make a request," R.C. cut in, as much to break up all the flirting as because he actually needed it, "would it be okay if we used that small office down the hall for planning? The same one you assigned Agents Neill and Ambry?"

"Of course. If there is anything else you need, please ask." Willy's tone made it clear that was a dismissal, so R.C. thanked him and the rest of the council again, then backed out of the chamber, Isabella preceding him. Once they were safely ensconced in the tiny office down the hall, R.C was finally able to relax and catch his breath.

"There, see?" he told Isabella as he sank down into the desk chair, leaning it back enough that he could rest his feet atop the small desk. "That went just fine."

"Only because you didn't say what sort of threat we are facing," came the rebuttal from the shadows as someone stepped into view. It was Jonathan. "But I think you're right not to," he continued. "They don't need to hear about tsiatko right now. It would only confuse them, and raise a lot more questions, questions you may not have the answer to."

"Exactly." R.C. gave the young detective a nod that was half thanks and half welcome, then stared at the white-erase board, which still bore Ted's neat, cramped notes spread across the smooth surface. So where to start?

When nothing else came to mind, R.C. levered himself out of his chair and approached the board. Picking up a rag there for that purpose, he cleared away a few notes at the top—they were initial thoughts and repeated below, so erasing them wasn't a problem. Once he had a clean swathe across the top he took one of the markers and drew a straight line. Then he started marking and labeling events, arranging them in order along that guide.

"We know Douglas sent his men up there on the sixteenth," he said, partially to himself. "Elk in the Trees was found on the seventeenth." He frowned as he noted the discovery. "We don't know exactly when he died, but we can assume the loggers would have noticed his body if he'd been dead when they arrived, so he probably died after they set up camp." He wrote down the other finds. "Peter Colman was found on the twentieth, Roger Tanner on the 23rd, and we showed up on the 24th." He did his past to rush past the "we" in that statement. "We've had three more deaths since then—Jeff Landis and Agent Frome on the 26th and now Gary Ostling on the 29th." It felt disloyal to call Nick by her last name, but at least it didn't hurt as much that way. "Plus we had the dead tsiatko on the 27th." He looked over the timeline and rubbed at his jaw. "Something doesn't make sense."

Jonathan had moved over to sit at the desk, and now he shook his head. "It looks right to me," he offered, and Isabella nodded. But something still felt off about it.

"Think about it," R.C. insisted. "Look, the logging started on the sixteenth, but the first person they kill is a local, and that's on the seventeenth? Why not one of the loggers? And why not the same day it started?"

"Because they did not attack until they were attacked in turn," Isabella pointed out. She was leaning against the table, the very picture of motion at rest, looking relaxed and stunning but coiled, ready to explode into action in an instant.

"Right!" R.C. added that in. "They killed that first tsiatko the second day they were working the site, Pat said. That would be the seventeenth, the same day Elk in the Trees was killed."

"So none of this would have happened if those loggers hadn't killed the tsiatko by accident." Jonathan pounded on the desk with one fist.

R.C. started to nod, but paused. "Maybe, maybe not. Why was it there in the first place? They'd already been logging for a day, and those chainsaws and whatever else they've got have got to make a ton of noise! Why wouldn't it steer clear instead? And if the tsiatko were just angry about Douglas Timber tramping through the woods, why not go after them when they were surveying the site, starting on the fourteenth? But Douglas would've been up in arms if any of his people'd been attacked before Landis—even if he'd tried to keep quiet about where it took place, he'd have raised a stink in general."

Thinking about that, R.C. pulled out his cell phone and dialed the FTPD—seemed like he might as well put that number on speed-dial, considering how often he was using it lately! "Yeah, hi, Special Agent Hayes here," he said once the communications officer answered, on the third ring. "Listen, can you check something for me? Has Salvador Douglas of Douglas Timber filed any missing persons reports two to three weeks ago? Sure, no problem." He waited impatiently while the officer checked. "Ah, okay—no, just wanted to check a hunch. Thanks."

Hanging up, he turned back to Jonathan and Isabella. "Nothing on that end—if Douglas did lose anybody early on, he didn't even mention it. The officer said there weren't any reports filed at all during that period, or at least not for missing people." He shook his head. "Damn, I thought that might have been the answer."

Isabella loosed one of her rich, throaty chuckles. "Is this man Douglas stupid?" she asked.

"Not at all," R.C. had to admit. "Slimy, greedy, unpleasant—but smart. Slick."

"Then why would he send his own people to survey when he could hire someone who knew the area better?" She glanced over at Jonathan, who straightened slightly now that her attention was on him. "Have any of your tribe gone missing lately?"

The young detective frowned. "I don't think so."

"Are you sure?" she persisted. "Perhaps someone you simply have not seen in a while? Someone who spends much time in the woods, maybe?"

"There is this one guy," Jonathan said slowly, scratching his chin. "Randall Brook. He's a bit of a loner, doesn't spend a lot of time in town but usually stops in once or twice a week to eat and buy groceries, that sort of thing. I don't know that I've seen him since you got here, though. Maybe not even right before that."

R.C. still had the dry-erase marker in his hand, and he tossed it from hand to hand now as he followed up on Isabella's suggestion. "What's this guy do, Randall Brook?"

"He's a scavenger," Jonathan answered. "He's got a little shack on the edge of town but he prefers a tent among the trees, or even just a hammock if it's nice out. He's a woodworker, so he's always collecting branches, but he picks berries and digs up roots and mushrooms and stuff, lives on that most of the time. Sometimes he hires out as a guide to tourists who want to go hiking." He stiffened, and glanced up at R.C. "And he's buddies with Thomas Peel."

Peel. The junior council member who'd cut a deal with Douglas Timber. Now things were starting to come together. R.C. tossed the marker onto the table and pulled open the office door. "Let's go ask if Thomas has seen his good friend Randall Brook lately."

The other two followed him down the hall and to the council chamber. R.C. was already opening the door as he knocked. "Excuse me," he called out as he entered and the elders looked up. "I just have a few questions—for Thomas Peel."

He thought the young, smarmy council member did a good impression of a deer caught in the headlights. "Y-yes," he asked hesitantly, not meeting R.C.'s eyes. "What can I do for you, Agent Hayes?"

R.C. didn't bother to correct his mistake. "Talk to me about Randall Brook," he demanded instead.

"Randall?" That surprised Peel enough that he did look up, but he quickly glanced away again. "What about him?"

"You tell me," R.C. insisted, leaning over the table with both hands planted firmly in front of him. "He's mixed up in this somehow, isn't he? Isn't he?"

Peel held out for a few more seconds, than crumbled. "Yes, okay, you're right!" he admitted. "Randall was working for Douglas!"

Aha! R.C. kept his excitement from bubbling out. Right now he had to stay the stern FBI agent. "Working for him doing what?"

"Douglas wanted someone who knew the area," Peel explained, his words directed down at the table and low enough that R.C. had to lean in further to hear. "To show him the best places to log. It had to be somebody who could keep their mouth shut. He asked me if I knew anyone. I suggested Randall."

That made sense. "And when was the last time you saw Mr. Brook?"

Now Peel frowned. "I don't know—a week or two, maybe. Why?"

R.C. pushed himself upright again. "Thank you, Mr. Peel." He pivoted and walked back out, not giving Peel or Willie or any of the others time to ask him anything else. He didn't feel like he had any answers yet anyway. But they were close by. He could feel it.

Back in the office, he added Randall's disappearance between the 14th and the 17th, with a question mark. "That would explain why a tsiatko was near the logging camp in the first place," he noted aloud. "Maybe they'd already done something to Randall Brook—

killed him, most likely—and now they wanted to get closer and get rid of anyone they could who was actually logging."

"But one of them got killed instead," Isabella commented, "and then it all spirals out of control."

"Exactly." R.C. stared at the board. Assuming Randall Brook's death, it did make a lot more sense. Though he still didn't know why the tsiatko had gone after him in the first place. From what Jonathan had said, Randall basically lived in the woods. Surely the tsiatko were long since used to him, like a class pet or a school mascot. Why kill him now? There was a piece missing still, but at least the puzzle was starting to take on a definite shape. And it was easier to fill in those last few spaces by studying the whole and seeing what they would have to be to plug those gaps. The problem was, a lot of those pieces kept winding up being dead people.

21

"Wow, it's cold!" R.C. commented as he entered the council building the next morning. After their revelation about Randall Brook the previous evening they hadn't come up with any other new information or any new ideas on how to deal with the situation, and eventually they'd decided to take a break for dinner and then call it a night and hope for a fresh outlook in the morning. Jonathan had apparently had other plans for the evening but he'd recommended the restaurant at the Kwataqnuk resort. "It is very good," Isabella had agreed. "They catch the fish fresh in the lake. We will go there."

So he'd found himself having dinner with Isabella that night. There were certainly far worse ways to spend an evening. She was beautiful, for one thing, with her rich laugh and her sharp eyes and those dangerous curves. Her Italian heritage showed through in her love of good food, and they ate well indeed, on grilled rainbow trout and striped bass, interspersed with salad and fresh brown bread and followed by some sort of dessert made of flour and nuts and honey, like a Native American version of baklava.

And the wine! She knew her wines, that was for sure! They'd had white to go with the fish, and red with dessert, and then an ice wine to finish it all off.

Somewhere along the way, they'd started trading stories. R.C. had a ton of them from his time in the MI, missions that took him all over Germany and most of central and Western Europe, even occasionally to Eastern Europe, plus lots of funny incidents that happened at Wiesbaden or some other base.

Isabella, it turned out, had even wilder tales to tell. Assuming you believed her when she talked about hunting Sasquatch or trolls or dark fey ("Redcaps are difficult, especially in a crowded mall," she explained as she drained her glass and refilled it. "Best to hide away until after hours and face them then, without distractions") or shapeshifters ("werewolves are simple enough," she'd claimed while spearing a piece of trout without looking. "They are men and they are wolves, and depending upon the form you hunt them as you would one or the other. As long as they do not have time to infect an entire village—or a monastery—they are not a problem. But true shapeshifters, their minds are as malleable as their form, they do not think like us, so you must not either if you hope to catch them."). Even if you didn't, they were riveting stories, and she proved to be a masterful storyteller, her voice dropping to a hush as the tension increased and then exploding with the action, coaxing a start out of him and then laughing at his surprise. They'd spent hours there, eating and drinking and talking, and R.C. knew that, were he a different man, he might have tried to follow her back to her room afterward. And he suspected she might even have let him. But Nancy was waiting patiently back in Denver, and their love and her trust were enough to guard him against even this fiery blonde's charms, so they'd said good night and he'd staggered back to his own hotel, where he'd crawled under the covers and had strange, muddled dreams of monsters and creatures and trees that threw branches at him like arrows, all while Nick looked on sadly and tried to tell him something but couldn't produce any words.

Waking up had been like a splash of cold water on his face—and the quick shower he'd managed had turned that into a literal truth. The lady at the front desk had apologized when he came down for breakfast—"we didn't have the furnace stoked up yet," she explained, "but we're working on it now, and you should have plenty of hot water by tonight." He'd settled for hot oatmeal and hotter coffee, and had felt nicely toasty by the time he'd exited the building and climbed into his truck.

That warm feeling had lasted all of two minutes, as the truck's heater stubbornly took its time warming up and the bitter cold outside chipped away at his remaining body heat bit by bit, starting with his fingers and toes and face and then creeping in along his arms and legs. By the time the council building had come into view even his chest felt cold, and each breath was like standing in front of a freezer, cold and crisp and sharp. Now that he was safely indoors he shook his hands and feet, trying to get feeling back into them and waiting for his flesh to warm again. Even with his coat and hat and gloves and the thick knitted scarf he'd bought from the Hawthorne House's tiny crafts store before setting out, he was still freezing. "Is it usually like this so early in the year?"

A few of the tribal elders were walking in as well, clearly about to start their day of deliberating and voting and whatever else a tribal council did, and one of them—an older gentleman R.C. had seen at the table, with a single long iron-gray braid that ran down his back and a trio of small triangular scars beneath his right eye that R.C. suspected were from a bird's talons—shook his head. "Waziya is coming," he muttered before brushing past and toward the stairs.

"Waziya," a few of the other elders agreed softly as they followed him. "Waziya is coming."

"Okay," R.C. asked nobody in particular, since most of the elders now seemed determined to ignore him and get upstairs as quickly as possible, "what exactly is a waziya?"

Typically, it was Jonathan who answered—R.C. hadn't noticed the young detective arriving, but was happy to see him nonetheless. "Waziya is the north wind," he explained, pulling off a heavy fur-lined glove to shake hands. "The name actually means 'Blower from snow pines.' He brings winter, and sometimes famine and disease as well." He shivered, his round, friendly face cloudy. "Waziya is not what you'd call a nice guy."

"Sounds like it," R.C. agreed. "But this is seriously early, even for here, right?"

"It is, and it's a problem," Jonathan said as they joined the line of men climbing the steps. "If this cold snap doesn't let up, it could kill all the remaining crops. We rely on those to get us through the winter, and to buy whatever else we need until spring. Things could become really tight without this last harvest." He shook his head. "We've had early winters before, but nothing like this—this is way too soon, and the sudden drop isn't normal, either." He managed a smile. "It's like Waziya is eager to visit this time around, and couldn't wait his turn."

"He did not have a choice," a deep voice offered, and both of them turned to see Nathaniel Bearwalker clomping up the stairs behind them. For a man of such advanced years his steps were strong and steady, and his eyes were bright and clear when he reached them, though he was breathing heavily. "Waziya has been summoned," he informed them once he'd caught his breath a little. "He has been called upon, and now he answers with his winds and his cold."

"Called upon?" R.C. stared at the old man. "You mean, there's really some Old Man Winter out there, and he'll come when he's called?"

"It is neither that simple nor that safe," Nathaniel told him. The steps were wide enough for the three of them to continue up to the second floor side by side, and he explained as they walked, "there are rituals, ancient rites, for summoning nature spirits. Waziya is such a spirit, though he is old and powerful, and most would never dare disturb his slumber." A deep frown creased his face. "But someone has done just that, and Waziya has answered their cries."

"That doesn't even make any sense," R.C. argued as they reached the top of the stairs and made their way down the corridor. "Even if the North Wind is real—and I'm not saying he is, or at least not as a person or a nature spirit or whatever—and he really could be summoned, why would anybody want to? Jonathan just said this could cost you guys your last harvest of the year—who would want that? Who would want an early, nasty winter, period?"

"No one in our tribe," Nathaniel agreed, but his tone made it clear that he believed someone did want exactly that. It only took R.C. a second to grasp his implication.

"The tsiatko?" The suggestion surprised him so much he stopped dead in the middle of the hall, and a few straggling elders had to detour around him. "You're saying they summoned the north wind?" He glared at the gnarled old man. "Look, I'm still having enough trouble believing they're real! Now you want me to accept that they're real, the North Wind is real, and they can somehow control it?"

"Not control it, no," Nathaniel corrected. "No one controls Waziya. But he hates us, and loves to bring pain and misery. If the tsiatko called to him for vengeance, he would answer them, because their request coincides with his own goals." He sighed. "They may discover that requesting Waziya's presence is a double-edged blade, however. Once summoned he is not easily dismissed, and he will not be discerning about who suffers under his weight."

"Great," R.C. complained as they covered the last few steps to the council door. "So now I've not only got to worry about a bunch of mythical tree-people trying to kill everyone, but I've got to deal with an angry North Wind on top of that? Fantastic."

Nathaniel patted him on the shoulder as he opened the door. "You are a strong man, Mister Hayes, and you have been touched by the other world once already. If anyone can find a way through this bleak time, it is you."

"Thanks for the vote of confidence," R.C. said after him as the elder moved across the chamber and toward the long table. "Let's hope you're right."

Jonathan entered next, and the grin he gave R.C. was both friendly and sympathetic. "Hey, there's always another spring, right?" he offered as he walked away.

"Yeah, sure," R.C. muttered, shutting the door behind them and continuing down the hall to his own temporary little office. The council chamber had a nice big fireplace, and he'd seen a merry blaze already going in there, and felt its heat, while the door was open. But now, out here in the hall, the chill was creeping in again, and he rubbed his hands together to keep them from going numb. "Let's just hope we don't all freeze to death before it gets here."

22

"**W**e should simply go after them," Isabella said again. "Before matters can get any worse."

How much worse can they get? R.C. wanted to ask. There's a whole race of tree-people out there trying to kill us, and now they've summoned Old Man Winter to do the job for them! He didn't say any of that, however. He and Isabella were alone in the little office, but he still couldn't bring himself to give voice to such pessimism.

Taking his silence for agreement or at least noncommittal interest, Isabella rose to her feet and stalked back and forth between the table and the dry-erase board, tapping the smooth white expanse of the board with her fingers each time she passed. "We know who we face," she pointed out. "The tsiatko, who may also be the seatco. We know where they are—in the Hog Heaven range. We know how they fight—they hide within the trees and loose arrows at us, always aiming for the throat. We know that they are quiet and stealthy and nocturnal, and that they attack at night and in deep shadow. They do not like daylight, or any strong light, and they do not like loud noises or open spaces. All this we know." She stopped and glared at him, hands on her hips, eyes flashing. "And we know, too, that this storm will come if we do not stop them first, and that it will lay waste to everyone and everything."

"I know all of that," R.C. assured her for what felt like the hundredth time. "But I still can't condone slaughtering an entire race of people!"

"They attacked first," she reminded him. "We are merely responding to the threat they pose."

"We don't know for certain that they did attack first," he countered. "Randall Brook is missing. We don't know he's dead."

"He is and you know it," she argued, and deep down R.C. had to admit she was right. He could feel it in his gut that the Salish scout and hermit had been the tsiatko's first victim. "They killed him when he did nothing to them. That makes them the aggressors. We are defending ourselves and the people around us, all the people of this reservation."

"If I thought for a second that they might erupt from the woods like an enraged anthill, I might agree," R.C. told her. "But nothing we've seen suggests that. Hell, they've never even left that one part of the woods. They've ignored plenty of targets in bordering areas. The only time they've ever attacked anyone"—he stood up as well, and leaned over to tap the map tacked to the board, right where a cluster of inked-in skulls indicated the victims—"has been right in here."

And then he froze, his fingers still resting against the cool, dry paper.

Could that be it? The answer, the missing piece of the puzzle? It just might be. Without another word he grabbed his coat off the desk chair and hurried out. Isabella stood staring at him, but he didn't have time to explain. Nor did he really want her with him. Not for this.

It had taken them roughly thirty-five minutes to get to Douglas Timber the last time. This time it took him under twenty. As R.C. pulled in, he braked hard, and managed to avoid hitting a rusty old Chevy pickup, sliding his own car to a stop right beside it. He shut off the engine and hopped out, noticing as he made for the building's front entrance that Douglas's Tesla Roadster was parked close to the wall. Good—he hadn't wanted to have to go chasing after the man.

The lobby looked exactly the same, right down to the same pretty, apparently bored young woman. Her eyes widened when he came through the door, and it was clear that she remembered their last encounter.

"Don't bother to announce me, Janice," R.C. told her as he breezed past her and through the big, polished doors behind her. "I already know which way to go."

He burst into Douglas's office, catching the wiry little lumber baron by surprise. "Agent Hayes?" Salvador Douglas half-rose from his comfortable leather seat as R.C. stormed toward him. "Have you discovered anything new about Gary's death?"

"I'm not here to talk about Gary," R.C. informed him. He marched right up to the heavy wooden desk and leaned across it, bearing down with both hands and causing the timber baron to shrink away from his shadow. "I want to know about your logging operation."

"What about it?" Douglas sank back into his chair. "I already showed you the files on it. And you shut me down, remember?" The last was said with bitterness and a trace of belligerence, but he quieted down and glanced away when R.C. glared at him.

"Tell me about the spot you picked," R.C. demanded. "Specifically, who picked it?"

"We worked with one of the locals," Douglas admitted. "He knew the area, so we told him what sort of things we were looking for—old-growth trees, lots of space between them, good sturdy trunks—and he found it for us."

"And who would that local be, exactly?" He already knew the answer, of course, but he needed to hear Douglas say it.

The shorter man sighed and glanced down at his hands. "Randall Brook."

"And when was the last time you saw or spoke to Mister Brook?"

"Right after the permits were signed," Douglas answered. "Part of the contract was for a bonus if we were able to secure the permits, so I paid him and he left. I haven't talked to him since." Now he frowned. "Why? Is he behind this somehow?"

"Not quite." R.C. looked at the papers and files scattered across Douglas's desk. As he'd hoped, one of them was a map of the area, with markers that he assumed showed various Douglas

Timber logging operations. "This is the one in Hog Heaven, right?" he asked, pointing at one.

Douglas studied it for a second before nodding. "That's right."

"And Randall Brook picked this?" R.C. shook his head. "Did he show you the spot personally?"

"No," the other man admitted. "He marked it on the map for us."

R.C. could feel that something wasn't right here, so he just kept hammering on it. "But did he hand you the map himself?"

Douglas frowned. "No, he gave it to Rick, and Rick passed it along to me."

Ah, now we were getting somewhere, R.C. thought. "Where's Rick now?"

"I don't know," Douglas claimed, but he didn't meet R.C.'s eye when he said it. "He's not currently on a job, so he could be anywhere."

R.C. loomed over the man again. "He's at the camp, isn't he?" he asked, letting his voice go low and gravely. It was gratifying to see the lumber baron gulp. "He's not supposed to be anywhere near there, but every time I look, there he is."

"I don't know anything about that," Douglas claimed, but his thin voice was even weaker and shakier than usual. "What he does on his own time is his own business."

"Well," R.C. warned, "if you call him and tell him I'm looking for him, it'll be your business, too—and not in a good way. Are we clear?" The other man nodded, and R.C. straightened up. "Good. We'll talk more later." He stalked out without a backward glance, hoping the intimidation would be enough to keep Douglas from actually warning his foreman, at least long enough for R.C. to find him. He wanted to catch the man before he had a chance to prepare any answers.

"Rick Marshall!"

The burly foreman started when R.C. appeared over the rise and shouted down at him, but he recovered quickly enough. "Yeah, whaddya want?"

"I want to talk to you." R.C. took the slope with quick, ground-eating strides, and reached the clearing in a minute. Marshall had stepped toward him as well, and met him right at the edge—next to the crime-scene tape that still roped off the entire area. "Not big on respecting authority, are you?" R.C. asked, indicating the bright yellow tape.

"I'm just keeping an eye on our gear," Marshall replied. If he was worried about being caught trespassing, his broad, bearded face didn't show it. "So what do you want?"

R.C. shook his head and forced himself to push aside his irritation. "I want to know who picked this spot."

"What? Randall Brook did—we hired him to tell us the best spots to log." But the foreman looked away when he said it.

"I know you hired him," R.C. agreed. "But I don't think that's all of it, is it? Douglas told me you handed him the map, not Brook. Did he really pick this location?" Marshall was big but so was he, and they were glaring eye to eye. The difference was, the foreman was used to cowing other loggers, maybe a few locals, possibly even a local cop or two. R.C. had faced down not only enemy combatants but drug dealers, murderers, kidnappers, rapists, terrorists—oh yeah, and a troll. After a second Marshall broke the staring contest and took a half-step back, both hands coming up splayed in surrender.

"Yeah, okay," he admitted, some of his bluster gone. "Brook did point out some spots, but they weren't any good. Too crowded, the trees were too young, and they were too close to the road." He shook his head. "We needed something older, denser. Like this one."

"So who picked it?" R.C. demanded.

"I did, okay?" Marshall snapped at him. "When he brought me out here to show me the spots he'd selected, we paused at that rise back there and I saw this little valley. It looked perfect. Brook said no, said we weren't supposed to be here, it was off-limits, even claimed it was protected." He snorted. "Protected by what, grizzly bears? It was just what the doctor ordered, so I marked it on the map, Douglas liked it, and we set up shop."

"Yeah, and you crossed a line when you did," R.C. told him, his own temper starting to rise. "Brook was right, it was protected—by the same things that've been killing your men and any local who got too close. The same ones who killed my partner!" He shoved Marshall hard, and the burly foreman stumbled back and almost fell but caught himself against a piece of equipment. "You were so busy being greedy, you didn't listen to the very guy you hired to steer you in the right direction! Do you know why every single one of the deaths out here has been right around the edge of this camp?"

He took a step forward and shoved the other man again. "Because you invaded their home! You and your saws and your axes and your chainsaws hacked down their trees, dug up their hidey-holes, tore away their refuges! You pissed them off! And so they came after you! They killed Brook—oh yeah, he's dead—and Jeff Landis and Gary Ostling, plus my partner and three locals who just had the bad luck to be in the wrong place at the wrong time."

Another step put him right in Marshall's face, and R.C. grabbed the other man by the shirt lapels and yanked him forward, rage giving him the strength to lift the big foreman almost off his feet. "And do you know what they've done now, smart guy? They've called down the winter on us all! That's right, the winter itself— they've summoned up the north wind to blow us down with the biggest, baddest storm you've ever seen. They're going to wipe all of us off the map, kill every single one of us. And. It's. All. Your. Fault!" He shook Marshall with each word, and finally hurled him away—the force of the blow tossed the other man back several feet, and he banged up against another piece that sent him spinning sideways, to land face-down on the ground, spitting out dirt and grass and blood.

"You're crazy!" Marshall managed after a second, shaking his head and levering himself up off the ground on his hands and knees. "They summoned a storm? They're using the winter to kill us? Man, you've lost it!" He managed to climb back to his feet, though he wobbled a little, and staggered close enough to glare at R.C. "Okay, maybe I changed the map! Maybe I crossed some invisible boundary to some nut-job hermit clan's backyard! And maybe, just maybe, they've been shooting us down with their hand-whittled bows and arrows every time we get too close to their patio and their sauna and their hidden Jacuzzi! And you think I'm not torn up about that?" His voice was growing louder and rougher, and his eyes were bleary as he stopped a few paces from R.C. "Those were my guys they killed!" he shouted. "And yeah, I feel bad about those Flatheads, and about your partner, too. But I didn't ask them to kill anybody! I didn't know there was anybody out here! And I sure as hell'm not responsible for the weather! Nobody is!" Shoving past R.C., he stormed off in the direction of the ridge, and the road beyond, where R.C. had parked his pickup next to a battered olive-green Range Rover he could only assume belonged to Marshall.

R.C. watched him go, but didn't move to stop him. He'd found out what he'd needed to know. The missing piece was now in place. Douglas had hired Randall Brook to find a suitable logging site, but Rick Marshall had overruled his suggestions and chosen a new spot—one that was within the tsiatko's own territory. They had killed Brook because they thought he'd led the loggers there, then they'd investigated the logging camp itself. But one of the tsiatko had gotten too close, and had been killed by accident, and that had set off the whole clan. Everything had fallen apart from there.

The problem was, even though he knew that now, what was he going to do about it? Especially now that they'd called on Waziya for reinforcements?

Feeling worn out and run down and tired, he slogged his way back up the hill and toward his truck. It was getting dark, and with the sun going down the cold was increasing. There wasn't anything more he could do here tonight beyond freezing to death, and right now he didn't want to give either Douglas or the tsiatko the satisfaction.

23

Isabella leaned forward across the table, the flickering candle light casting long shadows off her strong cheekbones, long, straight nose, and full lips. Her eyes glittered in that wavering darkness like the stare of a great cat, hungry and eager to feast. "You were right," she admitted, one index finger absently tracing a circle around the rim of her wine glass and producing a soft, humming tone. "The tsiatko did not start all of this. Their land was invaded, it felt threatened, so they tried to warn people away. Then one of their own was killed and they retaliated." But she shrugged. "It does not change matters much. They killed, and they will kill again—it is like a drug, now they are hooked on it and they will do anything to feel that rush again." Her fingers stopped circling and pounced, clasping the offending wine glass firmly and raising it to her lips. After an appreciative sip, she set the glass down and fixed R.C. with that unsettling emerald gaze of hers. "We must deal with them now, while we still can."

R.C. shook his head and concentrated on his food. Jonathan had recommended this place, and as with his two previous choices it was excellent—all they did here were chicken and salads, but the chicken was lightly charred outside but perfectly moist within and marinated in something both spicy and sweet, and the salad included things like walnuts and roasted yams. He was going to weigh ten pounds more by the time he got back to Denver—assuming he made it back at all. The thought sobered him, and he swallowed the bite he had been chewing before answering her.

"I can't 'deal with them,'" he explained. "And I can't let you, either." He took a long swig of his beer. "Here's the thing—they may not be human, exactly, but they were here before us. So as far as I'm concerned that means they get first dibs on things like uninhabited stretches of forest. And if someone trespasses, well, there are lots of farmers and other small-town or strictly rural types who'll do the same—if you cross them on their land they'll shoot you in a heartbeat and not feel a single stab of guilt." He waved his fork at her. "And a lot of the time, they won't even get arrested—they were defending their homes, which is a basic right. Same with the tsiatko." He took another sip of beer. "But I think I can talk to them. They've let me enter their woods a few times now without attacking me—I've told them who I am and what I'm doing here, and I think they've listened."

"They are more animal than man," Isabella argued then, lifting her knife and balancing it on her thumb, point down. "They may have basic cunning, and certain primal instincts, but you are saying they can reason like us. That may not be so."

"But it may be," he countered. "All those things you've fought, all those stories you've told me, are you telling me none of them were as smart as men? None of them could think and read and write and make plans?" A shudder caught him, and his hand shook slightly as he tightened his grip around his beer bottle. "I know that troll wasn't just an animal. It was careful. It laid traps—traps like a man would." A faint smile touched her full lip, and he glared at her. "What?"

"Nothing." She flipped the knife up and caught it by the handle, then set it down beside her plate. "Only, that is the first you have admitted it was a troll and not a homeless man or a wild beast or whatever other story you used to tell yourself."

Was it? R.C. searched his memory and realized she might be right. Somewhere during all this he'd finally admitted to himself that what he and his team had faced in Uppsala had not been human, or animal, but something . . . other.

"Okay, fine." He let go of the bottle and rubbed the bridge of his nose. "But that's my point—the tsiatko aren't animals. They're smart. And yeah, they're pissed off, and they're out for blood. But I think we can talk to them. I think we can work this out before anybody else has to get killed, especially any innocents wandering around beneath what they think are just normal, harmless trees."

Isabella leaned back in her chair and sighed. "I think you are wrong," she said, placing both hands flat on the table. "I think you hope too much for a peaceful resolution where there is none." She shook her head. "But I agreed to follow your lead. If this is how you wish it, I will not stop you."

A worry he hadn't even realized was pressing down on him suddenly lifted, and he straightened and smiled. "Thank you." Deep down, he really hadn't liked the idea of Isabella disagreeing with him—or trying to stop him. Now that he had her cooperation, however grudging, he decided not to waste it. He pulled out his cell phone and dialed a number. "Hello, Jonathan?" he said once the young detective answered. "Listen, I need you to do something for me. Can you get in touch with Nathaniel?"

The two Salish met him and Isabella out on the Hog Heaven range a few hours later. "This couldn't wait until morning?" Nathaniel asked as he climbed out of Jonathan's Jeep and tromped up the ridge to them, his usually deep voice sounding querulous and shaky for once, like the old man he actually was. But his step was strong and his eyes were bright, and the grip he offered R.C. was still firm, even if his skin was wrinkled and leathery.

"I'm sorry, no," R.C. answered as they shook. "The tsiatko prefer the night, so if we want to catch them in a good mood we're better off approaching them now."

"When they are strongest," Isabella couldn't help pointing out from beside him, where she stood wrapped in her long leather coat. "We are ceding them the advantage from the start. This is bad strategy."

"But good diplomacy," Nathaniel told her, and she dipped her head to acknowledge the wisdom behind those words. "You really think they'll be willing to treat with us?" he asked R.C. The heavy fur-lined coat he wore made him look like the bear that was his namesake, and for a second R.C. envied its warmth. The cold night air was cutting right through his own clothes, and he was just shy of shivering as he stomped his feet to keep them from going numb.

"I think it's our best bet," he answered after a second, nodding and shaking hands with Jonathan as well as the younger man joined them. "If they won't talk we may have to try it Isabella's way, but I'd rather not see any more bloodshed, human or tsiatko. They've lived here for centuries with very little trouble—I don't see why that can't continue."

Nathaniel nodded at that. "I agree. We may need to make a peace offering of some sort, but I've brought dried meat and berries and smoked fish, which we can set out for them. And as the eldest Salish on the reservation, and a senior member of the tribal council, I can speak to them with the full authority of our tribe behind me. I just hope they don't demand blood as their price for ending this feud." He glanced down at the logging camp below, and the woods that lay beyond it. "Shall we?"

The four of them traipsed down, taking care to find good footing in the narrow beams of their flashlights. At least walking helped generate a little more body heat, and between that and the adrenaline R.C. felt shaky but no longer freezing as they ducked under the police tape, crossed the clearing, and approached the woods.

"Let's stop here," he said quietly when they were still a dozen or so feet from the trees. "No sense giving up every advantage." He took another step as the others halted behind him, and raised his voice. "Hello!" The word echoed off the woods, and off the mountains beyond, ringing through the crisp night. "We have come to speak to the tsiatko! We mean you no harm!" He pulled out his gun, moving slowly and keeping his index finger well away from the trigger, and displayed it trapped between that finger and his thumb, holding it high and at arm's length. "Look," he called out, "I'm setting down my weapon!" And he crouched to lay it on the ground in front of his feet.

"What are you doing?" Isabella hissed behind him. "There are no doubt arrows trained on your throat even now! You wish to die as your partner did?"

The image of Nick, curled up and bleeding, flashed before his eyes again, but R.C. forced it away. "No," he responded carefully, not lowering his voice, "I don't want to die. But there's no way we can talk if we aren't willing to show them we can trust them." He glanced back at her over his shoulder. "All of us."

Nathaniel nodded. One hand went behind his back and under his heavy coat, and emerged a second later with a long-bladed hunting knife, its handle carved and polished wood, the pommel a bear head carved from what looked like turquoise. He set that down on the ground and stepped away from it. Jonathan drew a similar knife, though its cap was simple silver, and added it to the growing pile.

Isabella hadn't moved.

"Come on," R.C. urged her. "We have to show them we're serious about this."

"I do not surrender my weapons to anyone," she replied, her voice tight, her eyes flicking everywhere at once.

"I'm not asking you to surrender them," R.C. assured her—he hadn't missed the plural there. "Just to set them aside for a few minutes. If anything goes wrong, they'll be on the ground right in front of you."

"Yes, and I will use you as my human shield," she warned, but her hands had dipped under her coat anyway. A pair of pistols emerged in them a second later, and she placed those are the frozen earth by her feet. A pair of knives joined them next. Then a collapsible stun baton, the kind used by riot cops. Then a set of brass knuckles. Then a trio of small metal spheres R.C. didn't even want to ask about.

"Are you sure that's everything?" he asked her once those had joined her little mound or armaments, and she quirked an eyebrow and one corner of her mouth at him but nodded anyway. "Fine." He faced front again and rose to his full height. "My name is Special Agent Reed Christopher Hayes, of the Federal Bureau of Investigation," he called out. "I have been here before! You have seen me, and you know that I am only trying to end the conflict between you and the people who lived near you! Please, I ask that you come out and meet with us! Let us find a way to settle this before more lives are lost, on both sides!"

He waited, the trail of his words slowly fading away into the rocks and grass and dirt and trees all around them. Nothing moved, but there was a constant low buzz of noise all around, of the wind stirring leaves and grass and of small insects and of birds and other creatures shifting and stirring slightly. But there was no other reply.

"I told you," Isabella said after a moment, "they do not think as we do. This will not avail us any."

"Give it another minute," R.C. replied, not looking away from the woods. "Please!" he pleaded with it, and with the creatures he knew were hidden within it—he could feel their eyes upon him. "Please, meet with us! We have come in good faith, and set our weapons before us—you can see that we mean you no harm! There is no reason for further violence! And no one will invade your home again!"

For a second it was still quiet. Then his ears twitched. Was that a wind picking up somewhere past them, deeper in among the trees? He thought he heard the faint whisper of it among the leaves. Was that the sound of twigs breaking and branches swaying? Was he hearing birds calling softly to each other—or something else whistling in the shadows?

"Look!" Jonathan was the first to call out. "Right there!" He pointed ahead of him, a little to the right of where they stood, within the woods.

At first R.C. saw nothing. Then he thought a shadow shifted. Then another. They slid across each other, lengthening and darkening and moving, and it seemed as if tree branches were gliding from trunk to trunk, or the trees themselves were somehow rippling forward.

And then a tall, thin figure stepped out from the tree line. In the dim light of the moon and stars its skin matched the bark of the trunk beside it, and its long, narrow frame could have been just a sapling save that it moved with clear purpose and its feet rose off the ground as it walked. A second shape joined it, almost identical, and then a third.

R.C. felt his breath catch for a second and he felt momentarily lightheaded as the three tsiatko approached, and stopped only a few feet from where he stood. This close, it was impossible not to acknowledge that they were as much tree as human, with their roughened skin and their spindly fingers and their twig-like hair. But it was also impossible to miss the intelligence gleaming in their deep-set eyes, or the way they tilted their heads to the side as they studied him and his companions, and stood quietly, patiently, waiting for him to speak.

24

For the past two days R.C. had been hoping for something like this—a chance for attacker and attacked to meet and discuss the situation openly, peacefully, and possibly find some way to move past it that didn't require more death. But now that it was here, he found himself tongue-tied. He wasn't sure if it was the weight of the moment, knowing that the pressure was now on him to prove Isabella wrong, to show her that the tsiatko really could be reasoned with, could be trusted, or if it was just the strangeness of the situation, and of the tsiatko themselves, like the trees were standing in judgment on him, on the Salish, and on all mankind. Then again, the fact that it was late and dark and cold and that he hadn't been sleeping well was almost certainly adding to his discomfort.

Now was not the time to back down, however. He'd brought them all here, and now he had to help them see eye-to-eye—if that was possible. He owed that much to the people who'd already suffered from the mutual misunderstandings. He owed it to Nick. And it was because of her memory that he cleared his throat and raised his head to speak.

"Thank you," he told the trio of tsiatko first, fighting to keep his voice calm. "I know you didn't have to come out here, away from the trees. You could have just stayed in there and continued shooting at us. So thank you for taking this chance." The first of them might have inclined his head a little at that, as if acknowledging the compliment. Or perhaps it was just the chill winter wind bowing him, or a trick of the starlight.

Regardless, R.C. forced himself to continue. "Randall Brook led men here, to your woods," he acknowledged. "And so you killed him for that, because he should have known better. But it wasn't actually his fault." He took a breath, then pushed on despite the hard stares from the trio, stares that sent shivers through him and made him desperately want to run and hide somewhere, well away from these wild creatures of the forest. "He had actually marked several places for those men to cut down trees, and none of them were near you. But those men decided not to listen to him. They chose this spot, not him. They didn't know anything about you, and even if they had they might not have cared."

"This is true." Behind him, Nathaniel shifted, then stepped forward until he was standing beside R.C. Native American and tsiatko regarded one another, Nathaniel apparently not as squeamish about meeting their eyes, and with them side by side R.C. could definitely see the similarities in their eyes and noses and lips. It was as if someone had taken a thin sapling and carved the image of a Salish from its trunk. "I am Nathaniel Bearwalker," the old man announced, his voice once more deep and strong now that he'd awakened fully. "I am the oldest living Salish here on the Flathead Reservation, and a senior member of the tribal council, and I swear to you, on the graves of my ancestors and by all the holy spirits, that our people would never disturb your sanctuary. We knew nothing of this man Douglas's logging camp, and if we had we never would have let him place it in such an old and sacred region." He bowed slightly, his long white braids falling over his shoulders to dangle in front of him, and this time R.C. was certain he saw the first tsiatko bow back.

"Nine have died already," R.C. told them, holding up nine fingers to illustrate the point. "Two of your people and seven of ours. Of those seven"—again he used his fingers to show what he was saying—"one was Randall Brook. Two were loggers. But the other four were locals who had nothing to do with it, and my partner—we were sent here to find out why people were dying. We were here to see justice done." He had to fight to keep from closing his fingers into a fist. "And you killed her for nothing more than trying to do her job."

The tsiatko studied him, barely blinking, their narrow chests barely rising and falling. Thin tendrils of steam curled from their lips, showing that they were in fact breathing, but otherwise they did not move. Again R.C. shivered, and not from the cold. Did these strange creatures even understand what he was saying? Did they care? Did they feel anything besides rage when one of their own was hurt, and perverse delight when they tricked people or hurt them back?

Then the tallest of them, the one in front who had emerged from the woods, stepped closer and reached out before R.C. could reflexively pull away. His long, spindly hand closed around R.C.'s, the rough, bark-like skin scraping against his gloves. The grip was firm but not crushing, though he suspected those fingers had power to spare. The creature reached out with its other hand, and clasped R.C.'s second hand as well. It took every ounce of will for R.C. not to pull free, not to dive for his gun and come up shooting, and he shuddered at the strange touch of that inhuman flesh, but managed to hold himself still. Then he looked up, having to crane his neck to look it in the face now, and saw its eyes clearly. They glowed faintly, but from this range he could see that it was not the angry glow of a raging fire. It was closer to the soft glow of the dawn, and R.C. knew he wasn't imagining the softening around the edges of those lit orbs. It was an unmistakable look of sympathy, and it made his own eyes well up, though the cold turned the tears to ice the second they formed. The creature did understand, and it was saying it was sorry, in the only way it knew how.

"Thank you," he whispered, and the tsiatko nodded. A thin whistle emerged from between its lips, sad and slow.

They stood like that for a second longer before the creature released him, and then another second as R.C. wiped away the bits of ice upon his cheeks and made sure his voice wouldn't crack when he spoke. For the first time since they'd come out there that night he didn't feel he was in any danger—now it was just a matter of pushing away his grief long enough to see this through. "If humans had killed these people, we would bring them in to answer for their crimes," he explained finally. "But of course that isn't possible here, and exposing you to others would only make matters worse. We are prepared to—"

But he never got to his offer of mutual amnesty, because at that moment a loud crack shattered the night's calm.

Blam!

The third tsiatko, who was standing off to the first one's right, jerked back, its head whipping to the side. Then it toppled to the ground. When it hit, the sound of its impact was dry and crackling, like a bundle of sticks thrown against a stone wall.

Instantly the second tsiatko backed away, a bow appearing in its hands as if it had formed there from the cold around them. It had an arrow nocked and aimed at R.C. even as it retreated, and he didn't need a translator to tell him that its sharp, high whistling was saying something along the lines of "you see? They brought us out here to betray us! Kill them all and be done with it!"

But the first tsiatko hadn't moved, and it was watching R.C. closely, its eyes wide and sharp and waiting. "Please," he told it, raising both hands, fingers splayed to show he wasn't even thinking of reaching for a gun. "I don't know what that was, but we had nothing to do with it. We just want the killing to stop, on both sides!"

"Too late for that!" A voice called from behind him, and R.C. glanced back over his shoulder—and cursed. Two men had crested the ridge and were now walking down toward them, one big and burly, the other small and slight. He didn't need the moonlight glinting off the shorter one's silvered hair and glittering darkly in the first one's black beard to recognize them. Rick Marshall and Salvador Douglas.

"My god," Douglas whispered as he crossed the clearing, so transfixed he didn't even notice when he pushed right through the crime scene tape, leaving it to flutter free in his wake. "They're real!" He had a hunting rifle in his hands, but its barrel was pointing down and he was gripping it loosely. Marshall's rifle, on the other hand, was aimed straight at the first tsiatko, and its muzzle still steamed from releasing the bullet a second before.

"I gotta hand it to ya, Agent," the foreman said as he trailed after his boss, stopping a dozen feet back from them and off to one side so that he could clearly see and target the two remaining tsiatko. "When you claimed there were some kind of critters living out here, and that they were the ones doing all this, I thought you were off your rocker. But I told Mr. Douglas, and he was interested, so he had me follow you. When you came back out here, we decided to see just what was going on." He let out a low whistle, which produced an agitated cascade of whistles from the two tsiatko in response. "Guess you weren't making shit up after all."

Douglas hadn't stopped with his employee. He'd kept moving, walking slowly as if drawn without conscious thought, and didn't pause until he was even with R.C. and only a few feet from the lead tsiatko. "Amazing," he muttered, his eyes studying every inch of the woodland creature before him. "Half man, half tree—what are you?"

"They're trouble, is what they are," Marshall called out. "They killed Jeff and Gary, not to mention all those Flatheads." R.C. could feel the burly man's glare stabbing into him. "And your partner, the pretty little one. So why're you just standing around jawing with it? Or aren't you man enough to want revenge?"

That made his blood boil, but R.C. was careful to keep his voice level, and to direct his reply as much to the tsiatko as to Marshall. "I'm man enough to not need it," he said, stating each word cold and clear. "I'm man enough to know that Nick's death was a mistake caused by your greed and your selfishness. All the tsiatko did was defend themselves and their homes."

"Tsiatko." That was from Douglas. "Is that what they are? They're magnificent!" He glanced over at R.C. but only for a second before his eyes sought the stick-Indians again. "Do you have any idea what these creatures would be worth to the right people, Agent Hayes? An entire race of tree-men! It's fantastic!" His eyes were alight with greed. "We could make millions! Are there more? Listen, I'll need men to help me round them up, control them, keep them safe. I'll cut you in as a partner. What do you say?"

Marshall's response cut R.C. off from saying anything. "What? Didn't you hear what I said a minute ago?" the foreman shouted.

"They killed Jeff and Gary! They ain't pets, they're killers, wild beasts, and they need to be put down!"

"No, don't hurt them!" Douglas argued. "Who cares about a few idiot loggers? This will make us rich!"

"I don't want money," his employee snapped back. "I want payback for my friends!" He levered the action on his rifle, and there was a loud click as a new bullet slid into the chamber. Then he raised the gun to his cheek, sighting down it at the first tsiatko, who still had not moved.

"No!" Douglas actually threw himself in front of the creature, which was a comical sight since it topped him by three feet or more. "Don't shoot, you idiot!"

"Get out of my way, Mr. Douglas," Marshall warned, "or I'll shoot right through you." His voice had gone from loud to low and cold, though R.C. could hear the anger still coiled within his words, and he felt a chill run through him. The man meant it. He would kill Douglas, would kill them all, to get his revenge on the tsiatko—for a pair of murders that were ultimately his fault.

Which gave R.C. an idea of how to solve this problem before things got truly out of control.

"This is all your fault, Rick," he told the foreman, repressing the desire to flinch or cower as the rifle barrel swung in his direction. "You're the one who chose this spot, over Randall Brook's objections. You picked the tsiatko's home for logging, and all the people who died are on your head. If anyone deserves to pay for this, it's you." He looked up at the lead tsiatko as he said that, and thought he saw the creature's eyes tighten slightly.

Then it whistled, a short, sharp series of breathy little gusts.

Immediately there came a reply—from all around them. It was as if the night had come alive with a thousand tiny winds, each one blowing through the leaves of a different tree. They were surrounded!

Marshall realized that as well, evidently—R.C. was watching him and saw the foreman's eyes go wide. He jerked the rifle this way and that, trying to cover every angle at once, staring out into the night at the woods and their shadows, watching for any sign of movement.

There was a sound like a sudden, rushing rain, a rapid patter of soft, quick flurries, and the trees seemed to lose pine needles sideways, arcing them out into the clearing. R.C. had seen this once before, but this time the span was narrow, and all of those long, thin shafts had a single target—

—and he didn't move as Rick Marshall toppled without much more than a grunt that became a gargled sigh, a dozen or more arrows protruding from his neck. His rifle hit the ground beside him with a dull thud, and it didn't go off.

"No!" R.C. had all but forgotten Douglas standing beside him, but at the sight of his dead foreman the little timber baron snapped. His hands tightened on his own weapon, and he hauled it up and around, pointing it in the direction of the first tsiatko as if he meant to fire it from the hip.

"Put that down!" R.C. snapped at him, but the other man didn't seem to hear him.

"You killed him!" he shouted instead, aiming both his words and his weapon at the lead tsiatko. "Damn it, you killed him! You'll pay for that!"

The creature's eyes slid, not to Douglas, but to R.C., to his face. And R.C. hesitated only a second before nodding. That was all it took. There was another short whistle, and then a narrow breeze shot past R.C. along one side, ending in a muffled *thunk* and a gasp.

He didn't turn to watch as Douglas collapsed, his rifle dropping as well, the arrow in his neck snapping when he hit the ground.

Instead R.C. kept his eyes locked on the tsiatko leader.

"I'm sorry about that," he told the tree-creature. "These two men, they were the ones responsible for the logging and for choosing this location. We did not bring them here, nor did we want them here." He sighed. "They would never have stopped, especially once they saw you." He nodded as his thoughts finally settled and his racing heart began to slow. "And they attacked you first. You only defended yourself."

After a second the tsiatko nodded, and R.C. let out the breath he'd been holding. He relaxed still further when it whistled once more, a soft, undulating sigh, and its remaining companion straightened, put away its bow, and lifted their fallen companion in its arms instead. Then the two of them turned and walked back toward the trees.

"We won't let anyone else bother you," R.C. called after them, "if you will leave the people who do wander into this area alone."

The lead tsiatko paused just within the shadows of the trees and studied him. It nodded once, and whistled, but the sound was still wistful somehow, and its eyes seemed troubled. Then it disappeared into the dark woods, and the rustling faded with it.

"That was a lot more excitement than I've seen in decades," Nathaniel commented as R.C. turned back toward them. "And it could have gone a lot worse."

Isabella nodded, causing her long blonde hair to whip about her. "Yes, having them follow us proved to be a lucky stroke. Now those behind this are dead, and the project will die with them, plus the tsiatko were able to punish those responsible for their brethren's death." She gave R.C. a grudging smile. "You were correct. We did not need to hunt them."

"Yeah." But R.C. wasn't completely paying attention. He was still trying to parse the meaning behind the tsiatko's parting glance. "What do you think he meant?" he asked as they turned back toward the ridge. He would have to call the FTPD about Douglas and Marshall, of course, but right now he couldn't get the creature's last look out of his head. "Why did he look so sad, when he'd just gotten revenge on the ones who killed his people?"

"Because of Waziya," Nathaniel answered, panting slightly as they began the return climb. "They see now that you are a man of honor, and that we are not to blame for what happened, but it is too late. Once Waziya has answered, he cannot be turned away."

"That is a problem," Isabella agreed, reaching the top first and standing there, hands on hips, waiting for the rest of them to catch up. "I have fought nature spirits before, but only minor ones, and even then they were a challenge. The North Wind is far beyond us—it would be like a small puppy facing a grizzly bear." She frowned as her gaze swept over the wilderness all around them, her breath puffing out small bursts in the frigid air. "It will kill everyone when it comes," she warned. "Everyone and everything within a hundred miles. We must find a way to stop it."

R.C. nodded, but he couldn't think of anything to say as they trudged back down to their waiting cars. He was only just coming to terms with the fact that the tsiatko existed, and that he'd somehow negotiated a truce with them, albeit one that had required the lives of two men. The very idea of Waziya, much less facing it, was one he couldn't grasp right now. After all, how were they supposed to stop what was basically an angry nature god?

25

"This had better be good," R.C. groused as he stomped down the hill toward the small clearing. He had both hands tucked up into his armpits and his shoulders scrunched up around his neck and his bent head, his whole body curled in upon itself, but even so, and even with the new wool sweater he'd bought from the hotel gift shop and added on top of his flannel shirt and undershirt and long-sleeved T-shirt, he could still barely feel his extremities, and his whole body shook with shivers. Each breath was like a knife, a frigid blade that burned as it entered his lungs and burned only a little less as it exited, and his eyes burned as well as the cold froze them and caused his eyelids to stick to them with each blink. Even indoors he had felt the bite of it, huddled as he was before the big stone fireplace in the Hawthorne House's sitting room, with a mug of steaming tea cupped in both hands, but out here the weather was simply brutal.

"I think it is," Nathaniel Bearwalker replied. The old man was standing in the center of the clearing wrapped in an actual bear fur, its head still attached and atop his own like a hood so that it seemed a real bear stood there with Nathaniel's wrinkled face peeking out of its gaping mouth. "I have found something that might help us against Waziya."

"Is it a magic snow blower?" R.C. asked. Already a few stray flakes had begun to drift down, and if the white sky above was any indication they were in for a whole lot more.

"Not exactly," Nathaniel admitted, though his eyes twinkled

at the jest. "It is a ritual."

"What sort of ritual?" Isabella demanded. She and R.C. had driven there together, but his longer legs meant he'd reached the former logging camp first. He stopped by Nathaniel and she caught up, looking like the perfect ski bunny with her fur-lined but somehow still form-fitting parka, her thick boots, and her mirrored sunglasses, her long blond hair flowing out behind her in the cold wind. Of course, most ski bunnies didn't carry at least three guns and two knives, and those were just the ones R.C. had spotted so far. "I thought Waziya could not be dismissed once he had been summoned?"

"He cannot," the Salish elder agreed. "There are rituals that will shield against the wrath of the elements, but none that can banish them directly, for they are part of the great cycle of life, and beyond our power to control."

A fourth voice intruded from behind them, and R.C. glanced back to see Jonathan Couture making his way toward them. "I thought Waziya was too strong for even warding to protect us?"

"He is." Nathaniel waited until his great-nephew had reached the clearing. Jonathan was wearing a heavy fur-lined parka, R.C. noted with some envy, but his arms were laden with what looked like pine boughs, and he set these down atop one of the covered pieces of logging equipment with a sigh of relief. "But," the old man continued after that, "there are other ways to protect ourselves." He favored them with a brief, bleak grin. "When a bear attacks, you do not run, and if you cannot hide you must fight, facing aggression with aggression. But Man cannot hope to match the ferocity of a bear. That is why he has dogs by his side, to nip at the bear and drive him back with paws and teeth."

R.C. eyed the mound of pine needles dubiously. "We're gonna build ourselves a dog out of pine needles?" he asked.

"We are going to beseech another for aid against Waziya," Nathaniel corrected. He lifted several boughs from the pile, and then began marching around the clearing, laying them down at various points. As he did R.C. realized that the frozen ground was already covered with an elaborate array of chalk marks, forming a series of concentric circles with other patterns inscribed within them. Douglas's and Marshall's bodies were gone as well—he hadn't called Moran, but somebody must have. Which meant at least he wouldn't be tied to their deaths as well.

"There are only two who can stand against Waziya," Nathaniel explained as he worked, his deep voice carrying through the biting cold. "There is Okaga, the Spirit of the South, and there are the Wakinyan, the Thunderbirds. The Wakinyan are fierce and strong, but they are proud, and rarely take notice of the world below their wings or the people who crawl across it. If they were here they would no doubt battle Waziya, but it is unlikely they would heed our summons. Okaga, however—he is another matter. He is the South Wind just as Waziya is the North. Okaga embodies warmth and fertility, spring and growth and life. He is a nurturer, and may look upon us favorably and grant us his protection." With the last bough in place, he glanced up at R.C., Jonathan, and Isabella, and motioned them to join him as he stepped over some of the branches into the center of the circles. "We must call upon Okaga," he said, "and beg him to defend us from Waziya, or else we will all fall to the Blower from Snow Pines' wintry touch."

"Don't we need a drum circle to do this properly?" Jonathan asked as they moved in. "Or at least a few more people?"

"No time for that." Nathaniel held out his hands, and R.C. grasped one of them, Jonathan the other. When the elder frowned, both of them let go long enough to strip off their gloves and then interlaced fingers again. The old man's hand was as worn and supple and lined as old leather, and as cold as ice. Isabella took his other hand, and R.C. marveled again at the contrast in her, for her skin was silky and smooth overall but she had hard calluses along the top of her palm, at the tips of her fingers, and along the base of her hand. "Besides, most of our tribesmen would not be able to accept what we do, or the enormity of the threat we face. They do not truly believe, and so their pleas would not be sincere. We four have seen the tsiatko. We know Waziya is coming. We are the ones who must speak on the tribe's behalf."

"Tell us what to do," R.C. told him, his teeth chattering. "Quick, before we freeze to the ground." It felt as if it had become colder just in the time they had been standing there.

"Walk as I walk, gesture as I gesture," Nathaniel instructed. "And join your thoughts and your hearts to mine as we beg Okaga for help. Leave the rest to me."

With that he began stepping to the right, each leg raising so high the knee came up to his waist, his arms rising and falling in a counterpoint rhythm as a song began ululating from his lips. R.C. did his best to mimic both the steps and the arm gestures, and thought about Okaga. The South Wind, Nathaniel had said, and the Spirit of the South. Well, if anyone could help them it would be the warmth of spring.

They continued to pace around the circle, the constant motion at least keeping their limbs from freezing solid though R.C. felt as if his bare hands had simply become blocks of ice at the ends of his arms. Nathaniel kept chanting, though a sharp wind rose and began to swallow his words so that all R.C. could hear were the occasional syllable. If Okaga was listening, he gave no sign, and the clearing was definitely getting colder.

Then something shifted off to one side, just in the corner of his vision. They had stopped marching to the right and were now high-stepping back to the left, and R.C. turned his head as much as he could to glance toward that spot as they rotated around. The trees were moving! After a second he corrected himself, however. It wasn't the trees—those stayed stationary perhaps a dozen yards away.

It was the tsiatko.

A handful of them melted out of the forest, and then a handful more. R.C. thought he recognized the two who had treated with him the previous night, though he couldn't be certain. Especially since Nathaniel either hadn't seen them or wasn't willing to let them interrupt his attempted summoning. When he saw Isabella twitch slightly as she wound up with her back to the approaching stick-Indians, he knew she'd spotted them as well. What did they want, R.C. wondered. Had they decided that just killing Douglas and Marshall wasn't enough? Or perhaps they figured it was safest if anyone who had seen them clearly didn't survive to tell about it—and, conveniently enough, those four people were the ones standing out here in the open with nothing but some pine needles to defend themselves. R.C. had his pistol on him, of course, but he didn't dare let go of Nathaniel and Isabella's hands to draw it and shoot. He wasn't sure he had enough bullets for this many, anyway.

He debated whether he should say something to Nathaniel. Should they stop the ritual and take cover? Not that there was any-where to go—the tsiatko had spread out and circled around, and now the spindly figures surrounded the clearing. And, R.C. real-ized with a chill that for once had nothing to do with the dropping temperature, they were starting to close in.

The first of them—he was almost certain now it was the leader from the other night—stepped over the chalk marks of the outer-most circle. Several of the others followed suit. They breached the second circle, and every muscle in R.C.'s body tensed as he fought the urge to run. How could Nathaniel not notice what was going on around them? But the old man kept chanting and marching and swaying. If anything, his grip on R.C.'s hand tightened. Perhaps he did realize, and simply felt that four deaths would be a small price to pay if they managed to summon Okaga and fend off Waziya. *I'm sorry, Nancy*, R.C. projected toward his wife, safely back in Denver, as the tsiatko stepped over the last of the pine boughs and into the innermost circle. He tensed as the leading stick-Indian reached out with one long, gnarled, claw-like hand—

—and interlaced its sticklike fingers with his own.

The creature's other hand slid into Nathaniel's grasp, and sud-denly the tsiatko was part of the ritual, stepping with them, its gan-gly legs allowing it to effortlessly keep up with the elder's pace, its long arms rising and falling in time with their own. It raised its head and whistles rose from its narrow, toothy mouth, the tune mingling with Nathaniel's words to form a richer, more complex melody. R.C. glanced around, and realized that the other tsiatko had done like-wise, inserting themselves between his friends and expanding their circle. Where they had been four, they were now eight, four humans and four tsiatko, all clearly united in a common purpose:

To call upon Okaga for his aid in defeating Waziya.

Stunned, R.C. looked across the circle at Isabella. She surprised him by grinning and then giving him a deep nod back. It only took him a second to recall their conversation the night before and understand why. She had admitted, then, that he had been right to refuse to slaughter the tsiatko. Now his decision was proving doubly wise, because they had clearly felt guilty enough about bringing Waziya here that they were trying to atone by aiding the ritual to summon the North Wind's bitter foe. If they had killed the tsiatko, Waziya still would have brought winter crashing down upon them, but they would have had no help at defeating him. Now, because they had chosen mercy and mediation instead of murder, they might have a chance.

Then R.C. realized that he couldn't blink.

His eyes were burning, stinging, searing, but he couldn't close them, no matter how hard he tried. The lids were frozen to the flesh of his cheek and his brow. He tried to say something, but his lips were stuck fast as well, and sucking air in through his nostrils felt like a red-hot poker had been thrust up into his forehead.

The sky was glaringly white, blindingly so, and as he squinted, trying desperately to close his eyes even for a second, R.C. saw fluttering bits fall from above to land upon his head and shoulders and arms and to dust the tops of his feet.

It was snowing.

Nathaniel's voice faltered. He tried to take up the chant again, but the wind had risen to a fierce howl and drowned him out. The tsiatko's whistles were lost in the din as well, and all of them staggered together as the sharp air currents cut at them like a hail of razors.

"It is Waziya!" Jonathan managed to gasp as he dropped to one knee, only Isabella's grip on one hand and a tsiatko's on the other keeping him from face-planting in what was rapidly becoming a layer of glittering snow across the clearing. "He's here!"

R.C. pulled his hands free and slapped his face, barely feeling the impact through numb flesh. He tried again, and managed to shatter the seal binding his lips shut. "We need to find cover!"

he shouted as best he could through the sudden blizzard that had sprung up around them. Already it was hard to make out the others in the snow whipping about everywhere.

"This way!" Isabella gestured, her pale coat and blonde hair making her almost invisible, and turned back toward some of the equipment around them. One of the pieces was an enormous table saw, R.C. realized, presumably for cutting the felled tree trunks into shorter log segments. Isabella crouched under the tarp protecting the saw, and half-led, half-dragged Jonathan after her. R.C. put an arm around Nathaniel's shoulder and helped guide the old Salish to the makeshift shelter, and a minute later the four of them were huddling beneath the heavy table and its thick tarp. The tsiatko did not join them, and R.C. could only hope the stick-Indians had made it back to the relative safety of the tree line. All he could see past the tarp and the table's legs was swirling snow.

"We're in trouble," he muttered, rubbing savagely at his eyes and biting back a scream as the skin tore around them. He blinked reflexively from the pain, and then had to scrub again when the tears that formed instantly froze to his cheeks. "Waziya's got us but good, and there's no way we'll make it back to the cars before he turns us into popsicles."

"I have a flare and a lighter," Isabella offered quietly. "This table is made of wood. We could light it, perhaps break off pieces to use as torches. Fire and cold do not mix. Perhaps that would be enough to see us safely over the ridge."

But Nathaniel shook his head, sending his long braids all about. "It is too cold for that," he warned. "The fires would die in an instant, snuffed out by the snow and the wind and the ice. We should stay here and hope Waziya grows tired of battering at us and goes off to find easier prey."

R.C. gritted his teeth but nodded. He didn't like being stuck like this, especially under such flimsy shelter, but he didn't see that they had any other options. He started to say so, and paused as the sounds beyond the tarp dropped away.

"What the hell?" he managed, his voice unexpectedly loud in the sudden hush. Turning, he peered out beneath the tarp—and stared, his mouth dropping open.

The blizzard had not vanished, but it had moved to one side of the clearing, spinning about itself as if it were a small dog barely contained by its owner's fence. But on the other side of the clearing—he looked again, scarcely able to believe what he was seeing.

On the other side the snow had all melted away, only a few patches of white showing where it had been. In its place greenery was showing through the mud and dirt and fallen leaves, as new shoots of grass poked their way up into the sunlight. Even from here R.C. could smell the scent of plants and rich soil, and he thought he could feel a faint warmth on his face, caressing his flesh and restoring feeling the cold had stolen away.

"It's like winter on one side, and spring on the other," he said softly, sliding back out from under the table to study the strange scene. The others followed.

"Not just sides," Nathaniel corrected with a smile, his eyes gleaming again. "Winter to the north, spring to the south." The tribal elder laughed, the deep, rich sound filling the clearing.

"Okaga has heard our call. He has come to do battle with Waziya."

It did indeed resemble a wrestling or boxing ring, R.C. realized, and the two combatants were facing each other from opposing corners.

And he and Isabella and Jonathan and Nathaniel were caught right in the middle.

26

The whistling sound was the only warning R.C. got—a shrill keening, not like the soft trills of the tsiatko, and coming from his right. To the north. "Get down!" he shouted, and hurled himself to the ground, sweeping out one long arm to knock Nathaniel, who was next to him, off his feet as well. Jonathan and Isabella both dove for the frozen dirt as well, and just in time as what looked like a torrent of glittering little darts flew across the clearing, most of them to shatter upon impact, a few of the sturdier ones to imbed themselves, quivering, in the trees and rocks on the far side. R.C. didn't need to study the shards to know what he had seen, he had recognized the way the sun had caught on their sharp edges as they raced over his head. Ice. The North Wind had loosed a barrage of ice blades at them.

Or had it been at them? Peering back over his shoulder, R.C. noticed that the trees the ice had assaulted looked greener and straighter than their northern brethren, their trunks free of ice, their branches reaching up toward the sky and sun and showing green tips and buds and even a few petals. Spring had touched those trees, had stripped Winter's bitterness from their bark and breathed new life into them. Had those trees been the ice's true target? Or was it the being that had just embraced them?

Strain as he might, R.C. couldn't make out any sort of person or even figure near those trees. All he could see were branches and leaves and bark, nothing more. On the other side, however—

Perhaps his eyes were playing tricks on him. Certainly it was hard to look north, where the wind stung at him the moment he did, freezing his lids and lips and cheeks again with a single harsh caress. Still, there amid the swirling snow and ice at the north edge of the clearing, just in front of the dark, twisted, bare-limbed trees—was that a figure standing there, outlined against their dry and frozen bark? If so, it was tall but stooped, hunched like a vulture, with long arms and longer claws poised to strip flesh from bone, and piercing little eyes set in a narrow, sharp-planed face.

Waziya.

The wind howled, its pitch one of rage and defiance, and snow poured down into the clearing like an avalanche had just crashed in upon them. These were not the light flakes R.C. had seen earlier, but a veritable flood of snow, a thick wave of slush that blanketed everything in sight. Including him and his companions. He could feel the moisture seeping into his coat, his pants, his hat, even his boots, and with each inch it sucked away any warmth he had retained, leaving a sharp, fierce ache that threatened to shake him to pieces.

But then an answering breeze washed over him from the opposite direction. It seemed no match for the icy wind at first, for it was soft and subtle, slow and sweet, gliding and curving and in no particular hurry. But it carried with it the smell of fruit ripening and flowers blooming and vegetables poking up out of the earth, and with those scents R.C. found the pain in his chest receding. He could breathe again, and it was warm and rich and good. His clothes steamed gently as the golden sunlight cooked away the snow, and the ground hungrily drank the runoff, leaving not even puddles to show where the deluge had been seconds before.

Clearly, this round belonged to Okaga.

Isabella started to clamber to her feet, but R.C. motioned her back down. "I don't think this is over yet," he warned, and beside him Nathaniel nodded. "We're safer down here." Her scowl showed what she thought of that idea, but she did as she was told.

The day had started out cloudy but now it was bright and clear. Too bright. Looking up, R.C. saw only spots behind his eyes, and cursed as he ducked back down, blinking rapidly to clear his vision.

But the glare overhead wasn't from the sun, or any one source. It seemed to be coming from everywhere. The entire sky had gone snow-white, featureless and infinite and blinding.

This time the cold was not a sharp needle but a dull blanket, settling heavily upon them and slamming them into the ground upon which they lay. R.C. could feel the warmth struggling to compensate, but the sun couldn't pierce the whiteout and the chill sank in its teeth, taking up residence in his very bones as the ground seemed to turn to ice as well, so that they were being assaulted and frozen from both sides.

Waziya had demonstrated that he was not to be denied.

"They are too evenly matched," Nathaniel warned, his words puffing forth in clouds from his chapped blue lips. "We are midway between spring and winter, so neither has the advantage. And both were summoned, so neither has a stronger claim."

"So they'll battle it out forever?" Isabella asked. Her teeth were chattering, and it occurred to R.C. that southern Italy was warm year round. He at least knew how to handle a Denver winter, but for her this must be utter hell.

And it didn't help when Nathaniel shook his head. "Winter is implacable," the old Salish explained wearily, resting his head on the dirt before him. "Spring is more flighty. If the battle goes on too long, Okaga will lose focus, or direction, or simply weaken too much to continue. Waziya will conquer him, and us, and winter will sweep across the land."

"Okay, what can we do to help?" R.C. frowned when the elder didn't respond at first. "Come on, we have to do something! We can't just sit here!"

On Nathaniel's other side, Jonathan offered a worn smile, his usually cheerful face low. "What would you suggest?"

R.C. shook his head. Why ask him? This wasn't his sort of thing! All he knew was what Nathaniel had told them, about Waziya and Okaga and— "The Thunderbirds!"

Isabella was watching him closely. "What about them?"

"You said only two things could battle Waziya, right?" he asked Nathaniel, who nodded. "Okaga and the Thunderbirds. We have one"—he ducked as a thick branch, apparently frozen before its time, crashed to the ground only a few feet away, and hugged the ground even lower when a massive flurry of pine needles shot across the clearing, south to north— "what if we were to find the other?"

"We have no time," Nathaniel replied, shaking his head. "We would need to perform the ritual all over again, without interference. I doubt either wind would allow that to happen. Nor is there any guarantee they would even deign to appear—the Wakinyan, the Thunderbirds, soar high above us, and often the world of Man is beneath their notice."

"I know how to get their attention." R.C. rose to his hands and knees and began crawling toward the tree line. It didn't really matter which direction, but he wasn't stupid enough to head for north and he didn't want to be too obvious he wanted south so he chose "west" instead. All around him, over him, and even under him the ground and the animals and the trees pushed back and forth for the two candidates, ice and snow against warmth and greenery, each side trying to undermine the other.

R.C. remained focused. He crawled through winter and spring alike, ignoring freezing rain and snowstorms and deadly wind but also newborn plants and warm breezes and cheerful sunlight, his only goal to reach the relative safety of the trees. At last thick roots appeared before his hands and tall shadows loomed over him, their foliage blocking out much of the spiritual battle that still raged on all around. R.C. looked up. The trees jutted up like towering cliffs from this angle, their thick bark seemingly proof against the winds that assaulted them though their branches shook and leaves tumbled down here and there. It felt almost as if the trees were watching him, but R.C. didn't mind. It was actually what he'd been hoping for.

"We need your help," he called out. He couldn't see anyone there in the shadows, but he could tell they hadn't left. "Okaga can't beat Waziya alone. We need the Thunderbirds. And you need to call them to us. We can't do it, not in the middle of all this."

The trees stayed still and silent amid the wind. R.C. waited, even as icy fingers speared him in the back right through his layers of clothing.

"Please," he whispered, his voice shaky from the pain. "It's the only way to make things right again."

He slumped down on the ground, the last of his energy spent, waves of heat and cold washing over him, his body too tired even to shiver.

And, as his eyes fluttered closed, he heard the whistling begin again. It was fast and insistent, high and demanding, and it rang all around the clearing, the echoes rising even over the winds, even up through the leaden sky, up above the snowy covering and into the clouds.

And just as R.C. thought he was finished, a spark of light lanced down, so bright it left afterimages even against the snow.

Another flash followed, and another, each one a jagged slice of pure illumination that shattered the cold and let darker clouds roll in.

Then came the boom.

The first one left R.C.'s head ringing and his body vibrating like he had been thrust inside a massive bell just as it was struck from the outside. A second titanic crack came a second later, shivering its way up through him but not from cold. He even managed to smile with aching lips and tingling teeth, because he knew what these were.

They were thunderclaps.

The clouds were sweeping across the sky now, lightning flickering within them as they flew straight for that angular figure in the north. R.C. couldn't make out much to the clouds themselves, but he thought he saw shadows above and alongside them, and those dark impressions slid up and down like wings beating the air. Lightning flashed from the front and he had the notion of a long, hooked beak outlined by the blue-white glow. The clouds puffed out below, and more lightning crackled at the bottom, many-forked and curved like great claws outspread to rend and tear. He saw four clouds in all, each one distinct and each a different shade of grey. One was blue-gray, one was soot-black, one was shot with red, and one was a baleful yellow.

He rolled onto his back and stared up in awe as the Thunderbirds took the fight to Waziya, their claws and beaks ripping into his wintery flesh.

Nor did they attack alone. A strong wave of warmth followed them, adding to their momentum and carrying along the scents of growth and life and flowers. Okaga was lending his strength to the Thunderbirds, making common cause with them to defeat their mutual enemy.

The icy figure to the north recoiled from the thunder, and flinched back from the lightning. Snow and ice thrust toward the clouds but were batted aside by great shadowy wings. Freezing winds were torn to shreds by sharp crackling beaks and claws. Then the heat and the sunlight struck, shriveling the figure where it stood, forcing it back even as it shrank, until it retreated back beyond the clearing and vanished into the woods there. The clouds circled once and then vanished, taking the last vestiges of snow and overcast skies with them. The sun shone down instead, beaming from a clear blue field, and R.C. sat up, the golden beams driving the last of the chill from his bones and spreading a gentle warmth through him in its place.

"Waziya is gone," Nathaniel announced as he stomped over to R.C. and offered him a hand up. "Okaga and the Wakinyan defeated him. He will not return until his appointed time, and it will be a long while before he attempts again to overstep his traditional bounds."

R.C. nodded, using the older man's still-strong grip to help him regain his feet. He stood and stretched, joints popping in a satisfying way where moments before they had been frozen solid. Peering back toward the trees, he thought he saw a glimmer of sunlight reflecting off deep-set eyes, and nodded his thanks. The faint reflection seemed to bob once in reply. Then it vanished.

With a deep sigh, R.C. turned back toward Isabella, Nathaniel, and Jonathan. They all grinned at each other like fools for a second, then turned without a word and began to make their way back toward the ridge, and the cars that waited beyond. They had won. The reservation and its people were safe.

27

"You cannot go back."

R.C. took a deep breath to calm himself and twisted to look down at Isabella, who stood on the curb just behind him. "Sure I can," he argued.

"You cannot," she insisted. "You have seen too much. You know too much of what is truly out there. You cannot pretend any longer. The world is different for you now, and those around you will see it. You do not belong among them anymore."

"We'll see." He unlocked the truck's door and tossed his duffel onto the passenger seat to avoid continuing the conversation Isabella had started this morning when she'd found him at the hotel and discovered that he was planning to return to Denver.

"Why shouldn't I?" he'd asked when she'd shaken her head. "The problem's solved, everybody's safe, justice was served. Time to go home, try my damnedest to get my job back, and go back to work."

Which was when she'd started going on about how he was different now, and had to move on.

Nor was she the only one.

"You have been marked," Nathaniel had warned when R.C. had gone up to the tribal council to say good-bye—for real this time. "No one could witness what you did and not be touched by the power that swirled around you. In particular, the Wakinyan. They are not meant for mortal eyes. To catch even a glimpse of them is to make one *heyoka*, a mixed-up man, filled with vision and power but forever a step off from the regular world. You stared up at them and saw them fully. You will never be the same."

"You saw them too," R.C. had pointed out, and the old Salish had laughed.

"Yes, but I am already *heyoka*," he explained. His eyes had twinkled. "That's why so many people think I'm bug-nuts crazy."

R.C. had shaken hands with him anyway, sorry to be leaving the funny, wise old man behind, and with Jonathan as well, knowing he'd miss the junior tribal member's quiet cheer. He'd accepted Willy Silverstream's thanks for ridding them of the threat—even if the rest of the tribal council didn't know all the details, they had taken Nathaniel's word that there would be no more deaths in that corner of the woods, provided people were respectful when they walked among the trees—and said farewells to the other council members as well.

Isabella had been waiting for him outside.

"I've got a wife and a home and friends and a job and a life waiting for me," he explained to her now. "I'm not about to walk away from it all just because I saw some weird shit." Though of course the "job" part was definitely still in question—he wasn't looking forward to the FBI investigation he knew was waiting for him back in Denver, or to having to justify his actions to a boss who had already labeled him a major screw-up and put him on leave. But he'd cross that bridge when he came to it.

Isabella shook her head. "You can try to fit back into that old life," she warned, "but it will not work. Not anymore."

"We'll see." R.C. held out his hand, and she accepted it. Her handshake was as firm and no-nonsense as always. "Take care, Isabella Ferrara. It was nice working with you, and thanks for saving my life however many times you did."

That at least got a smile out of her, a slow, sensual one that transformed her from irate hunter to stunning model in a heartbeat. "You saved my life at least as many times," she pointed out, "and you kept me from killing people who had done nothing worse than defend themselves and seek revenge for the deaths of their loved ones." Still holding his hand, she leaned in and kissed him quickly on each cheek. "Take care, Reed Christopher Hayes. And may you find the path that suits you."

R.C. nodded and climbed into his truck. Isabella stayed where she was. Quick glances in his rearview mirror confirmed that she watched, motionless, as he drove away.

"Come."

R.C. stepped into the office and shut the door behind him. Ebling was sitting behind her desk as usual, her arms in front of her, elbows on the blotter, fingers laced and just tapping her lower lip. The look she graced him with seemed less angry than the one she'd scoured him with when he'd left her presence the last time, and more tinged with uncertainty, concern—and maybe even a little fear.

"Sit." He sat. "I've read Agents Neill and Ambry's report," she informed him, her eyes flicking to a folder by her right elbow. All of their reports were done electronically, of course, but Ebling liked to have everything printed out and stored in hardcopy as well. That way if an electromagnetic pulse should short out all of the computer systems in the world, she'd explained, their office would still have all of its case files. Though R.C. and Nick had joked that, if there was a pulse, checking notes on a cold case probably wasn't going to be their biggest concern. He tried not to let that thought make him smile now, since he was trying to be as professional and serious and respectful as possible. He hadn't expected to get called into the office again so quickly—he'd only gotten back last night— but he was hoping that was a good sign.

"According to them, the case was closed," Ebling continued. "The killer was mortally wounded, and dead in the woods some- where. So why is it, Mister Hayes, that three more people died after they left? Gary Ostling, Rick Marshall, and Salvador Douglas— the owner of Douglas Timber, his foreman, and one of his loggers. What can you tell me about that, seeing as how you decided to stay on the reservation even after the case was done?"

"Tragic hunting accidents," R.C. replied, struggling to keep from grinning. "Unfortunately, it happens. All three men were upset by recent events, so they probably weren't as careful as they should have been. Honestly, they shouldn't have been handling firearms in their state, but they weren't the kind of men who listened to warnings or took advice." Especially when it had to do with hunting down the supernaturals that had killed their friends and co-workers, he added in his head. In a way, everything he'd just said was true. They had been tragic accidents, and they shouldn't have been hunting. Maybe if Douglas and Marshall, in particular, had listened to him, they'd still be alive.

"I see." It was clear from her tone that the AD knew there was more to the story than he was telling. "And you just happened to still be around when these deaths occurred?"

"I did." He spread his hands wide, then rested them on his knees. "Mr. Douglas called me after Gary Ostling was found dead because he still had my card from when I'd been heading up the case. I didn't know he and Rick Marshall had died until the FTPD called to let me know, just as a courtesy." Jonathan had called those in, he'd later found out.

"And you have no idea what happened beyond a series of 'accidents'?" Her tone was sharp, biting. "Did Agents Neill and Ambry perhaps decide to leave too soon?"

He shook his head. "No, the case is closed." He put as much sincerity as he could muster into his tone. "There won't be any more deaths up there." Of that, at least, he was fairly certain.

"I see." Ebling lowered her hands at last, and he watched as she lifted the folder, flipped it open to study its contents—and then set it aside. "Fine. Which just leaves us with one last loose end." Her eyes bored into his skull. "You."

"Yes, sir." He knew she had more to say, so he just waited.

But for once, she didn't get straight to the point. "Did you know," she said instead, "that some of the Salish on the reservation claimed to see strange things the day before last—the day before you finally left and returned to Denver? They said they saw thunderclouds that flew like birds, and winds from the north and the south that contained faces. And then there was the weather. A flash-blizzard? Even for Montana, that's unusual this early in the year. And it was so localized, not more than fifty miles across—and centered right on the Hog Heaven range. Doesn't that strike you as strange?"

He didn't like this new tack of hers, or the way her voice had gotten lighter, as if she were forcing herself to sound casual just before she pounced, but he knew if he wanted even the vaguest chance at getting his job back, he had to play along. "It is strange, sir," he agreed. "I had to buy a whole new wardrobe."

"This isn't the first time you've encountered something strange, is it, Mister Hayes?" The steel was starting to show beneath the silk as she lifted a second folder from her desk. R.C.'s stomach lurched upon seeing the Army seal on its front. He didn't have to read the typing along the tab to know that it said two words: "Uppsala Incident."

"You remember this, don't you, Mister Hayes?" The sharp, clipped words were the clang of the trap snapping shut. "Of course you do. You lost your entire team that time, not just a partner. You said that an "enormous, crazed homeless man" killed them. Four trained Army officers, slaughtered by some European hobo? Astounding. There were inconsistencies in that case as well, weren't there? You were found innocent of any wrongdoing, and never charged with anything, but you were put on psych eval and taken off active duty." She tossed the file back onto her desk. "Just like now."

R.C. swallowed, trying to stay calm. "Yes, sir. It was a bad time, sir. Just like now." He already had a good idea where this was going, and part of him wanted to rip apart that desk, those files, and her smug expression all at once, but he forced himself to stay seated, though his hands did clench into fists.

"The Salish tribal council contacted me about you," Ebling told him next. "They seem to think you're directly responsible for saving them from any further problems. And someone up in the DoJ likes you, or else you'd never have gotten that consultant status." There was that frown again, and the tightening around her eyes spoke or real, deep anger again, too. "Which puts me in a delicate position, Mister Hayes. If I fire you now, or bring you up on charges, it'll be bad publicity for us, plus it could anger certain people who seem to have taken a liking to you. On the other hand"—she leaned forward, her eyes blazing now, her voice losing its calm—"I think you're, at best, a crazed lunatic whose wild delusions get the people around him killed, and, at worst, a psycho killer who masks his own brutal murders within violent cases he's investigating. I don't want you within a hundred yards of my other agents—they aren't safe with you around."

"I'm sorry you feel that way, sir," R.C. managed to reply through gritted teeth. "I have never deliberately put anyone else at risk." He shoved away the memory of the tsiatko watching him after Douglas' attack, and of him nodding.

She waved aside his claim. "You are hereby placed on indefinite leave, pending a full psych eval and possibly a follow-up investigation. You will receive sick pay until such time as your case has been decided conclusively." The look she gave him would have shriveled a bug on the sidewalk without the benefit of a lens or sunlight. "I promise you, Mister Hayes, you will never handle a case again. You'll fester and mould while I invent new reasons to keep you on inactive status, until you either quit, die, or screw up so badly I can finally nail you. Now get out of my office and out of my bureau."

R.C. rose to his feet. He started to turn away, but stopped and took a step back instead, the rage within him enjoying the brief look of terror that crossed his former boss's face as he leaned in over the desk, both hands planted in front of him, and shoved his face within a few inches of hers. "You have no idea the things I've seen," he told her, his voice a low, gravely rasp he barely recognized. "You have no idea what I've faced. And everything I've done, I've done to protect people, even pathetic little paper-pushers like you. So you can take this job, you prissy little bitch, and you can shove it up your puckered ass. But the next time something comes down the pike and starts killing people, and nobody can figure out what it is or how to stop it, don't come looking for me. You're on your own."

Then he turned and stormed out, making sure to slam the door properly behind him.

He hadn't parked in the Bureau's garage this time—a premonition, perhaps?—and so when he emerged from the building through the front doors R.C. turned and made his way down the block toward where he'd left his pick-up. Slung over his shoulder was the small duffel bag he'd kept in his desk, with its spare change of clothes, extra ammo, and basic toiletries—a mini go-bag, in case he and Nick had caught a case and had needed to leave too quickly to stop off at home and grab their larger ones. The bag now held the other things that had been on his desk—his coffee mug, his and Nance's wedding photo, a shot of him and Nick at her last birthday bash, a finger-basketball set, the pen set he'd gotten long ago as a college graduation gift, a few other odds and ends. He'd taken the time to collect those on his way out because he knew that there was no way he was ever going back. Not after Ebling's decision—or the way he'd lit into her. That had been unprofessional of him, and stupid to boot, but damn, it had felt good!

R.C. was so busy beating himself up over that career-ending tirade that he didn't hear the car pulling up alongside him. He only noticed it when it slowed and its passenger-side window lowered. The car was a sleek European sports car of some sort, done in a gleaming red, and peering out at him was a familiar face, blond hair swaying about her striking features.

"It did not go well, I take it?" Isabella asked.

Despite the oddity of her just showing up like this, R.C. couldn't help but laugh. "You could say that," he admitted, stepping onto the grass and approaching her car.

"I told you it would not," she reminded him. He just nodded. "Well, the past is the past. Time to move forward." She reached over and unlocked the door, then pushed it open. "Come with me."

He only hesitated a second before tossing his duffel bag into the back and sliding onto the low-slung leather seat. She peeled away from the curb before the door had even clicked back into place.

28

"**W**here are we going, exactly?" R.C. asked finally. They'd been driving for about twenty minutes, and Isabella showed no signs of slowing down. She handled the car like a pro, taking tight turns and gunning the engine at every possible occasion, shooting through narrow gaps in the traffic and evading street lights as if they were enemies bearing down on her. Perhaps it was her Italian blood. She even had on leather racing gloves!

But her only reply now was to smile and shake her head. Evidently it was a big mystery.

Briefly he wondered what he was doing, getting into a flash sports car with a strange woman he'd only met a week or so earlier, and who he knew for a fact went heavily armed and enjoyed hunting and killing things. But he trusted Isabella almost as much as he'd trusted Nick, and she had already saved his life at least once if not more. So he decided to just lean back in the smooth leather, enjoy the calming thrum of the powerful motor, and let her take him wherever it was they were going.

The sound of the engine changed as she finally downshifted, slowed, and pulled off the road into a parking lot. A quick glance at the dash revealed it had only been another ten minutes, but even so R.C. judged that they'd left Denver proper and were somewhere on the city's outskirts, probably still too close to technically be in another town. The parking lot Isabella was now cruising through was large and empty save for a single vehicle up ahead, some sort of off-roader from the silhouette. It was parked right in front of a sprawling office building, and the sign planted in the clearly untended stretch of lawn running between the building and the sidewalk said "EnterWeb."

"I remember this place," he said slowly, wracking his brain for details as Isabella pulled up beside the other vehicle—an old Jeep Grand Cherokee, he saw. "It was one of those big Internet start-ups, a few years back. They made a big splash, had full-page ads in all the papers, even sponsored a float in the city's annual parade. And then they folded a few weeks later."

Isabella shrugged as she shut off the sports car. "I know nothing of that," she admitted. "But this is the place." She slid out of her seat and peered back at him. "Come. Your future awaits."

"What kind of future hides out in the Ghost of Internets Past?" R.C. muttered to himself, but he clambered up and to his feet anyway. She was already striding toward the building's wide front doors, and he caught up to her after a few paces. "Still not going to tell me what we're doing here?" he asked, glancing sideways at her. Again she smiled but shook her head.

"She won't," a new voice called out. "But I will."

The doors had opened, and a man was waiting for them just inside. Isabella nodded hello as she glided past, and R.C. followed her, then turned and studied the new speaker. He was young, maybe thirty, almost as tall as R.C. but leaner, with thick blonde hair and the deep tan of someone who spent a lot of time outdoors. Good looks and a ready smile, along with the unseasonable board shorts and T-shirt he wore, completed the look of an avid surfer, but his eyes were sharp and restless as he offered a hand. "Good to finally meet you in person, R.C." Then he grinned rather impishly. "Too bad you didn't reply to me that first time—could have saved us both a lot of trouble."

"I'm sorry?" R.C. shook hands with him—the guy had a good solid grip. "Have we met?" He didn't look or sound at all familiar.

"You don't remember? I'm hurt!" And the stranger did actually seem upset for a second, his lips even forming a pout before he shook it off. "Well, it was a long time ago. I told you I was a friend, remember? Warned you not to let them convince you it was all in your head?" He paused, obviously waiting for that to spark something, then finally added, "The trolls?"

"Wait a second!" Now it came back to him. After the Uppsala incident, he'd found a note slipped under his door back at Wiesbaden. It had told him not to believe their claims that trolls didn't exist, and to keep his wits about him. It had been signed "a friend," and below that there had been a strange marking. An odd symbol, with letters woven through it. The letters "o," "c," "l," and "t."

OCLT.

"That's why it sounded familiar!" he told Isabella, who nodded. Then he looked over at the surfer dude again. "You sent that?"

"I sure did. Macklemore's the name, but you can call me Mack." Mack clapped him on the back. "Now come on, let's give you the grand tour."

"So this is the organization you work for?" R.C. asked Isabella as they passed through the main lobby and headed for the doors beyond the reception desk. The whole place smelled of stale air, cobwebs, and rats, but layered atop those smells were newer ones—ozone and rubber and plastic and paint, much of that matching the renovations he could see taking place all around. "You didn't tell me you were based in Denver!"

"We weren't," Mack answered for her. "Hell, we weren't really based anywhere, unless you count my trailer, and that wasn't going to be big enough for what we have in mind." He laughed at some inside joke, then pushed open the doors and gestured proudly. "Behold, the new heart of O.C.L.T.!"

R.C. stared. "Um, okay," he said after a minute. "Great. So what's O.C.L.T., exactly? And why're you guys TPing an old office building with cables?" Because that's what it looked like. Beyond the doors was an open floor plan, a single vast chamber with small offices ringed around the edges, but even that much was difficult to make out thanks to the profusion of wires everywhere. They hung down from the ceiling, draped over cubicles, snaked across the carpeting, and tangled up along the walls—it was like a jungle explosion, only the plants were made of metal and plastic and fiber-optics.

"Okay, it's a little messy," Mack agreed, surveying the chaos. "But it's a work in progress. I got out here as fast as I could, but even I can only do so much. Just wait until it's finished, though. This baby's going to be state of the art! It's going to put places like NORAD to shame!" Then he seemed to register the rest of what R.C. had said. "Wait, what'd you mean, 'what's O.C.L.T. exactly? 'bella, you didn't tell him?"

"There was not the time," she answered. "And do not call me that." There was definite warning in both her tone and her eyes, but Mack shrugged them off.

"Okay, fine." He took a deep breath, and for a second his face turned serious. "O.C.L.T. stands for the Orphic Crisis Liaison Taskforce," he explained, stating each word slowly and clearly. "We take care of the problems nobody else can handle—the stuff most people don't even know exists." R.C.'s confusion must have shown on his face, because Mack sighed and rubbed a hand through his unruly hair. "Okay, listen. Years back, I started an email list, right? There were lots of bizarre things happening all over the world, things most people wouldn't believe, and I wanted to keep tabs on them. So I set up a network to keep me informed, and to share that information with like-minded individuals. That was the original O.C.L.T."

"That's what contacted me after Uppsala," R.C. offered, and Mack nodded.

"Precisely. But that's all we were, a loose group of associates who shared info from time to time. We couldn't do much about anything—we didn't have any direct resources, no mandate, nothing. Just the intel." He grinned again—R.C. could already tell that this was a guy who didn't like to stand still very long, and that his mind was always racing as well. "Fortunately, I'd gotten noticed. A few people came to me with an interest in taking O.C.L.T. to the next level. And after a problem a couple months back, when a friend of mine almost died because we didn't have anyone we could turn to for real help, I took them up on it. And voila!" he waved his arms at the large room. "Here we are!"

"You still haven't told me what you do, though," R.C. pointed out. He leaned against the wall beside the door back to the lobby and folded his arms across his chest. "Exactly."

"You always talk in circles," Isabella agreed with a huff. She turned toward R.C. "There are monsters, yes? Trolls, tsiatko, yeti, many others." He had to nod—after their recent experiences there was no way he could deny it any longer. "Many other things out there, too—aliens, fey, vampires, mutants. The police, they cannot handle such things. The military, either. FBI, CIA, MI6, Mossad—fine for terrorists and kidnappers and bombs, not so much for aliens and werewolves and Redcaps. Someone needs to step in. That is us."

"So you hunt and kill monsters." She'd said as much before, and started to nod now, but Mack cut her off.

"No. We're not killers." He cast a quick glance at Isabella. "Well, not all of us. We're a taskforce. We deal with the problem, whatever it is, whatever it takes. Sometimes that means killing. Sometimes, it's just talking." The grin was back but it wasn't as wild now, and it held a tinge of respect. "Like you did up at Flathead."

R.C. frowned, thinking about what they'd just said, these two strangers who talked about aliens and monsters as if they were everyday fixtures. And maybe, for them, they were. "Okay, so you take care of the problems. You protect people from the things they don't understand. I'm cool with that. And now you've set up shop in Denver?" He smiled at the slight widening of the other man's eyes. "Yeah, I caught that—you said you got here as soon as you could, and you don't talk like you're from here. I already know she's not." He jerked a thumb at Isabella, who smiled, apparently taking that as a compliment. "So why here?"

"We're still a small group, at our core," Mack said by way of an answer. He grabbed a hanging cable and swung from it absently, reaching for a second one to pull himself up off the ground. "We've each got some unique skills—you've already seen Isabella's, and you can probably guess at mine. But the one thing we don't have?" He dropped back down, his eyes locked on R.C. "A leader."

R.C. couldn't help himself—a short bark of laughter burst out of him. "So, what, you're offering me a job? You've got one hell of a sales pitch!"

"This is no joke," Isabella insisted, grabbing him by the arm. "This is the path you were meant for. Deep down, you know that."

Mack just watched him. "It's a lot to take in," he said finally, and for once he seemed still and at rest and serious. "But this is the real deal, R.C. Isabella's right, this is where you've been heading your whole life." Then he smiled. "But don't just take it from me. Come and meet the bosses."

With that, he turned and started weaving his way through the tangle of wires and cables and old office equipment. Isabella glanced at R.C., one eyebrow raised in query, before following.

R.C. watched them go. What to do, he wondered. He trusted Isabella, and there was something likable about Mack, but what did he know about either of them, really? And now they revealed they were part of some weird shadow organization that, what, handled aliens and mutants and monsters? How crazy was that?

Then again, if someone had told him two weeks ago that he'd be siding with a bunch of tree-people to summon the South Wind and the Thunderbirds to defend them against the North Wind, he'd have said the same thing. Crazy.

And there was the letter from the DoJ. That had been real. Whoever these guys were, they had some major pull.

Fighting monsters. The ones he'd met so far, yeah, somebody sure as hell needed to get on that.

And, really, what else did he have to do?

With a sigh, he shoved off from the wall and marched into the mess, sprinting through the open patches to catch up.

"Right in here," Mack said as he opened a door and flipped on the light switch. The room proved to be a large conference room, and unlike the rest of the building it was tidy, its wood-paneled wall handsome and stately, its thick carpet clearly new and unmarred, its ceiling high and smooth. Sconces along the walls provided an even, subtle light, and a long oval table of polished wood took up most of the space, with comfortable-looking high-backed leather chairs spaced all around. "Go on in," Mack added. "They'll be right with you."

R.C. nodded and stepped in, only half-surprised when the door *snick*ed shut behind him. He moved over to the chair at the end of the table, pulled it out, and sat down. And waited.

"Mister Hayes." The voice came from the other end of the room, and as R.C. glanced up he was surprised to see someone sitting there. And even more surprised when he realized he could see right through the man's head, to the wall beyond. What the—?

"Thank you for coming." This was a woman in the chair beside the man, and if he squinted he could see through her as well. More figures began to appear, populating several other chairs, and in each case R.C. could tell they weren't really there—they didn't have any dimension to them, no solidity, and despite the lights their faces were in shadow. It was like looking at people in a bunch of computer monitors, only without the monitors. He mentally revised his estimate of Mack's skills—maybe the man hadn't been making empty boasts after all!

"We've been watching you for some time," another man said, and R.C. detected a definite European accent in his crisp, clear tones. "Ever since we established O.C.L.T., in fact. You were one of a very select group we considered for entry."

"The way you handled yourself in Uppsala put you on our radar," another woman added, her voice sounding Asian though he couldn't make out her features. "You kept your head and deal with the situation, despite the loss of your friends. That was impressive."

"We were pleased when we heard about the situation in Flathead and discovered that you had been assigned to it." That was the first man again. He, at least, sounded American.

R.C. nodded. "You got me that consultant gig after Ebling benched me," he guessed. "Because you wanted me back on the case."

"Precisely. Consider it a trial run," a different man said. His accent—Russian, maybe? "And you passed with flying colors."

The first woman leaned in slightly, revealing strong features that had a decidedly English cast to them, even if they were still digitally blurred. "Understand, Mister Hayes, that not every situation will call for combat. We need someone who can dish out violence when it is necessary—but who doesn't always turn to that as a solution. Someone who considers every option and goes for the best one, not just the most obvious. Someone like you."

"You said 'we,'" R.C. replied. "But who are you, exactly?" He hoped he wasn't crossing a line, but he wasn't about to even consider working for people if he didn't know who they were and what they really wanted.

"We can't tell you that," one of the others answered. "I'm sorry. Each of us represents a different nation, and our countries all agreed to participate in creating and funding O.C.L.T. But for obvious reasons we need to have plausible deniability, so no names."

"That also means no interference, though," the Asian woman added. "You'll be free to run O.C.L.T. as you see fit. We'll provide you with equipment, resources, money, even government access— you'll be bumped up from the Bureau, and loaned out by the DoJ for a "special project," so you'll keep your agency affiliations but not have to report to anyone there. You and your crew will have actual government status within each country involved, and we've got agreements for consultant status with many others. We'll keep tabs on what you're doing, and we'll let you know if we hear of anything we think you should handle, but we won't assign missions, or evaluate progress, or demand budget approval. This is your show."

"We're just your biggest fans, who're giving you the tools to do the job." That was the first man again, and R.C. could tell he was smiling from the sound of his voice. "It's a big job, Mister Hayes, but we think you're the right man for it. What do you say?"

"What about the rest of the team?" R.C. asked instead of answering right away. "Mack and Isabella, and anyone else already involved—won't they get annoyed if you just appoint me to take charge over them?"

"Unlikely," the English woman answered. "Each of the team is supremely talented, but none of them are cut out for command. They're each much more accustomed to working alone, but they recognize that some situations are too big for them by themselves. They'll be happy to have someone to help them figure out which are which, to organize everything and determine strategies and use each of them to their best advantage."

"Mack was the person who first brought you to our attention," the possible Russian gentleman added. "And Isabella approves of you as well."

"She does?" That surprised him a little. "But she wanted to handle things one way, and I vetoed that and went for another."

"And you were right," the first man pointed out. "She admitted as much in her report, and said she respected you for standing firm. This team needs a strong hand, Mister Hayes. Anyone weak won't be able to control such distinct personalities. You would be a tremendous asset, and with you at its head O.C.L.T. could make a major difference. What do you say?"

R.C. thought about it for a second. It was crazy, of course. A secretive multi-national agency of oddballs and geniuses and loners, and they wanted to put him in charge? Then again, things would have been a lot worse in Flathead if he hadn't taken charge. And that troll would still be running around Uppsala if he hadn't stepped in. So maybe it wasn't that crazy.

Maybe it was just where he was meant to be.

"So?" Mack asked as R.C. stepped out of the conference room. He was doing gymnastics using two of the cables, rocking between them like they were rings and he was at the Olympics. Isabella, on the other hand, was sitting cross-legged on a clear patch of floor, sharpening the edge of an already wicked looking stiletto. "How'd it go?"

"I want a full rundown on our current activities," R.C. replied. "I need a full roster, too—who we've got, where they are, what they can do. And I want a list of any and all possible missions, tagged by location, date, and danger level."

Mack grinned. "You took the job. Awesome!" He dismounted, sticking the landing perfectly, and held out his hand. R.C. accepted it.

"I also need a floor plan," R.C. told him. "I want to know what this place is going to look like when it's done, and where my office will be." He laughed. "Good thing I've already got my stuff in the car." He paused. "I still want to know, though—why Denver?"

That got a laugh from both of the others. "Because you were here," Isabella answered, rising smoothly to her feet and sheathing the stiletto somewhere R.C. didn't want to know. "It seemed unlikely you would move—did you not say you had a life, friends, and a home here?" She shrugged. "So O.C.L.T. had to come to you instead."

"It's cool," Mack agreed as they turned and began making their way back toward the front doors. "We needed a new base anyway, and this place is perfect! Plus it's near the center of the country, so you can get anywhere in a rush."

R.C. nodded, his eyes on the floor as he picked his way along. "I'll also need a list of our resources," he decided. "I need to know how fast we can get to those places, and what options we have."

"You got it, boss man." Mack's tone was slightly facetious, but his smile said he was kidding, and R.C. had a feeling the man in the conference room had been right. These people needed someone to tell them what to do. Well, he could handle that.

He allowed himself to grin as well, as he slapped Mack on the back, and then turned to smile at Isabella. "Let's get to work."

Want more O.C.L.T.?
Turn the page for a sample
from the first book in the series:

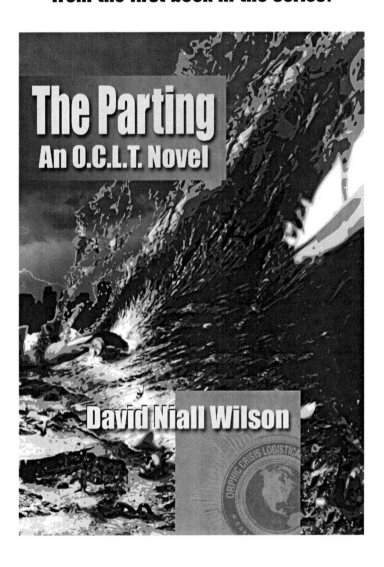

The Parting
An O.C.L.T. Novel

David Niall Wilson

1

In a low bunker in the desert near the border of Jordan and the Dead Sea, a dozen men gathered. They arrived over a period of hours, none too close to behind the other to avoid any chance, even in this remote location, of being recognized together. They were not men given to solitary excursions, but each had left comrades and security behind in the interest of secrecy. They were robed, and their faces were covered against the whipping desert sand. Far above, the moon shone, pale and cloaked in clouds.

Salt clusters along the bank of the water glimmered oddly, almost glowing in the dim light. The water was as flat and lifeless as a sheet of glass. None of the twelve even glanced at it, though the last of them stopped and gazed directly across the surface toward Jerusalem. He stood there for only a moment, and then passed between the two squat, expressionless guards stationed outside the door. The two were associated with none of the twelve. They were carefully vetted mercenaries without affiliation. They didn't know who they guarded, or why, and they didn't care, as long as they were paid well, and on time.

Inside the building was a single long room. There was a small kitchenette, and a bathroom, relics of previous owners, but these were sealed. The room was centered by a rectangular table set very low to the ground. The twelve gathered around it. There was water, and tea, but for the most part the drinks were ignored. The room was lit by a single lamp on the table, as if those present weren't even comfortable knowing one another, let alone getting a good look.

When they were all seated, the man at the head of the table leaned back, glanced around at the others, and shook his head.

"We represent," he began, "an incredible gathering of power. The resources we command should be able to move mountains—with or without faith. We can, and have, bought kings and ambassadors."

"And for all of that," one of those to his left growled, "we have failed once again at the one task we must accomplish before all others."

There were mumbles of agreement all around. None of those gathered was happy, and each secretly blamed the others for their failure. They were not men accustomed to failure, or the denial of their desires. They dealt in blood, fortunes, and power. The one thing they shared—the one central binding power—was the passion of their faith. They were from a variety of nationalities, but theirs was a common enemy and a holy cause.

"Sometimes," the man who'd first spoken continued, "I feel as if we have lost our way. Allah places more obstacles in our way than he removes, and despite our unwavering loyalty, the Holy City is yet in the hands of the unclean. They have proclaimed themselves God's People to the world. What have we been proclaimed?"

"Killers," one of the others said.

"Terrorists," a third cut in. "They say that we care about nothing but the shedding of innocent blood. No matter that our beliefs are those of our fathers, and our father's fathers. No matter that the blasphemy of our most Holy City being handed by Western dogs to the unclean cuts us to the very soul."

He slammed his fist on the table. As sturdy as it was, the glasses and lamp jumped. Still, none of them rose. Their passion simmered, but it didn't boil over. Nothing that had been said was new. Theirs was an old hatred, and it burned slowly, but with great heat. It was fueled by frustration and the futility of their efforts.

"There must be a way," the first man spoke again. "Allah will show us that way."

The grim semi-silence of the gathering was broken by a peal of rich, feminine laughter. They spun as a single unit, drawing blades, and guns and diving back from the table with cries of surprise.

They were leaders, but each of them had earned their position through years in the field. None of them was privileged by birth, and if they'd been compromised, every man of them would fight to the death.

There was no invading force. It was a lone woman, wrapped from head to foot in traditional Arab robes. Her head was swathed in a dark Hijab, covering all but her face. It was a remarkable face. Despite the dim light, her eyes glittered, and the grim line of her mouth was bent in a scornful frown. She stood with her arms crossed, glaring down at them as if she belonged—as if her presence did not break every law of their faith. As if all their security was so much dust in the desert.

"So," she said at last. "You have come to wallow in your defeat. How clever of you. How proud you must be. Allah would be pleased."

The first of the men back to his feet closed on her, his dagger raised.

The woman cocked her head and watched him, making no move to retreat.

"Who are you?" he asked. "How do you come here?"

"I came on the wind," she replied. "I come because you have called me. I come—because you have failed."

"You will not leave this place alive," the man said.

"I will," she said. "I will leave as I came, and I will leave with your promise, and your aid. You may call me Amunet."

The man closed on her quickly. He was not in the mood for idle chatter. He drove the dagger straight at her heart, but she only smiled. She spoke a single word—a word none of them heard clearly, and that none of them would have understood had they heard it.

The dagger shimmered and lost its rigidity. It coiled and turned back on itself, writhed and squirmed in the man's grip. He screamed, and tried to release it, but—now a serpent—it had coiled back around his wrist and moved up his arm toward his face. It was fast, and he staggered back, crashing into the table and falling across it, reaching to grab the snake behind its head and prevent it from reaching his face.

Two of the others ran to his side. One gripped the serpent behind its head, and the other dragged it free of his wrist. They held it—and then—with a cry of his own, the man gripping the neck cried out and backed away. His hand dripped blood where the sharp dagger blade had cut him. He stared at the wound in shock.

The dagger fell to the floor between them. The twelve turned and stared. Amunet gazed back at them, unperturbed.

"You will listen to me," she said. "You will help me, and I will help you. Though I am certain that my words are wasted, I will tell you this—there is nothing you can do to prevent it."

"Sorceress!" one of the men cried. "Allah protect us!"

Despite what they'd just witnessed, these were hard men. They were not going to be taken down by a simple illusion, and they were unused to being spoken to as lackeys—or for that matter, by women. Most of them were unaccustomed to a woman speaking to them at all if they had not addressed her first. The frustration of their recent endeavors, coupled with the ignominy of the situation was too much. They spread out and moved in quickly. They did not speak, they acted, but the woman, Amunet, did not back away. She raised both of her hands and spoke in clear, cutting tones.

Again, her words were lost to them. She seemed to speak in tongues, though now and then a phrase made the ghost of sense. The already dim light darkened, and there was a rising wail from outside the building. They ignored it. Before any of them could reach where the woman stood, the wailing was joined by twin screams.

They hesitated and turned toward the single door. There were no further screams, but the wail had grown to a roar, as if the desert had lifted up to sweep them away.

"What is it?" one of them cried. "What is happening?"

"Sandstorm!" another yelled. "It must be a storm. What else could . . . ?"

The door slammed inward as if struck by a huge hammer. It crashed open and hit the wall so hard the stout wood cracked. A dark cloud roared through and spread like smoke. The wail they'd heard was now a droning, pulsing mass of sound. Before they could even back away, the wall of locusts struck them. They were driven back, pounded into the walls, covered head to foot in biting, buzzing death. They screamed, and as they did, their mouths were filled. They tumbled back, scrambled for cover that did not exist, and through it all, Amunet stood, untouched, unmoving.

When the twelve were down, covered and helpless, crawling with her plague, she clapped her hands and shouted a single word.

In that second, there was absolute silence. The locusts had vanished. The door swung loose on its hinges. The light flickered once, threatened to go out, and then grew steady once more. Amunet walked to the table and straightened it. The twelve scuttled back against the walls, watching her in terror-stricken awe. She met their gaze, not smiling, not angry. When she saw they would not speak again, she nodded very slightly.

"Now," she said, "you will listen. There is work to be done, and if you hope to know the glory of your vision, you will act swiftly and exactly as I command. You have prayed, and you have maintained your faith. I am here. Your ancestors, long ago, faced off with the Hebrew sorcerer Moses—and their hearts were weak. Mine is strong, and I offer that strength to you. In exchange, you will bring me what I need. The Holy Land will grow powerful once again. You will be great in the eyes of Allah, and of the world. I will have what is mine."

One by one, the men rose from where they'd fallen. They checked themselves for dangers that were not there. One of them walked to the door and, after glancing out to see that the two guards lay dead in the sand, closed it as well as he could. They righted the chairs and returned to their seats. When they were ready, Amunet began to speak, and they listened very carefully. They listened long into the night, and then, when she was finished, they dispersed as randomly and as quietly as they'd arrived.

When she was alone in the room, Amunet finally allowed her lip to curl in a dark, enigmatic smile. She turned out the lamp, and as the light drained from the room—she was gone.

**And here's a few pages from
an O.C.L.T.-related occult thriller:**

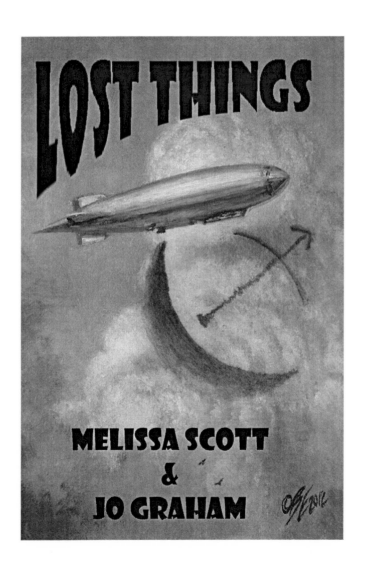

LOST THINGS

MELISSA SCOTT
&
JO GRAHAM

Prologue–May, 1929

The bowl of the lake reflected nothing. On bright nights the full moon seemed magnified by the water, as though it had come to rest in the dark pool. That was why the Romans had called Lake Nemi Diana's Mirror.

The sounds of the massive pumps covered any noise it might make, working night and day to drain the lake. It was the most significant archaeological site in a generation – two Roman ships from the reign of Caligula, resting beneath the waters of Lake Nemi in almost pristine condition. But then It knew all about the ships. It had known them for a very long time.

They were ruins in the mud, a few beams exposed as the lake drained. They were gone like the Sanctuary of Diana that had once graced the shore. But She was still here. Far away in the woods the man heard it and stiffened – the faint baying of hounds.

It inhabited this man. It wore him, frail thing though he was, already weakening in Its grasp. They were running, he and the man, his sedentary feet made fleet by fear. They were running through the woods while briars grabbed at them, while moonlight mistook their path before them. The hounds were louder. They were coming. The hunters were behind. They could see the flashes of their strange torches, incandescent in the darkness, silver against the trees. A white hound led the pack, sharp nosed and keen, the others following her. It was She who led.

The man's breathing was harsh. They were being driven. Out of the trees, out of the wild wood. Now there were shouts behind, calls from one hunter to another in strange, bastard Latin. The hunters had seen them. The ground was muddy and they slipped. This man was no hunter, no soldier, and he had been run hard. He slipped and slid down the bank, one leg catching beneath him, knee twisting. He was down. The white hound crested the bank, beautiful and implacable.

And then She was not there. It was two brown ones, bloodhounds, the man thought, and they stopped and set up a cry. It was only a moment before the hunters came up. Silver lights played over their face, and they cringed, It and this man, hiding from the brightness.

"Poor soul," one of the hunters said, sliding down the bank. "It's Signore Gadda all right."

They wore blue uniforms, all the hunters. A second one climbed down, lifted this man's hands from his face. "Signore Gadda? Can you understand me, sir? Do you know what has happened?"

This man would reply, but It would not let him. It could see the white hound behind the hunter, and It screamed.

The first hunter spoke again. "I thought we'd never find him. His wife is frantic. God help him." He moved his hand across his chest, as though making some sign of warding.

Another man climbed down, a tall man in middle age, wearing black rather than the blue uniforms, and the second hunter spoke to him. "Signore Davenport, it is definitely your man. But I do not think he understands a word."

"It is a terrible tragedy," Davenport said, and he leaned over them. This man knew him. This was his leader, his patron. He was afraid he would lose his job. But he could not speak. "Vittorio? Can you hear me?"

It screamed. There was the smell of incense on this one. He reeked of Her.

"We should take him to the hospital in Rome," one of the hunters said. "I will send a man to tell his wife that we have found him but that he is very ill."

"Yes, definitely the hospital," Davenport said. "Vittorio...."

The hunters hauled them to their feet, dragging them from the wood, from the ships, from the wild, but It did not resist. To Rome. That had potential.

One of the hunters shook his head to the other. "What makes a man do this? Suddenly go mad and dash into the woods to live like an animal?"

"Perhaps they can help him at the hospital," Davenport said. "Some kind of seizure or stroke, I do not know." He looked at this man again, his face a study in concern. "Perhaps he will know his wife when she comes."

"To Rome," they whispered. "To Rome."

Chapter One

Five thousand miles away, Lewis Segura jerked awake. Not a dream of barbed wire and trenches this time, or even the sickening lurch a plane makes when it stalls, the nose beginning to dip down. It had been worse than that, weirder than that. There had been a lake, and things like snakes, like giant eels, moving through the depths, screams underwater that wakened echoes where there couldn't be any; a dark wood, and shapes within it, and at the last a white hound appeared between trees, waiting for him, her head raised, her eyes as blue as the summer sky. His heart rang with familiar certainty: this was coming, this was true.

He sat up, craning his neck to see the clock on the table. Not even midnight. Alma slept next to him, burrowed into her nest of blankets, the pale sheen of her blond hair against the darkness. Her breathing was even and steady. Whatever had wakened him hadn't bothered her, and heaven knew Alma had her own ghosts.

He hugged his knees to his chest, hoping Alma would wake. He'd always dreamed like this, even before the war, but since then—since then there had been more nightmares, tinged with smoke and the sound of guns, but the true dreams had remained, clear and distinct. If this was one of them—well, it was a warning, surely?

He closed his eyes, trying to make sense of the sequence of images, of the struggle under the water, the serpent twining around a drowning man, rings of flesh and scale like a hundred clutching hands. And then there had been the screams, silent and mindless and horrible, bubbling with icy water. He'd run toward the woods like a man pursued until he'd checked, seeing the white dog. And behind her.... Behind her stood three women, caught in moonlight, one with a bow strung and ready in her hand, another with a poppy as scarlet as fresh blood, the thin petals resting gently against her white-robed shoulder. Between them stood a third woman, hands upturned, a veil covering her hair. They were all the same, he realized, the same fine-boned face, serene and stern at the same time; their eyes were blue, implacable. In the water behind him something roiled beneath the surface, and the dog bared teeth in a silent snarl.

He crossed himself like a child, but the images were still vivid, the silent women, the snarling dog, the thing beneath the water and the thrashing terror.

Lewis took a deep breath, trying to put the emotion behind him. If it was a true dream, a warning, what did it actually mean? Stay away from water? The closest lake was a good five miles away, and he didn't swim anyway. Beware a white dog? No, the dog had been hunting the thing in the water, the same as the women. They hadn't been interested in him, just the lake and its secret. Bow and poppy and veil, three identical women, or one woman seen three times…. He couldn't make sense of it, and the fear was still heavy in his gut.

Alma was still asleep, her back to him, curled around her pillow. He thought for a second about nudging her awake and pretending he'd done it by mistake, but she'd had a busy day, taking a charter to Grand Junction and back. It wasn't a long flight, but it meant threading the passes, and for a guy who didn't like letting a woman fly him even when she did own the company. Lewis didn't want to wake her.

Instead he turned over carefully, listening to the faint strains of the radio coming up from downstairs. Jerry was awake, or maybe it was Mitch. Jerry had lived there for years, maybe since the operation that had taken part of his right leg after the war, and Mitch lived over the garage until he could get a place of his own, which Lewis figured would happen about the same time that Jerry went back to teaching, which was to say never. But his bosses' living arrangements were none of his business, especially since Mitch was part owner in Gilchrist Aviation and he was just a hired pilot. Even if he shared Alma's bed.

Lewis turned over. Alma's soft breathing was slow and soothing.

Sometimes the dreams were all right, like the one that had led him to Alma. It had been a good dream, too: a plane that he'd never flown, shaped like one of the Stahltaubes he'd seen before the War, but every bit as maneuverable as the bird it mimicked, so that he had swirled and spun, not in defense but in sheer joy of flight. Below him stretched Long Beach, the airfield and its lines of planes, the crowd with their heads tipped back to see him dance.

The flare had gone up to call him in, and he'd taken the plane up toward the cloud deck, which made no sense in retrospect, but at the time had seemed the most reasonable thing in the world. He'd risen through the clouds into sunlight and blue sky and a sweet green runway stretching straight and clear before him, the windsock barely twitching on its stake beside a hanger like a young cathedral. He'd brought the bird-plane down, felt wheels kiss the sod, brought it gently to a stop beside the hanger, and a fair woman in a blue dress turned away from a scarlet biplane. It was for him, he thought, his plane, his freedom, and the woman smiled. Our Lady, the Queen of Heaven, and he'd awakened with the joy still sounding in his bones.

At the time he'd been out of work three weeks and was starting to think he knew how a dope fiend felt when he couldn't get his fix. He still might not have gone to the airshow except that at the Legion meeting Frankie Onslow had said that he'd heard that a guy named Peters, who belonged to a Post up-state, had a crop-dusting service and might be looking for a pilot. The combination of the news and the dream seemed to be telling him something, so he'd taken a couple of dollars from his last pay packet and ridden the trolley out to the show.

Of course, Peters hadn't been hiring, but he'd mentioned a man named Stalkey who'd taken Lewis's name and the phone number of the boarding house, and mentioned another guy named Wiggins. Wiggins was equally non-committal, but said he'd heard that Jeff Forrest had a new mail contract, and wrote the name and hanger number on a scrap of paper.

"But he's got a couple of planes in the stunt show," Wiggins said. "I wouldn't go over there till after."

That made good sense, and anyway Lewis was hungry by

then, and his feet were getting sore, so he found himself a spot in the grandstand to unwrap his sandwiches. Bologna wasn't his favorite, but it was cheap and ok with a lot of mustard. He ate both of them and folded the waxed paper into a triangle, watching the stunt plane swirl and dive. With the right plane he could do pretty much everything he was seeing. He could do better than most of the pilots—if it were a combat situation, he could take them all.

That way lay danger. He fished in his pocket for a nickel instead, bought a Coke, and climbed out of the stands to watch the rest of the show. The white Jenny just finishing its loop was Forrest's, and if that was his best pilot, Lewis figured he stood a chance at any jobs that were going.

He wouldn't go over there yet, though, would wait until the crowds cleared out a little. He shaded his eyes, squinting, found the next plane as it dropped down out of the high blue, lining up on the runway. The loudspeaker crackled, the whine of the plane's engine already swallowing the words.

"—Al Gilchrist—Cherry—"

Weird name for a plane, Lewis thought.